The Lost Princess

Joy Lewis

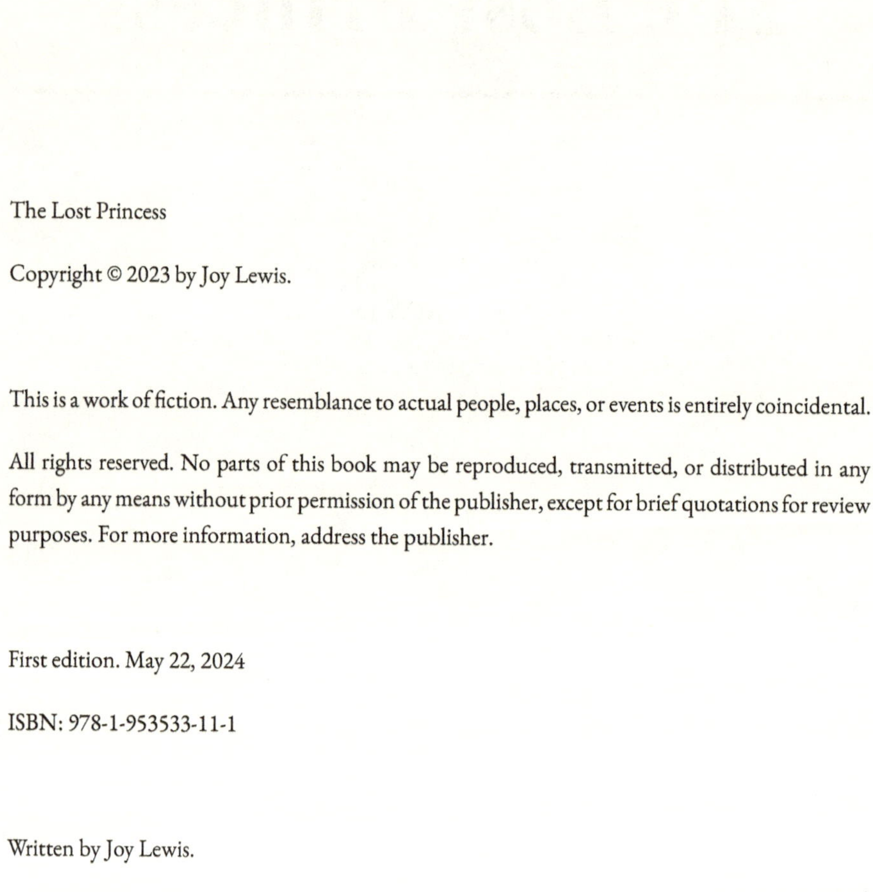

The Lost Princess

Copyright © 2023 by Joy Lewis.

This is a work of fiction. Any resemblance to actual people, places, or events is entirely coincidental.

All rights reserved. No parts of this book may be reproduced, transmitted, or distributed in any form by any means without prior permission of the publisher, except for brief quotations for review purposes. For more information, address the publisher.

First edition. May 22, 2024

ISBN: 978-1-953533-11-1

Written by Joy Lewis.

www.joylewisauthor.com

Cover Design by Artscandare Book Cover Design.

https://artscandarebookcoverdesign.com

Chapter One

Dogfight

Malik hoped to all the gods that Hell at least had no corpse flies.

Because he had no illusions as to exactly where his soul would be sent when he got to the front of this line. It was where people like him belonged.

And as long as the next world had none of *these*, he reasoned it would be a better place.

The fat, black fly in question landed on his nose as if he were already dead.

Go find one of the rotting ones. His teeth grinded in the back of his mouth as he stared at its multifaceted eyes.

The chains around his wrists weighed him down, but it was a comfortable weight. One of his first lessons had been that everything was a weapon.

For a moment, he indulged in the thought of using the length of iron chain that he and the rest of the condemned dragged in a line to take hostage the man in front of him.

He's going to die anyway, he reminded himself. *They wouldn't care if I did it.*

Everyone in this line was going to meet the same fate at the end of it. It was why they'd chained them together. Panic and aggression were the best of bedmates.

At the very least, if taking a hostage didn't work, he could choke him. It wouldn't help, but it might've made him feel better.

Only one way to find out, Malik considered.

But the more he watched his target, the more obvious it was. They both hailed from the same kingdom. Or rather, what had been their kingdom.

The back of his neck was the same tanned shade, his hair the same deep brown. He hadn't noticed past his scars.

Malik casted his eyes elsewhere as he gave up the thought. They expected his people to act like brutes. Why should he prove them right in their last moments?

Even if he craved an excuse to scare them. His lips came up at the edges as he gave it some thought.

He was going to die. That was a given. But couldn't he have some fun first? He could attack the guard who read him his last rites. Now that would be useless—at the most, he'd manage a headbutt.

But how *gratifying* it would be.

Malik focused on that thought and only that. It helped take the edge off of what would come after.

There would be no getting out of it. He'd admitted to what they'd accused him of.

Aisha's going to be pissed.

The thought of his sister was almost enough to make Malik lose it, so he stopped thinking altogether.

The sound of the irons clanging against each other drowned out the shouts and cries of those behind him. He was second to the front of the line.

The heat rose off the land in waves. It blurred the figures standing among the crumbling stone arena around him, but he couldn't help but see the pile of unmoving men in one corner of the arena's ground. A cloud of corpse flies fought each other above.

Belnya prisons were multifunctional. Above was the arena and a venue for both sentencing and the executions that inevitably followed. For someone to land his sorry ass here, he had to have pissed off someone important. Or done something the rest of the kingdom considered too sickening but to kill you for.

Underneath the hot surface of the earth was where sand and the prisoners who were cursed to live were. Though, there was a saying about that.

The lucky ones die by the executioner's axe. The others die below.

As Malik squinted past the heatwaves, he recognized someone other than his executioner.

Of course, his family wasn't here. Aisha had been misinformed as to his whereabouts. It was the only reason she wasn't picking up the pace in chains behind him. If she knew, she would have tried something hollow-headed to follow him here or break him out.

And his father ... Well, Malik was here instead of him. That should've been good enough.

No, the man who he recognized was none other than the damned king. Guards flanked him on every side where he sat in the arena's raised seating.

As his fellow prisoner was prodded forward with the end of a soldier's blade, Malik's eyes went again to the pile. Someone had done a very good job of pissing off the king himself.

Whoever it is, he's still in line, he realized.

The king would have left already otherwise. This close to the dead, the smell and heat were enough to make vomit rise in his throat.

He turned his gaze back to watch the man in front of him. Even if they both had to die today, at least his body would rot beside someone of the same earth as his.

But a rough grip as his shoulder forced him to his knees.

"Yes. That's the one." The voice came from the other side of the arena, but he couldn't mistake it.

It was the king. And he was here for Malik himself.

Malik supposed he shouldn't have been surprised that the king was here for him.

He had admitted to killing no less than a dozen healers trying to cure somnus. He hadn't been shy about that.

Even if he hadn't done it, he'd done plenty of other things deserving of such recognition. It was why Malik was so sure of where his soul was destined for once they drained him of blood.

"Unchain him." Malik's head whipped up at the king's command.

No one questioned the order, but Malik could feel the guard's agitation. Malik smiled at the man in his shadow so that the rest of the arena couldn't see.

"Maybe he wants us to switch," Malik proposed to his guard in a whisper. "You be the prisoner. I'll be the big man with a sharp stick this time."

He could feel the eyes of the arena on them. The guard seemed to take longer than was necessary to unchain him.

Under his breath, he spat at Malik, "Monster."

Malik came to his feet as soon as his part of the chains slipped to the ground in a loud clatter. He looked down to see the stain of the previous prisoner's blood still seeping into the earth.

Some paces from him stood the man who came from the same earth as him, the Karsian prisoner who had marched in line before him.

Karsia doesn't exist anymore, Malik reminded himself. *It was conquered and its fruit was ground into something more palatable. Swallowable.*

Malik let the thought pass from him. None of that mattered now. Besides, it wasn't as if their supposed shared blood made them friends. This man was a stranger to him.

The man of Karsian descent across from him been similarly unchained and was standing still before the blade of a guard.

His head pounded with blood. He didn't like surprises. "I'll tell you where their bodies are if my word isn't enough to prove it," Malik announced to the general assembly in a shout.

While he hadn't committed those murders, he certainly knew his father's favorite disposal spots.

To his surprise, the king answered from where he sat. "No, I quite believe you. The problem lies in the waste." He paused and addressed the other prisoner. "If you kill him, you will walk free from here."

Malik's body thundered with anticipation. He could always feel fights before they happened. A look from the Alostran king, and the other prisoner was armed with a long knife.

Now that they were face-to-face, Malik could see more of the other man who was of Karsian descent. The rest of him was just as scarred as the back of him had been. He'd had his fair share of fights on the street.

He recognized Malik at once. He could see it in his eyes. He couldn't say the same of the man across from him.

He could also see what he thought of Malik. There was no kinsmanship there, or he would have been a fool to assume so.

The prisoners still chained behind him bayed at the sight. Malik had to agree. A spectacle before death was better than death alone.

The Alostran king turned his gaze back to him. There was something about the way he looked at him that he hated.

"Win against him, and you'll walk free."

Malik waited for his knife, but they didn't give him one. The guards merely moved their blades so they weren't pointed at their throats and backs any longer.

They aren't fool enough to arm me, then.

Somewhere in his brain, the corpse flies buzzed loud enough to smother his thoughts.

He ran.

Chapter Two

First Kiss

As Penrose sat as still as possible, she rehearsed the plan in her head for ending her marriage before it began. Her maidservant's deft fingers laced glittering jewels and preserved flowers through her plaits. She was almost convinced the woman could hear the hum of her mind as she worked on her plan, but she tried to smother the thought.

Don't be crazy, Penrose bade herself.

There was no concrete reason not to go through with it, she knew. Her feelings weren't enough to put a stop to this alliance forged from so many years ago.

You just don't want to, she thought.

Sheriline was done with her work and staring at their reflections in the mirror. She was smiling at what she'd done. Penrose copied her expression.

"Thank you," Penrose said. "It looks ..."

There was no other word for it. The maidservant had made her look stunning. Almost too much so—like a doll. Her straw-colored hair that usually knotted at the base of her skull without provocation was braided and wrapped around her head like a crown.

Safe from rat kings and their nests.

She wanted to snigger at the thought but thought better of it. Sheriline would have asked and that would have led to a conversation she didn't wish to have. Or more likely, an interrogation of where she'd learned of such a thing.

Penrose's smile faltered for a fraction of a second. She watched herself plaster it back on her face.

She needed her glasses back. None of the prince's servants seemed to know where they'd been misplaced after her journey here four weeks ago.

Missing glasses are not a reason to cancel a wedding, she reminded herself.

Rapping knuckles against her wooden door interrupted her thoughts and relieved her of finishing her sentence.

"The princess is—" Sheriline didn't even get to finish her declaration before he walked in.

Sheriline blushed for her. The crown prince Cassius—and if the fates had their way, her husband in a matter of two hours—walked inside her bedroom.

"Your Majesty, you can't be in here," Sheriline gasped. "You shouldn't see her before your wedding—"

He smiled at her maidservant. "It's a good thing I've seen her now. There's something I'd like to change." He added a meaningful look for emphasis.

Sheriline's blush spread to her throat before she bowed her head and acquiesced to his unspoken wish for her to leave.

Penrose swallowed. It would be a lie to say he wasn't attractive. He was beautiful. His chestnut hair was perfectly styled so it caught the sun's rays angled through her window, highlighting it in places. He looked like his people. Strong. Unburdened.

This was a good thing. She—her kingdom—needed this marriage. Her people did.

"Prince—" She started.

"Rose," he interrupted. His hand came behind her neck. His lips hovered at her ear. No one called her that except him.

He'd never touched her like this in the month she'd been here, preparing for today. Or in the meetings they'd shared leading up to today. Her heart hammered through her dress obscenely.

Boys never touched her like this. Not that she'd bothered getting close to any of them since she'd been promised to someone else already.

For *him*.

His lips were on hers before she knew it. Her first kiss was urgent. Pounding.

Is this so terrible? A voice asked inside her.

She had no answer. Her blood was pounding too much to think.

After a moment, Penrose found her response. She kissed him back until her knees lost their strength.

She pulled back abruptly, gasping for air. She needed her medicine. Now.

"I—" Her chest was too tight to speak. She needed the inhalant and the device her father had manufactured for her.

Red invaded her face worse than Sheriline's blush. Her traitor body had revealed its weaknesses again. And during her first kiss.

Of course.

Breath had fled her lungs, and she felt as if some goblin crouched on her chest.

Penrose flew from the prince's arms to the chests she'd brought with her. Her breathing had been reduced to wheezes—like she was breathing through a cloth.

Where is the medicine?

She'd already used what little she'd had left in the device. Penrose pushed aside one of the piles of books she'd brought with her only to find useless clothes instead of medicine. Her chest tightened.

Strong arms clasped her to him. "Rose. Shh. It's okay."

Her wheezing allowed only for a few words at a time. "Sorry," she managed. He wasn't supposed to have seen this.

Her father, the king of Aloster, had been very careful to keep her condition hidden from everyone but their most trusted servants. Or as best as he could've.

The magnifying glasses for reading couldn't be helped. From the time she'd learned to read, and after her tutors eventually found the answer to her difficult start into literacy, Penrose had been inseparable from her books. Her parents had commissioned the spectacles because doing so had been easier than keeping Penrose from reading.

Besides, as their child and now only heir, it wouldn't have been fit for her not to have been able to read scrolls of their land's laws or communications from other kingdoms.

Minutes passed, and Penrose's chest slowly released its hold on her airways. "It's not contagious," she explained when she could speak again. "And not related to ..."

Saying the name of it isn't going to spread the sleeping curse, she reminded herself.

But before she completed the thought, Prince Cassius said, "Your parents informed us of your condition. Our doctors are working on formulating a similar inhalant medicine."

Penrose stilled. She swallowed down the lump in her throat that came with the mention of her parents.

I know they care. Mother and Father have never stopped caring. It would be silly to think otherwise.

Something sparked inside her chest at the rest of his words. This was the king her people needed. Giving. Kind.

Out loud, she said, "That's very generous of you. Thank you."

As she moved, her hair fell about her face. Sometime when they'd kissed, the prince had unpinned the braids that Sheriline had fixed her hair into. Her hair fell into waves as the gems and preserved flowers scattered around them.

His mouth found her ear again. Bumps rose across her skin from his whispered breath.

"Will you come to marry me like this?" he asked.

Her throat was tight for a different reason this time. She thought of her country and the cure her people needed.

But she also thought of the heat rising to her skin at his touch.

"Yes."

Chapter Three

Sorrowtail

"Don't touch it. The prince wants it this way," Sheriline admonished the servant girl who had attempted to braid Penrose's hair again.

The room wasn't big enough for her and the four servants fastening different parts of her dress. And the dress.

Excess fabric gathered in piles behind her feet. Penrose wondered how long it would take them to respect her again if she tripped over it during the ceremony.

The word caused her heartbeat to quicken and her skin to slick with new sweat. To calm herself, she focused on evening her breathing. It was a technique she'd learned early in her life to help her deal with her sudden breathing attacks.

My people need this alliance. We all need him, she reminded herself.

Within Penrose's lifetime, his kingdom had developed a closely-guarded cure to the deadly sleeping curse.

The wars are over, she reminded herself. *Today will mark a new day. The future.*

And she had plans for this cure. Penrose swallowed as the servants started to tighten the bodice of her snow-white dress.

She was going to release it to the world. Even if she had to leak the secret to spies from the kingdoms that bordered theirs, she would get the cure into as many hands as possible.

Even if her new husband brought her to trial for releasing the kingdom's secrets to their enemies.

It was time to end this suffering.

Something tells me he'll understand. Penrose remembered his words earlier. He'd ordered his healers to formulate a new medicine for her breathing attacks.

For *her*.

Penrose gasped. Her breath stopped in her chest.

"Princess, it's going to be alright," Sheriline assured her. "It's perfectly normal to be nervous."

"My dress," she said through a cough. "It's too tight."

Her fingers fumbled with the ties along her spine before her new maidservants nearly tore apart the dress to loosen it.

"My lady." Sheriline's eyes were wide and her eyebrows scrunched together. "You're not well—"

Two in one day. It's getting worse.

Red crept up her throat. Penrose shook her head. She couldn't let them guess that something was wrong with her. The rumors of her weaknesses would spread.

They might even try to stop the wedding.

She needed to channel her mother and the air of undisputed authority that she carried about her like a shawl.

"I'm fine," she said in a low voice. It was easier to mask the wheeze that infiltrated her voice during her attacks when she spoke like this. "A moment of air will be enough."

Before another fit took her entirely, Penrose pushed through Sheriline's crowded room to her balcony. Perhaps it was rude, but she couldn't care about that now.

Sheriline's balcony was smaller than hers, but just as high into the air. She focused on not looking directly down.

Penrose breathed in the clear air as the evening sun warmed her skin. The prince lived in the hold he'd been given by his parents, a swath of land in the southern reaches of his kingdom. The hold towered tall enough to overlook much of his lands. The prairieland stretched impossibly far, and as she let it guide her vision, she could almost see her home, Aloster.

She blinked and summoned her last letter from her parents in her mind's vision. The letters had been blurred to her unassisted eyes, but her father's handwriting was familiar enough to decipher.

Despite not having her glasses, she'd written to them almost every day. She was getting better at writing neater without being able to see well what she wrote. Reading their responses was harder, but not impossible with a lamp and some time.

Penrose was fairly certain she'd communicated her doubts about today clearly enough. She frowned.

And yet, they hadn't seem concerned in their correspondence to her. They commented on the other things she wrote on—the droll topics of weather and what sort of ruler she'd make.

She knew well enough that they were trying to quell her fears and doubts. Penrose breathed as her chest loosened its grip on her lungs some. She didn't have to be reminded of the risks that rode on today.

A shadow swept across the small balcony. At once, Penrose's heart soared. She hadn't thought him healed enough for this.

She whistled into the wind buffeting the side of the tower. Her fingers clung to the rusted metal railing as she searched the endless blue above her. The notes had almost certainly been snatched by the relentless gales that plagued this part of the sky, but she couldn't help hoping.

With a flutter of dark blue feathers, he landed on the balcony's railing like he belonged there. Penrose smiled back at him. Sorrowtail belonged wherever he was.

That was just the kind of creature he was.

His eyes were bright black and fixed on her, and his feathered head took her in at an angle.

She felt one of her eyebrows arch. "You're well enough to fly all this way? Are you certain of that?"

It was quite a distance to the bottom of the tower for a finch to fly, especially one with an injured wing. But he looked back at her as if to say, *I got here, didn't I?*

She shook her head at him. "You're much too proud to admit any sort of failing, are you? Silly bird."

Penrose dug into the inside of her dress to find the secret pocket that had probably been meant for a hidden dagger in case of assassins. For the possibility of this occasion, she'd filled it with bird seed instead.

Despite her words, she held out her hand with the treat anyway. She wasn't just going to allow her closest companion to fly away from her just because she'd insulted his pride.

Sorrowtail looked back at her for several seconds. Perhaps she'd gone too far this time. A bird's pride was a serious thing, she'd learned.

But the seed did the trick. Or perhaps it was the fact that she hadn't seen her feathered friend in nearly a month. His talons were a familiar pressure against her palm as he picked at her peace offering.

When he'd had his fill, Sorrowtail angled his head up to look at her. With a gentle touch, Penrose rubbed against his blue head. His eyes closed as she did so, and he chirped softly. The muscles around her heart tightened.

She'd missed this.

Shortly after the two of them had arrived here, Sorrowtail had sustained an injury to his wing no doubt from the high winds that pummeled the tower's exterior.

He was born in the wild, though he'd adapted to live with Penrose in her room within her parent's castle by coming and going when he pleased through her open windows. It had been a difficult choice, but she couldn't in good conscience keep him so high in the sky when there were no trees or other perches for him to safely land on between her balcony and the ground.

When she'd been reasonably sure that he could fly short distances, she'd accompanied him to the bottom of the tower to find him a structure to nest inside while he recovered fully.

The prince's servants had to beg her to come back with them. She'd used almost all of what she'd brought of her inhalant medicine to get to the bottom of the tower's endless steps.

There had been no going back down to see him, at least until her stay was over here. And she'd used the absolute rest of her medicine stowed in her inhalant device in the weeks between then and today.

Penrose's eyebrows came together.

I must be hallucinating.

It was if the thought had summoned the smell of it. The medicine itself was odorless, though it had to be burned to be inhaled, like incense, and the process gave off a faint odor almost like burning paper.

She smelled it now.

Her eyes scoured the lands around them. The vast part of his territory was uninhabited grasslands. There was nothing to suggest anything like it was being burnt nearby.

Penrose looked up and saw something she hadn't noticed before, though she still didn't understand. It was a balcony. Not hers—her room was on the opposite side of the tower. Her eyes went back to the countryside around her. Perhaps there was a manufacturing plant nearby?

But as she wondered at what it all meant, Sorrowtail startled from where he'd been perched on her hand. Before she could calm him with reassuring words, he began to circle her head and squawk at her.

"Sorrowtail—" Penrose stepped out of the way of his low dive, and something crashed into the balcony floor where they'd been moments ago.

Though all that was left were broken pieces and bits, it was clear enough what the object had been before it had fallen.

At the same time, she recalled whose room the balcony above likely belonged. Penrose darted under the eaves of the doorway as she caught her breath and stared at what had been the device her father had manufactured for her breathing condition.

It had been, as far as she knew, one-of-a-kind.

And she suddenly knew whose room was on the opposite side of hers in the tower—the one that had an attached balcony above this one.

Prince Cassius's.

There was no time to process it all. Someone was coming through the doors. She had to hide it.

"Princess—"

Penrose shoved herself into Sheriline as she came through the balcony doors, knocking the woman over.

"Princess!" Sheriline said, this time with a touch of indignation.

As she righted herself, Penrose kicked the biggest pieces of her broken inhalant device off the balcony. It was the only way she could keep the maidservant from seeing it after she'd opened the balcony door.

And if there was any chance of keeping her condition a secret, she needed to take it.

Besides, smashing into the balcony one staircase down had been enough to break it beyond repair. Penrose didn't have the knowledge or skill or materials for such a thing.

"Beg your pardon, my lady, but what are you doing?" She didn't sound like she wanted Penrose's pardon at all.

"My apologies, Sheriline," she said in a gasp. "I didn't see you there."

Sheriline looked to believe her words as much as she would have believed her had she said the sky was green.

But she needed her and the rest of the servants to leave. Penrose had an already half-formed plan in mind for what came next, though she wasn't sure at all if it was going to work.

But one thing was certain to her. She couldn't marry the prince. She couldn't tie the future of her country to him.

Because he'd been lying. He wasn't developing a new formula for her medicine.

He'd known about her breathing condition. And he planned to use it against her to keep her in his tower. He must have realized that walking down so many flights of stairs aggravated her ability to breathe.

This place was nothing more than a gilded birdcage for her.

As her fingers went habitually to the bridge of her nose to massage where her glasses usually dug into the skin, she realized he'd likely destroyed something else of hers.

She hadn't misplaced her glasses at all. Her first night here, she'd left them beside her bed on a table full of books. In the morning, they'd been gone.

I'd blamed myself.

The twin feelings of danger and dread knotted in her throat. The only thing she didn't know yet was *why* he'd done it.

Penrose clung to the fact that she knew: the prince was not the person who he seemed to be.

The words came out of her mouth as she formulated the rest of her plan. "I'm so sorry. I think I was just nervous about his request."

Sheriline's eyes narrowed on her. She looked back to the other servants. "I will call you when you are needed. Go to the ballroom and assist Relsoff." When she returned her eyes on her, she said, "What request?"

Penrose swallowed. Her nerves and inexperience were honest enough, so why not focus on those?

"The request to see him before the wedding." Penrose bit into her tongue. "I thought this sort of thing ... came after."

Sheriline's eyes widened, and she could see that she believed her.

Likely, she was remembering what the prince had said and done with her hair earlier. The way he'd entered her room without regard.

"That's highly—" She broke off, as if remembering that they were talking about a prince who could do what he wanted. "What did he say, child?"

Penrose bit into her tongue more at the epithet. "To meet him an hour before the wedding in his rooms," Penrose said in a whisper.

Her maidservant took a long look at her, as if deciding something. Finally, she said, "Do you know how to please a man?"

Penrose could have gagged. She'd read all there was to *that* topic about two summers ago. Somewhere between the medical books in her parent's library and the novels she'd bribed Lesabeth to bring her from outside the castle, she'd inferred enough.

The reminder of *her* made her stomach cramp unexpectedly, but Penrose shoved the thought away.

Sheriline was late.

Even so, her cheeks burned. "I think I know enough of it."

Sheriline turned her back to her to look through her drawers, though Penrose could see her shaking her head. "The wedding is barely an hour away. Surely, he could have found a better time for this."

When she turned around, she was shoving a plant root into a sachet. She pushed it into Penrose's palm.

"Should you not want to produce an heir so quickly, chew on this for a bit afterward. You'll have to have one eventually, of course. I was going to give you this after, but ..." Sheriline went silent.

Penrose's mouth hung open at the gesture. She took the small pouch in her fist and thanked her before slipping out of the room. On her way out, she heard Sheriline say, "Tell him you two can't be late. Even prince and princesses must show up to their weddings on time."

Not if I have anything to say about it, she thought.

Penrose was going to steal the cure ahead of schedule.

Chapter Four

The Prince of Grime

Malik's shoeless feet pounded against the scorched earth that gave to sand in spots.

His opponent lunged for him at once, but that was a mistake. His open, unprotected swing to his face told Malik exactly the kind of opponent the scarred man was.

He'd learned to fight on the street somewhere. No formal training, which wasn't a bad thing by itself. But it made him easy to predict.

Malik's leg connected with the man's gut, and he lurched forward. But in the instant before he could steal his long knife, the man spat into Malik's eyes to blind him.

He felt warm blood trickle down his tricep as he jerked out of his opponent's reach and wiped his eyes with the back of his hand. He'd gotten first blood on Malik.

In a fight to the death, there were no rules. And in Malik's experience, all fights were to the death.

At the appearance of blood, the spectators there to watch the executions roared. They hadn't expected a fight, but they loved it.

The man's eyes flitted from the wound to Malik's face. "They will call me a hero for killing you. The prince of grime."

He said the title like it was a dribble of grease in his mouth. Indigestible and fetid. The sun slanted down on them, baking them inside the arena.

He looked at his opponent. Fools harbored hope that their enemies would give them grace in the end. They convinced themselves that, when it came to it, even the people who hated them didn't hate them enough to kill them.

Malik harbored no such illusions.

He'd been going to die today. There'd been nothing else for him. No way out.

His teeth clenched. Malik had taken the blame for the murders as punishment. Was it worth trying to win this fight?

Would there be punishment, too, in evading death?

As his opponent got another slash on him—this time along his chest—his body answered for him. When it came to it, he wanted to live.

Damn the consequences.

He'd confessed to it, hadn't he? It wasn't his business if the king wanted a blood spectacle.

Nor that he was so good at such things.

As soon as he decided, it became easy for Malik. He allowed the other man to gain ground. Malik's blood dotted the ground as he dodged the long knife.

One strike. It was all he needed. He could smell the sweat on the other man now. It was almost time.

"People like you are the reason they treat us like this." His opponent's teeth were bared as he jabbed straight through the air where Malik's chest had been moments ago.

"The reason for the slums. The reason they spit on us," the other man said. Each of his words was punctuated by a new slash.

Malik's black hair had loosened from the tie at the base of his head. Loose, sweat-soaked strands fell across his field of vision.

The scarred man's next words were a roar. "I will walk proud among my people." He aimed one final slash, too close to miss, at Malik's throat.

Malik repeated the man's words in his mind. *My people. Not ours.*

But he barely registered the words. His body had taken over.

There was no getting out of the way of the strike. It was the exact moment when his opponent was most vulnerable.

It was also the exact spot where Malik had been freed of his prisoner's chains.

Malik moved, by his own estimation, faster than the wind. Sight, sound, and pain blurred around him, but he used them all to his advantage.

The iron chains were in his hands at the same time that the searing pain raced up his cheek. He'd had to take the strike in order to accomplish something better.

Malik had invited him to chase him, to close the distance between them—and to do it on his own coin, too. The man's energy was well spent from chasing Malik and stabbing at him.

The iron pressed tight into his opponent's skin as Malik pulled it harder against the man's neck. The knife hit the earth uneventfully. The stands of people above watched in a new silence.

There was no cheering. Instead, his opponent's gurgling and gasping filled the arena.

The scarred prisoner had fallen to his knees, his hands clawing uselessly at the chains Malik had gotten around his neck. He managed a few scratches into his skin before he slumped forward.

Malik allowed the chain to fall from around the man's neck, but he didn't drop it. Whether or not he still needed it remained to be seen. He looked at the king.

Though sweat had dripped into Malik's eyes, he saw something on the king's face that made him think what had happened—or perhaps *how*—hadn't necessarily displeased him.

"Bring him forward."

***

The healer was stitching together Malik's face where the now-dead prisoner had sliced it open. Pain pricked along the nerves. Blood had dried into the shirt he'd thought he was going to die in—a prisoner's tunic.

"Why?" Malik asked again. It must have been the tenth time he'd asked it. His voice was rough as he repeated it. "Why the effort?"

The king of Aloster looked at him archly from where he sat at the other side of a table. It appeared to have been the Belnya prisons warden's office. "Considering your position, do you really expect to get a reason?"

Malik breathed. He couldn't concentrate with the pain. He gripped the healer's hand where it was still stitching his face. "That's enough," he told him.

The healer's face went white. His eyes flickered to where the king sat, but no one insisted that he should stay. He stood, packed his tools, and left the room.

Malik returned his attention to the king. "This wasn't for the sake of seeing a dog fight."

It didn't sit right with him. Miracles weren't real. The gods didn't care about people, least of all him. And kings didn't allow murderers to live without cause.

No, he'd been allowed to live for a reason. And Malik would have it from him, one way or another.

This time, the king gave a sharp glance at the other people in the room which was too hot without a dozen people filling it.

"Everyone but my guards will leave us."

When the king met his stare again, there was something new to it. He was sizing him up, Malik realized. As the others left, only two of his kingsguard remained.

"You're not wrong to be suspicious." He stood, and though his guards barely moved, they moved enough so that they protected him from all angles again. "We've wanted to destroy you and yours for longer than you've lived." The king stopped. "It's a great sacrifice not to kill you where you stand."

The truth was plain on his face. It wasn't a matter of insult or intimidation. It was merely a matter of fact.

Though Malik was only one arm of House Ezar, he wasn't without a considerable reputation on his own. It was a reputation that he'd honed for nothing short of seventeen years.

The Prince of Grime. It was what they'd taken to calling him. He handled the worst of what Ezar family dealt in. Their hands were in many pockets, doing things such as collecting dues, feeding, and stealing where it suited them. But his father had refined in his son a talent for getting things done.

Whatever that required.

So, the king's words were nothing short of the truth. Regarding the safety of the common citizen, Aloster would have been better off without him roaming its streets.

The king sighed. "I almost had the distinction of executing his son."

Malik leaned forward. He was well aware of the blades and pistols that followed the movement, aiming at his chest and head.

"My living is not without conditions," Malik guessed, spitting the words.

For the first time since he'd seen the king in person, the man smiled. It was strange to see on his face, lined with the stress of ruling a sprawling kingdom glued together from three broken ones. And the stress of coming into rule as the *bastard king*.

"Of course, people like you operate under the premise of debts and payments," he said. Malik wasn't a fool and didn't interpret the smile as a sign of amiability. He didn't miss the way he said *people like you*, either.

Taking his time, the king sat down at the table and met his gaze. "I have a proposal. An agreement. I believe you're familiar with them?"

This time, Malik smiled. "You want me to kill someone."

He had wanted to unnerve him. Psychologically, gaining the upper hand was almost as important as figuring out your opponent's motives. He needed to do both here.

But instead of balking at what he'd said, the king only leaned forward.

"Of course." A heartbeat passed before the king added, "Why else would I risk letting you live?"

Chapter Five

The Thief and the Cure

When the door closed behind Penrose, she went to work at once. Her wedding to him was to be in an hour, but she wasn't so naïve as to believe they wouldn't come looking for her sooner.

All she needed was a few good minutes. She started with his desk first, which she knew was the most hopeful scenario. But as her eyes started to ache, squinting at the third piece of correspondence she'd pulled out of his stack of letters, she forced herself to move through them faster.

In her haste, a bundle of parchment slipped through her fingers and fell to the floor. It was a tightly wound scroll with a broken wax seal. She recognized it as the symbol for kingdom of Cavana—the insignia for the prince's family.

Penrose's heart lodged inside her throat. *There has to be something here. Somewhere.*

A migraine built behind her eyes. The letters were difficult to read, but she could make out one word that was repeated throughout the piece of correspondence.

Sleeping curse.

Her hands gripping the piece of parchment trembled. She needed to take this back to her room at once.

There's no time. I'll have to keep it on me.

Slipping one hand into her dress, she fished out the sachet with the root in it to replace it with the tightly rolled paper when the sound of metal on metal rang through her ears.

Penrose froze.

"Drop the items," a familiar voice behind her said. "And turn around. Slowly."

She did as she was commanded, turning around to come face to face with Sheriline and the armed guard beside her.

Her maidservant's expression was unlike one she'd ever seen on her face before. Penrose fought the instinct to pull back from the woman. Somehow, it unsettled her more than the guard and his drawn weapon, though she couldn't stop looking at the keenness of his blade, either.

Sheriline took a few paces forward, bringing them within touching distance of each other. Penrose's heart hammered through her wedding dress. Her plans and clever daydreams left her now, abandoning her like melting snow at daybreak.

Sheriline had discovered her lie. And maybe more.

Maybe even her intent to steal the cure.

Her hand touched the edge of Penrose's jaw, and she fought against the cringe springing to her muscles at the touch. But all she did was move Penrose's face from one side to the other, as if examining it for some mark or flaw.

"Such an attractive, obedient girl. The perfect end to such grisly wars—a pretty gift with a bow on top. But I suppose looks can be deceiving," she said, pulling her hand away.

Penrose's stomach clenched. She wasn't just some peace offering.

Was she?

In the same moment that Sheriline stepped back from her, her foot came down, hard, on the pouch she'd left on the floor. The root was ground into dirt underneath her boot.

"I lost a brother to your side," Sheriline said after she'd crushed the root. "He was killed after surrendering."

Her mouth was dry. She wanted to protest that such a thing would have ever happened—that her people wouldn't have done that. But the worst part of the wars had happened before she'd even been born.

It could've.

"Give me a reason," Sheriline said.

Her breath froze in her throat. "A reason," Penrose repeated back dully. Her heartbeat drummed in her ears.

This was all wrong. This wasn't why she was here at all.

"To think you're not a spy."

"I'm not here to start a war," Penrose countered. She couldn't say it. *Spy* was too close to what she'd only moments ago been. "I'm here for the cure."

What she was doing was dangerous, but she needed to convince her.

"I need this alliance. My people need the cure to the sleeping curse." Penrose drew in a breath and let it flow through her lungs. "I need to know he'll share it with me when we're married."

"Trust is a funny thing," Sheriline said. "When it appears, it seems to come from nowhere. But when it breaks, it doesn't reappear near as easily." She came closer to her. "Our people worked tirelessly to develop it and safeguard it."

Penrose swallowed. She was so close to it. She couldn't jeopardize her mission any more than she had. It could be catastrophic.

She couldn't tell her she was stealing it and escaping her wedding. There was no time left for that, anyway.

Her final hope sat in her mind, and it was like the highest, reddest apple on the tree. Her last hope. It had to work.

Penrose said in a too quiet voice, "I'm not here to cause strife. Or hurt anyone. I want what you want—a peaceful future."

Sheriline stared at her for a long while before she commanded the guard, "Put away your weapon. We're making the princess late to her own wedding." To her surprise, Sheriline stepped behind her, running a brush quickly through her hair that she hadn't seen on her person a moment ago.

Her hands worked lightning-fast. Penrose wasn't sure how she'd done it, but her messy hair had been transformed yet again. She ran her fingers through it and found it mostly loose, though gems and flower buds had been fixed in small, tight braids hidden throughout. Nearly invisible.

She breathed out. "Thank you."

It was a custom of her people's. Heirs to the crown that married before they'd ascended couldn't wear the crown itself, but they were always wed in gleaming jewels and flowers from their homeland.

Sheriline stayed behind her, fixing pieces of her dress and hair as she spoke. "I've been a maidservant to royals before you, so I know something of your kind. Something most of you would rather not admit."

Penrose stiffened. "And that would be?"

"Duty doesn't necessarily accompany the heart, though I hope in your case, it does." Sheriline adjusted one of her tiny braids, and Penrose guessed they were both remembering the same thing: when the prince demanded to see her in her rooms hours ago. "While not openly encouraged in any kingdom, dalliances may be had."

The princess's mouth hung open for a moment. Whatever she'd expected, it hadn't been this. But Sheriline wasn't done.

The maidservant added after a moment, "One way or another, a person doesn't survive long without their heart."

Sentimental, Penrose considered. *I suppose weddings make everyone behave in unexpected ways.*

She hoped her actions would be viewed similarly—nerves for the wedding, nerves for her people's wellbeing, nerves for a new future.

Penrose's eyebrows came together at Sheriline's strange urge to speak on this, but she kept her mouth shut. She was just glad they were off the topic of her being here. Even if she dreaded what had to come next.

As Sheriline worked, the guard cleaned up what remained of the mess on the floor. Sheriline spun her around, made a few final adjustments to the ground-up, rosy pigmentation on her cheeks, and pushed her out of the prince's chambers.

As they raced down the halls of the tower, she saw a flutter of blue move past a window. She kept her smile to herself.

Sorrowtail was here, too, she reminded herself. And soon, she would have more help.

At the least, her parents would be here. And if her father had correctly interpreted the code she'd written into the last of her letters, he'd know her concerns for today.

And even if she had to marry him, her father could procure her a new breathing mechanism. They would confront him together about his actions or whomever he'd ordered to destroy her things.

She had help. Even if her wedding dress fit too tight. Even if she felt like she was the offering walking into the jaws of some gaping monster instead of a wedding ceremony.

Her father's words came to her.

Take stock of everything you know. Then take stock of what you need to know—and why you don't. Only then can you hope to control the situation.

No matter what happened, she was getting that cure.

Chapter Six

The Wedding

Penrose felt like she was dreaming.

The flames of lit candles danced all along the walls of the great hall where they hung in lanterns. The smell of peonies perfumed the air, and she saw the reason why soon enough.

Among the officials and other important individuals from all over the three kingdoms, several stone fountains had been erected in the hall. Penrose couldn't imagine how they'd gotten them up here. It made her legs ache thinking of it.

Bobbing on the surface of each was an uncountable number of peonies. They floated like white and pink clouds on the rippling water. The scent filled her lungs with honeyed air as Penrose stalked past.

She should be speaking to the priest with her intended, she knew, but she had to find—

"Princess!" Their voices clamored over the hum of the conversations around her.

Penrose didn't bother turning around. It would mean she'd have to acknowledge them, but she had to find him first—

A firm grasp found her arm. The swarm of people around them stopped their conversations mid-word.

"My love, there you are." The prince's breath tickled the back of her neck.

The priest had slipped between the stunned guests to catch up with the prince. He was decades older than her fiancé, but had been as fast as him in getting to her. He leaned between them.

"Your pardon, your Majesties, but the three of us have somewhere to be."

But Penrose hadn't stopped scanning the crowd staring back at her. Diplomats, retired war generals, and representatives from the other kingdoms had come to witness the historic wedding between their nations.

But something was missing.

"We can't start yet. They're not here yet," she said to them.

The only tell on the Prince Cassius's face was a slight tightening around his mouth. "Who isn't here, my darling?"

"My parents," she said while looking over the heads of the crowd around them. "I don't see them anywhere. Their carriage must be late."

But the priest was already ushering them both to the edge of the room where two crowned individuals stood. Her heart rose for a second before she realized they were the prince's parents and not hers.

Penrose dug her feet into her shoes to stop the procession forward. This was all wrong. She needed to speak with her father. Even her mother would have put a halt to this for her.

But you can't just say no. The future—a good future—is what we're all getting out of this.

But she needed his insight. She needed to know she had an ally here. Someone on her side. She breathed as she thought of the unending staircase below her feet.

Someone to get her out.

"They said they'd be here." She hadn't realized she was gripping the prince's arm back just as hard. They'd stopped.

She heard him speak to a servant. "Are you certain you've checked the entire area? They would be heading from the west."

The servant's nod was stiff, his eyes never leaving the prince. "Your Majesty. There's nothing out there. All coaches have arrived."

Penrose took her chance. She slipped out of his grip to move to the wide window overlooking his kingdom.

Although a tall railing kept her from the edge, the open air came to greet her suddenly. She wrapped her fingers around the metal as she scoured the landscape.

Where are you? What happened?

Her heart lurched. *You said you'd be here.*

A mass of blue feathers fluttered in front of her face. Sorrowtail landed between her fists.

She could hear them behind her. Soon, all pretense of choice would be gone. Something told her they'd drag her to the altar if necessary.

The warmth that spread in her chest at seeing a friendly face was short-lived. He would have seen.

"Sorrowtail ... did you see them?" she said in a whisper.

But as he looked up at her, his soft feathers lightly ruffled by the wind, his eyes were cold and sad.

They weren't coming.

A peace offering. The words echoed inside her.

She was the daughter of a warrior—yet too weak for the field of battle. She was also the daughter of a great queen, descended from a long line of royalty. Yet she was no commander and went generally disregarded by those in power around her.

Penrose had known all her life that she wasn't what they'd hoped her to be. That she wasn't like either of them.

Her mother had chosen her father, one of Penrose's grandparents' top generals in the wars, to rule with her. And this was what they'd gotten.

And with her difficult birth, she'd left her mother unable to produce more heirs.

It only made the most sense that they'd then utilize her at least as a peace offering.

The future is without more bloodshed. Without more war and curses. It's my duty to make that future.

Unshed tears pricked at her eyes, and she blinked them quickly back. Queens didn't cry. Not even princesses cried.

Penrose glanced back at the wedding behind her. It was all wrong.

He was hiding things from her. Keeping her here. She needed to know why.

Behind her, screams suddenly pierced the air like the strings of a harpsichord, building over each one with fresh horror. Penrose's heart shoved into her throat as she spun on her feet and saw it. Spilled wine spread like blood on the ground.

The bodies remained still on the floor, unmoving.

And then, a dead silence.

She was frozen.

Penrose had never seen so much of the sleeping curse at once. And, if the screams of horror were any indication, neither had any of the rest of the room.

Diplomats pushed over themselves to get to the barred windows. She didn't want to think about what they were trying to do.

Penrose nearly missed it, but a gesture from the king directed a swarm of guards to block the entry to the staircase out of the hall and the windows.

A strange calm overtook her. Even if the gods had chosen this day and time to claim them all with their curse, at least her parents hadn't shown up. Her heart felt like it had been stuffed inside a bird cage, beating and bloody.

Even if she died here, they would live.

Even if she had become a liability to them, something more valuable when traded away, she still loved them.

"Stay close to me." The prince brought her close to his chest as he ordered the healers who had flooded the hall from his rooms above. "Give them all the medicine we have available." To the rest of the room, his raised voice said, "Calm yourselves. There is enough of the cure for everyone here. Rest assured that the gods have allowed us to survive this."

Penrose's throat felt tight. Despite his word—and despite the fact that they were in the safest place they could have been, considering his kingdom was the only one with a cure—she couldn't stop shaking with the fear.

The sleeping curse was said to the be gods' punishment for transgressing their favor. The slumber came on suddenly. The withering death came on slowly and painfully.

The terror of it was that those stricken with the curse were still alive as they decomposed. Still breathing, still able to bleed. But unable to wake.

It was said to be worse for their loved ones—to have to watch the victim die a slow death.

Penrose felt numb as he pulled them to the closest body on the floor. The healer was leaning over her, a woman dressed in fine silk robes with a sling attached to her dress. It looked specially made. Her hair was in an elaborate style often worn by Karsian ladies.

She must be an important Karsian official.

She realized what the sling was for a moment later. A few paces from them, another woman held a baby close as she tried to rock his cries away. He had the same shade of black hair that his mother had.

As the healer tilted her head back and gave the sleeping woman a vial of clear liquid, the prince crouched on her other side.

He moved the hair out of the unconscious woman's face and he told her, "You will live. The gods want you to live. Stay with us."

Penrose tried to stop her hands from shaking, but she couldn't.

In that moment, she didn't see the Karsian diplomat and mother to the infant boy.

She saw her older sister. She saw Lesabeth.

Soon enough, Penrose was on the floor. Her entire body was shaking as she pulled her knees to her face, and she couldn't stop it.

If only Lesabeth could have been here. She would have known what to do. The answer to it all.

And then, the thought that crushed her.

If only she'd have lived a little longer. I could have cured her.

Penrose wasn't sure when she'd started breathing shallower and shallower, but she was gasping quietly on the floor now. The healers had attended to nearly all the curse victims. She hadn't even seen how it had happened and how the medicine worked.

Stupid. Stupid.

Belatedly, Penrose realized that the wedding had started again without her. Their wedding guests were in tears at the miracle that had happened all around them.

While it was a common enough medicine to get in Cavana, Penrose knew that for the rest of them, they'd never witnessed anything like it. But she couldn't go back to pretending everything was fine and dancing around.

"Lessa. Why couldn't you hold on for a bit longer?" she whispered. "Lessa."

Penrose was drawing too much attention to herself. The king and queen of Cavana were staring. She had to seem normal. Whole.

A whisper grazed her ear. "I told them we wanted a private ceremony." The prince planted a kiss behind her ear as he held her close. From the outside, it would likely be hard to tell they were talking.

"Our witnesses have signed the documentation already," he added. "Meet me in my rooms."

After he stepped back from the embrace, Penrose realized that he'd been concealing his mouth to keep anyone from reading his lips.

Chapter Seven

Eyes of the Gods

There was no going back.

As she walked inside the prince's rooms, Penrose's stomach knotted. It was clear to her now more than ever this was the most important thing she could do with her life—stop the sleeping curse from claiming more lives.

She had to marry him.

But before the priest could follow them inside, the prince closed and locked his door.

She should have found out more of what was going on here, but so far, she'd only found more questions. Despite all her clever codes and strange knowledge gleaned from her books, Penrose hadn't been clever enough to uncover this.

The princess of Aloster spun around to face him. "What are you doing? Our marriage will be null without his word," she reminded him.

A priest or priestess was said to be the eyes of the gods. Wherever they were, so were they. It was sacrilege to marry in the absence of one.

The prince smiled at her. "I think you'll find they'll believe me. The gods are with me where I go, too."

Penrose took a step backward. His room was dim except for fading lanterns hanging from the walls in a few places. The curtains on the windows had been drawn. The entryway to the balcony was open, however, and the last of the sun's rays limned the room in a golden light.

He crossed the distance between them. Suddenly, his hand was in her hair, stroking through it.

"I thought I told her not to do this," he murmured, shaking out the flowers and gems woven into the small strands hidden in her hair. His thumb stopped and slid from her strands towards the edge of her jaw to bring her face to his.

"So, Penrose, are you going to marry me?"

Penrose took another step back, this time towards one of his hanging lanterns. More ornaments fell from her loosened strands as she moved.

Her heartbeat was louder than her words. "Give me the secret to the medicine, and I'll agree to marry you here and now. I'll excuse the other things."

The prince looked at her askance. "Other things? What do you mean?"

Her cheeks burned. Had she been wrong? Had she assumed malice when there had been nothing but unhappy accidents?

"You've been keeping me here," she said, though her voice shook far too much for her liking. Penrose swallowed. Embarrassment was not a strong enough word.

They hadn't even married yet, and she was acting like a paranoid ass and generally assuming the worst of others.

The prince's eyebrows came together. "What do you mean? You've been free to leave anytime, my love. Never have I posted guards outside your room or kept you locked away in some dungeon."

"Of course not—"

Penrose bit into her tongue. She'd done it. She'd ruined things.

It was then that she saw something glimmer in the stone fire pit on his balcony. But neither coal nor ashes glimmered.

As the evening sunlight hit it, it prismed for barely a moment. But Penrose knew what it was—or rather, once had been.

Her reading glasses.

The problem was, he'd followed her gaze and realized what she knew. The knowledge that couldn't be convinced away.

"If you could have remained the good girl you were supposed to be, it wouldn't have come to this," he said.

She couldn't move. She couldn't do anything. Penrose felt a shiver come over her skin. Her breath was locked in her lungs.

As he angled his head to the side, Penrose watched as the flame of the nearest lantern cast a strange, flickering light over his face. Part of the light reached his eyes, but it seemed as if the dark color of his irises absorbed it without reflecting it. "There will be no terms. No conditions."

He was within arm's distance of her now.

"Marry me," he continued, "or the prisoners—our guests—will die. I'll let the cure fail."

Penrose was in a nightmare. It was the only explanation before her.

But her brain showed her the answer before her body could even draw breath.

This is why he accompanied every dosage of the curse's medicine. She stared. *He controls it. But how?*

Eventually, her mouth forced words out. "Who are you?"

The prince's tight expression suddenly dissolved into a half-grin. He walked around his room, around her, like they were having a conversation about trade routes or the direction of the wind.

"All that matters to you, my rose, is that I'm the one with power." His fingers grazed the spines of the books lined up on his bookshelves. "And whether you're going to allow those below to die a horrible death."

"You can't—" It was impossible. She stared at him. Was it?

She needed to buy more time. She needed to think.

"The medicine," she said as she started backing away from him in the same manner as his casual gait. "You have a way of reversing it. Nulling it."

He only smiled. "Try again."

She thought harder. Penrose remembered what she'd read about the antidote to poisons like belladonna.

"They need a second dose," she guessed. Her back hit the bookcase.

He was too close to slip away from, but he merely stopped in front of her. Out of his silver and black tailored coat, he pulled a vial with clear liquid.

The cure.

He tossed the glass to her, and she barely caught it before it hit the books behind her. She stared down at it. Shaking it in her fist revealed the same thing. She unstoppered the bottle, but there was no smell.

She looked from him to the glass. It couldn't be true.

The words were tight in her throat. "Is this a joke?"

None of it made sense. She'd seen the sleeping curse before. If they'd all been acting, they were damn good at it.

There was nothing but water in the glass.

His eyelids closed halfway as he took in the fit of her wedding dress. "Nothing I do is a joke."

She felt herself go cold like she'd been standing outside the castle in a snowstorm. "Why are you keeping me here? How did you find out about my condition? My parents would have never told you that."

"You think yourself sharp, but you don't see what's in front of you." His eyebrows rose. "You're here, my rose, because I need you. I couldn't risk the chance that you'd leave me. You're here because I chose you."

"Our parents chose—"

"Would have preferred such an alliance for their eldest, wouldn't they have?" he interrupted.

Penrose stared until she could respond. It took her several seconds, though it was only one word.

"Lesabeth."

Somehow, he'd done it. He'd hurt her sister.

Perhaps he'd even caused her to become cursed with the sleeping disease.

He didn't speak. Instead, he smiled at her like they were still having a pleasant conversation.

Penrose's blood throbbed in her veins. It was time to act. She was no warrior like Lesabeth had been.

But maybe she could borrow her sister's courage.

"My rose." At once, his fingers were lifting her chin. Wildly, Penrose wondered how he couldn't see her plan in her eyes. He continued, "Since you don't seem to be moved for the lives of our hostages, I am aggrieved to inform you that there is another."

In the same second that Penrose jerked her arm towards the prince's head—the same arm that held the glass of useless water—the prince pulled the curtain from what she'd assumed to be a window.

He'd underestimated her. It was the only explanation for how she'd gotten the hit so squarely against his head.

Glass shards rained on the floor like diamonds. The water soaked both their wedding outfits.

On the other side of the curtain was an iron bird cage hanging from the ceiling. Inside it was Sorrowtail.

In the dimness, the glint of cold steel caught on the firelight.

Chapter Eight

The Lost Tower and the Truth

Malik tested his binds again. By now, it was more from habit than hope of escape. This was the king he was dealing with, not one of his father's competitors.

His hands were bound at the base of his back. It was only by the grip strength of his thighs that kept him upright on the horse they'd saddled him to. Kingsguard surrounded their caravan party on all sides.

Night had fallen since they'd set out, and there seemed no hope of stopping until they got wherever in the hell the king was leading him to. In addition to treating his wounds, they'd fed him and given him water, but Malik suspected that was only because they couldn't have their hired mercenary passing out.

It had been a hard day's ride from Belnya prisons, but they hadn't gone due north into the cities of Aloster like he'd anticipated. Instead, the sun had receded too quickly into its hiding place. As if even it couldn't bear to look upon him for longer than was necessary.

They were headed east.

He could feel it in the air when they passed through the last of the badlands surrounding Belnya.

Shadows fell across them. The rough, scarred earth gave to grasslands. They were close to what had once been the kingdom of Cavana. About a century ago, a single king united them under one rule. After years of inter-warring and other politics that Malik didn't bother himself with, the-then prince of Cavana had married the crown princess of Aloster. She'd succumbed shortly after to somnus. Soon after that, the joint forces under one banner of the king had half-conquered, half-negotiated-the-surrender-of what was his ancestors' homeland.

His Karsian ancestors had fought in the wars, too, but none of them had been lucky enough to marry a royal from another country and die young, ensuring a peaceful transfer of power. No, his people had been forced into this place. It had been the only way not to die out from the sleeping disease.

Not that doing any of that had stopped somnus.

"Keep a loose perimeter about us for the moment. He has no weapon."

Malik looked over to see the king's mount ride up to his horse. As he'd commanded, his kingsguard spread to a wide and loose circle around the two of them.

Malik took it in with interest. Secrets were always worth something, even if only for blackmail.

Especially for blackmail, he considered while side-eyeing the king. Also, there was the assumption that he wasn't a weapon in himself.

Malik didn't bother bowing or showing deference to the king of Aloster. He was tied up. If he wanted a groveling dog, perhaps he shouldn't have tied him up so effectively.

Besides, he was a convicted man. Why should he act differently?

"Have you heard of the Lost Tower?" the king asked after a moment passed in which it was clear Malik wasn't going to initiate a conversation or attempt a bow.

Malik swept a quick look around. Night had fallen properly by now and he'd only had the angle of the sun to go on, but he was fairly certain of which corner of the map they were in.

There wasn't supposed to be anything here. It used to be the holding for the previous king of united Aloster—this man's father—before he'd been crowned. Malik didn't particularly care about that.

"No," he said honestly.

The king kept his gaze forward. "The tower is ensorcelled by an old spell which makes it nearly impenetrable. The magic is strong. Enough so that you should consider the tower one of your opponents. The other is a witch, deep inside its heart. Gain entry inside, kill her, and you're a free man."

Malik was silent for several paces. Flying insects buzzed at his feet and eventually made their way to his face.

"How many?" he asked.

"You're referring to …?"

"How many condemned men have died before me?" Malik said, his voice flat. "How many have you come to this arrangement with?"

It was the only answer that made sense. It was clear in the way they treated him that they all would have been more comfortable leaving him in the pile of rotting bodies back in Belnya prisons.

The answer was that he was their last choice. Malik had seen the almost-routine way they'd gone about this. There'd been little discussion as to the route they'd take. The king had barely offered orders to his guard.

"The way has been travelled before," Malik said, his chin pointing to the ground ahead of them. "Too recently for coincidence."

In the silence between them, Malik continued, "It would have been easy at first. Pull any prisoner slated for execution that had shown any preference for getting his hands bloody." He paused and guessed some more. "But they've all failed."

The bugs threw their hard carapaces against Malik. They felt like pebbles with wings.

Hell better not have these, either.

"What do you want?" The king's voice was dull. It was clear that he hated having to deal with the likes of him.

Malik resisted a smile at that. *Good.*

"What I require is not immunity for crimes I have committed alone. What I require is a blind eye to the business proceedings of my entire family," Malik said. "No arrests. No charges. No investigations. They will go untouched."

At this, the king glanced at him. It was a quick thing and barely noticeable in the dark, but he didn't miss it.

The beetles trying to swarm around him crawled in Malik's hair. He let the quiet stretch between them. Too many people were uncomfortable with silence, which made it a valuable weapon.

Before Malik gave up on hearing his answer, the king spoke again. He looked forward this time, as if their conversation was over and he were speaking to someone else now.

"A century ago, my young father imprisoned her to seal her power. She is not the source of somnus. But she is the reason for the curse's degradation from what it once was—a deadly but merciful disease. Instead of the torture it now is."

"She sleeps, but she absorbs the nightmares of those afflicted with somnus. She has grown in power from them. She has stewed in them for years." The king paused before adding, "What we've observed is that the only way to kill her before she kills you is to slit her throat while she still slumbers in her magicked trance."

"The truth is," the king said, looking at him at last, "is that it doesn't matter what I concede to you for this. I could promise you the position of my right hand in my court. I could promise you my as-of-yet unconceived heir. I could promise you a droplet of moonlight nectar."

The king's words hung in the air as he spurred his mount forward. They were done talking. His meaning was clear.

Through the darkness, Malik saw the tower rise from against the black night sky where it touched the bottom of some low-hanging clouds. The temperature dropped. It felt as if the sun had left this place for longer than a few hours.

For the first time in a long while, Malik couldn't think of an answer to his opponent's taunts.

Chapter Nine

A Promise in the Dim

Prince Cassius's smile was gone. A line of blood ran from somewhere near his temple to the edge of his jaw. It hadn't knocked him unconscious like she'd intended.

She'd only pissed him off, it seemed. But a part of her wanted to do more than that. If what he said about Lesabeth meant anything, she wanted to do much more.

The knife he'd produced was small, but even from paces away, Penrose guessed that it was sharp enough.

Sorrowtail was at the bottom of the cage, his eyes closed and his injured wing pressed tight to his body while his other one was spread near his head. He wasn't moving.

A sickly feeling lifted in Penrose's stomach. He was healthy and flying not long ago at her wedding ceremony.

"What have you done to him?" The words came from somewhere deep inside of her that she hadn't known existed.

"Nothing that's permanent, though that can be remedied." The prince drew the edge of the knife against the base of his thumb. The small nick dewed blood.

"The Karsian woman with the child. You wanted to help her, didn't you?" He'd walked to her side as he talked.

She couldn't speak. There was a way out of this. There was a way she could save them and escape with Sorrowtail. She just hadn't seen it yet.

A bead of his blood landed on her dress. She watched as it soaked through it, spreading through the gauzy layers.

This time, he used the flat edge of the knife to lift her chin and force her gaze on him. "I don't need a blade to hurt them, Penrose." He waved it in front of her face. "This is just so you understand me clearly. You do, don't you?"

I have to escape. I'll take the cage and run.

But I can't make it down all those stairs to get out of here. He's ensured that.

"Yes." She breathed. "How long?" Her throat was tight, but she forced herself to say more. "How long have you planned this?"

She was going to try to get to the hostages first. A group of them against the prince ... or even the prince and his parents ... *It might be possible.*

He smiled, and the dribble of blood ran into the dimple of his cheek made by the expression. The effect was grisly.

"Long enough. You were too important to me not to get."

She had to keep him talking. It was her only chance to get out.

"And why would that be?" She glared at him. "If it's Aloster you want, I haven't even been crowned yet. The king and queen aren't going to just surrender the rule of their country like this." She pulled in an unsteady breath. "They will fight. I can promise that."

It was her only gleam of hope. Her parents couldn't be threatened. Penrose shifted towards the bird cage as she spoke, praying that he didn't notice the movement.

"Perhaps you're right," Cassius said, "but I have even more uses for you than simply as my queen."

She froze. It was worse if she didn't know what was to be her fate, she decided. Much worse.

Her eyes went to Sorrowtail's cage. It didn't matter. She was getting them both out, and they were freeing the hostages.

Her heart skipped a beat. She'd gone too long without disguising her intent with more conversation.

But he didn't seem concerned. "If you're going to try it, then you'd better get on with it. We don't have all day to be wed, I'm afraid."

That was when she realized. The knowledge sat inside her and turned her stomach like poorly prepared food.

All those people out there … None of them will believe me.

Penrose remembered their stares and the barely concealed whispers that ran from behind their hands. And then there had been her outburst about her parents. They already thought her an emotional mess.

And Sheriline does, too.

If she reneged on this agreement now, Penrose realized what it would have looked like. Sheriline would have to tell them that she'd seen Penrose in his rooms and lied about it.

That she'd been trying to steal secrets.

But beyond those reasons and the lives of the hostages, Penrose knew she couldn't turn away from this. She'd never been able to.

Somnus had spread exponentially through her kingdom throughout the past several years. If there was any hope of curing it or—gods' will—stopping it for good, Penrose had to pursue it.

Even if it meant sacrificing her happiness.

Penrose removed the golden ring from around her finger that had been given to her by her mother for this reason many years ago. She stepped forward.

"My Rose." His eyes absorbed the light of the dying lanterns around them. "Finally."

"I will marry you." She held her opposite hand out for his ring. She thought of her sister. Of Sorrowtail. "But assure yourself that I will never love you."

In the back of her mind, she made a silent vow to accompany the spoken one.

And I'm going to stop you from hurting more people. As long as I live, I will always foil you.

Even if it kills me.

His ring was silver and cold as she took it. As Penrose moved to fix hers onto his digit, biting into her tongue all the while, something happened.

He acted too quickly. In a blur, his hand was in a vice grip around her wrist, cutting off the circulation to her hand.

Penrose cried out in pain, her other hand going for his face to scratch at it, when he pinned both of her arms behind her back.

"What are you *doing*?" She wheezed the words.

The emotion had rippled across his features with ferocity. There was no other word for it besides wrath.

Where she'd expected a scream came words out of his tightly controlled lips.

"What did you say, Penrose?"

Because of the tone he took when he said her name, it sounded unfamiliar to her ears. She'd been playing with fire before.

This was a bonfire.

Her blood thundered in her ears. *Go back to who you were before. Back to ignorance.*

But she couldn't. Not when the one who'd understood her the best had left this world … because of *him*.

Penrose bared her teeth. "I vow it on my life."

"Take it back!" When the prince roared the words in her face, the lights struggling in the lanterns around them flickered out at once.

Penrose swallowed her fear. Her thoughts were stronger than the terror coursing through her, and she simply had to remember it.

I will use the darkness to my advantage. At the same time, she started to pull against his hold on her.

"I will *never*," she growled back.

But he worked faster than she could. The thumb of his free hand found the center of her forehead. Penrose didn't dare breathe as she watched something happen that she couldn't explain.

From the empty air came a haze of blue light that hovered over her head. Slowly, like it was dripping over an invisible sphere that circled them, it seeped to the floor.

"Then here you'll stay to the end of your cursed days ... until something loves *you* back." Without stopping to breathe, he added, "And may that something be a monster even worse than me."

Although Penrose didn't stop fighting until she slid to the floor in a slump, her eyes closed well before that.

In the seconds before the sleeping curse took her, she thought of the emptiness waiting on the other side of it and craved it.

Chapter Ten

Shattered

Malik's muscles strained with the effort of pulling his weight up the rope they'd *graciously* given him to scale the structure. The entrance at the base had been long ago blocked, according to the king.

Holy hells, but this damned tower was tall.

Sweat prickled at the back of his neck. He didn't need to turn around to see his men training their weapons on his back. He could almost smell the gunpowder that they so wished they could use on him.

If he gave up, they were going to shoot him. If he indicated for any moment that he was going to run tail and escape, they were going to hunt him down.

But there was no need. Killing was what Malik did best.

The rope he'd scaled already hung under him, swaying against the tower in the breeze. Already, deep calluses had formed into his hands. He'd be surprised if they weren't bloody by the end of this.

The tower's exterior had been battered by the winds and elements for decades. Parts of it had crumbled, though Malik suspected there was more to it above him where the vines that encircled it were thickest.

He shoved himself to the left suddenly, nearly scraping half his face on one such thorn-laden vine. He swore into the wind.

It wasn't enough that his mark was a murderous witch. No, the entire—

Pain slashed through him, and Malik hung in the wind from the force of the attack. His teeth grinded in the back of his head as his hand went to the knife they'd supplied him for the witch.

But there was no sign of the king's soldiers attacking him from below. It would have been nothing short of a miracle to make that shot on the first try.

Because Malik was looking for it, he saw it when it happened for the second time. The cluster of thorny vines clinging to the tower's exterior shivered.

Malik drew the knife in the seconds before a length of vine broke from the cluster and whipped at him. The rope swayed from the force of their meeting, shoving Malik's body against the unforgiving side of the tower, but the thorns weren't done.

More of the vines broke from their cluster, moving like snakes on the wind as they lashed at him from all directions. Malik's palm dug into the rope as he held tight to it with one hand and slashed back at them with his other.

He didn't have enough hands. The vines broke past his one-handed defense and switched at his skin, dragging their thorns into his exposed flesh and cutting him.

Damn you and your unborn progeny.

This was what the king had meant when he'd said the tower would be as much of an opponent as the witch.

Malik swung at the vines lashing at him. The blade caught on some, but not enough. More of his blood dropped in *plops* below.

I can't do this. This is how they all died. Malik's teeth grinded together. He hadn't been hired to cut off the vining from the side of the tower. Even if it attacked him.

Malik slipped the long knife into the waist of his pants and hauled himself even faster up the rope that he dangled from.

He'd be damned if he was going to die here. He'd survived smotherings, strangulations, and fights worse than this. He wasn't going to let *plants* kill him.

Malik pushed himself harder up the rope. Either he'd make it or he wouldn't. Maybe, if he dropped, they'd shoot at him.

Though what was more likely was that they wouldn't waste their bullets just to spare him from being aware when his bones shattered on impact of the ground.

At least, he wouldn't.

But as he pulled himself another arms-length up, he felt a prickly, searing pain around his throat. Malik thrashed against it, and his body smacked into the castle. The thorns tore into the skin at his throat as they tightened around him. The pain of the thorns digging into his skin merged with the loss of air in his lungs.

He couldn't decide if it would saw off his head first or choke him.

This was how they'd all died. Malik saw the pile of bodies again. He smelled the baking stench from Belnya.

His eyes rolled to the heavens, and he saw something.

One more stretch upward. If he could last that long, maybe there was a way inside. It was a window. Metal bars had lined it long ago, but part of the structure had rusted and fallen apart in the wind.

White spots danced in his vision, but he ignored them. Blood ran into his tunic as the vines tried to keep him in place by his throat. He jerked his body up the rope without breathing.

Before he could question whether or not he'd make it, Malik aimed and threw himself against the section of glass not protected by iron.

Glass shattered under his body.

Malik was still gasping for breath when he stopped rolling. Red splotches dotted the ground, and he shoved a hand at his neck.

Still attached.

He pulled out the thorns as much as he could and threw them on the ground where the glass had rained. He was in. But at a cost.

A shard from the window had buried itself into his forearm. A deep throbbing warned him against removing it—at least not without the price of significant blood loss.

Malik looked around for the first time since he'd landed on the floor inside one of the tower's rooms. His hand remained like a cage around the wound.

This ... was a wedding.

What the hell?

Distrust buzzed in his skull, but he ignored it for now. All around was dust and banners from forgotten kingdoms. Aloster still existed, of course, though it was the old emblem. But there were also the emblems from what had once been Cavana and Karsia.

Malik needed to press forward. He didn't have time for this.

He tore a piece of Aloster's banner as he passed by the hanging tapestry. He gritted his teeth, and, before he could change his mind, his fingers dove into the wound. They fumbled in the warmth until he found the shard. At once, he wrapped the cloth around it tight enough to staunch it. His fingers on that arm tingled.

It would do for now. Ragged breath filled him.

Malik ran to the doorway out of the room which led to a winding stairway. A new plot was forming in his mind. If he got out of this alive—a heavy *if*—he was going to force the king's hand.

He would get what he wanted.

No matter what.

This witch was in for a big surprise.

Chapter Eleven

Greedy

Malik ignored the pain screaming through his body. He'd woken a day ago prepared to die. So why was living so much harder?

It's always harder, he considered.

As the last of his energy gave, he reached what he realized was the final stair. Puffs of air left his lips.

She'd better truly be enchanted to sleep. This lumbering is enough to wake corpses.

A cavernous room stretched before him. Among shelves were lanterns long extinguished. They hung along the walls in regular intervals, though they weren't necessary.

Windows that stretched from the ceiling to the floor let in moonlight, that, against the inky sky, gave the room a blue cast. It was enough to clearly illuminate the bed in the center of the room.

She was as still as a corpse, and as Malik watched, she didn't even breathe.

His fist clenched around the handle of the long knife they'd given him. Was this some sort of joke? A test?

Maybe, he considered. *Maybe not.*

He couldn't hope that she was dead already. Malik had to proceed as if she could wake at any second.

Her long, blonde hair fell on either side of her. Her lashes were thick and the same color as her hair. They looked feathery on her face, and Malik wondered what color eyes were framed by them. She looked as if she were dreaming—and not like she had somnus, either. She was ... peaceful.

Malik's eyebrows came together. It was time to stop being an idiot.

If this was the witch responsible for the torture that was somnus, then he'd best not forget that if he liked his sanity. Nevermind how she looked.

Malik crouched and fully pulled the knife out of his pants' waist. She faced the other direction, but he didn't want to take any chances.

Not if he was going to take her hostage.

It was the only way he could guarantee he got what he wanted from the king. Otherwise, if his family wasn't safe, his body might as well have been rotting in the sun in the pile at Belnya prisons.

His feet were careful and practically noiseless. He needed to be quick if he was going to pull this off, like a spring-release trigger.

The moonlight from the windows had spread across the floor like bath-water. One more step, and he'd leave the last of the room's thick shadows and come into the only source of light. Malik didn't have to think. There was no other way forward for him.

As he stretched a boot towards the light, he heard a noise in the center of the room. Malik clenched his teeth together and pulled himself against the shadows once more.

He waited, but nothing happened. He considered the possibility that he'd imagined the noise.

But then he noticed it. Where there had been a crushing silence before ... *there* it was. It was the sound of air moving.

She was breathing.

Malik's nostrils flared. He'd wasted too much time. The witch was awake, and his plan was going to fail.

He was going to die. And not in a way in which his father would have reclaimed him, post-mortem. He was going to die like a dog here. Alone, nameless, and disavowed by his own family.

Screw the plan. There's only one way out.

Sudden motion stopped him. Malik froze as he watched something rise up into the air above the witch. In a flurry of blue feathers, a bird had appeared from nowhere.

Malik could hardly see from where he'd shoved himself behind a writing desk just past the light of the moon. He knew that as soon as he exposed his position, it would be over.

What the hell?

But he couldn't stop himself from doing it. He didn't understand the noises that had suddenly filled the silent, cavernous room.

As he watched, Malik realized that the bird had landed on the witch and woken her fully. But she …

She was *laughing*.

The girl was scratching at the bird's feathers, and his black eyes were fixed entirely on her until he closed them in what seemed to be pleasure.

"You're healed now. I don't understand," she said with a shake of her head. She brought herself to a sitting position, and Malik almost lost sight of her face.

When the bird opened his eyes again and narrowed them at her, she snorted at him. "Sorrowtail, you prideful creature. To be injured is not a failing."

The small songbird gave a noise that sounded like the closest thing it could manage to a squawk, bouncing backwards from her chest to her leg like it had been mortally wounded.

The part of him that wasn't an idiot screamed at him to do it now. He was a fair shot when it came to darts. He was confident he could throw the knife into the back of her head from this distance. It would be instant.

He'd have to reckon with her familiar afterward, but he thought he could handle the bird.

He would be free. His family, too, possibly.

And yet, he couldn't move. Something worse—something utterly nonsensical occurred to him then.

He didn't want to kill her.

He wanted to protect her.

He wanted ... her.

Not in the way that his father had tried to procure women for him before. The ones who bartered the use of their body for his father's funds. The ones who saw him as nothing but the spawned devil of House Ezar. The ones who drugged themselves to get through with fucking him.

No, this wasn't the same at all.

She was whole. Laughing. Happy. And she'd pissed off the most powerful man in Aloster enough to make him want to kill her.

No matter who she was, to command that much anger was power.

Don't be dense. She'll gut you as soon as you make yourself known.

But if that wasn't the way to go, what was?

Yesterday, he thought his death would come as his severed head hit the blood-stained ground of Belnya prisons with the stench of bodies still filling his nostrils.

Even if he had to go, how much preferable would it be to die with the boot of a beautiful girl on his neck, crushing his windpipe?

Malik smiled. He was definitely going to Hell.

He stood out of his crouch and walked forward.

Chapter Twelve

Hired Mercenary

Sorrowtail jumped into the air where he'd been perched on her thigh. A sharp, unnaturally aggressive chirp left his beak.

In one motion, Penrose jerked upward, coming to her feet.

She'd thought this was more of her dream that she'd been having. Her body had felt heavy and her senses felt dim like they were in dreams. But as she blinked past the shadows enveloping the room's edges, she saw she'd been grievously mistaken.

She was awake. And not alone.

Her last memory assaulted her. Her betrothed—gods, her husband, now—had tricked her. He'd ...

What had he done to her? She'd been sleeping. Had that been ...

She bared her teeth at the prince. "You'll stay there until you can explain yourself."

Although she had no weapon and no real threat other than the keenness of her words, Penrose couldn't back down. He'd know how scared and utterly defenseless she was if she did that.

To her surprise, he stopped at her words. As the moonlight touched his face, she saw she'd been wrong.

This wasn't Cassius at all.

His hair was a dark brown, matching the tone of his sun-kissed skin that was occasionally marred by a stretch of scar tissue. From his features, she could see he was clearly Karsian.

Even at stillness, it was impossible to ignore the muscles under his clothes. The clothes themselves were ragged and barely holding a stitch before her eyes, and a handmade tourniquet was wrapped around his upper arm. But it was his eyes that arrested her most of all.

They were a warm chocolate brown and probably a source of annoyance for someone who otherwise held himself like he would and could strangle a bear.

Penrose stopped herself. It was the adrenaline that had fueled such thoughts, and she needed to start thinking rationally. She needed to do something.

Who is he? Her heartbeat thundered too fast. She felt like she was going to pass out. *How did he get here? What does he want?*

She didn't recognize him from the wedding party below. *And he shouldn't have snuck in if his intentions were benevolent.*

But instead of rushing her like she was sure he would, the strange boy turned his hands so that what was in them was exposed to her. He was holding a long knife in one of them that looked to have been used recently.

"The king of Aloster sent me," the stranger said. "He wants you dead."

Before she could do anything or even think about those words, he continued, "But I don't feel like getting my ass handed to me. So, I came to you with an alternative solution."

He dropped the knife, and the sound echoed loudly in the prince's room.

No. Father would never. He wouldn't.

Penrose couldn't believe him. Even if her father and mother had missed her wedding and her pleas for help written in code to them, they didn't want her dead.

Even if they used me as a peace offering. So what? She swallowed. That didn't mean this.

Maybe ... Maybe the agreement between our countries fell through.

But her father would never want her dead. She was sure of that. Surer than anything.

"I don't believe you," she said between her teeth.

She was prepared for his attack, but instead, he kicked the knife on the floor so that it spun in a slow arc to her. Her boot caught its handle.

Without taking her eyes off him, she bent to pick up the weapon.

You're not that smart of an assassin, are you? But she bit her tongue when she looked down at it.

Carved into the pommel was a most familiar emblem. It was her family's crest—the one worn exclusively by members of the Alostran royal family.

There could be no doubt. Only three people were allowed to possess such an object.

Her. Her mother. And her father.

Penrose closed her fist around the dagger to keep her hands from shaking. It was hers by right, anyway.

She looked up at him. She was going to get to the bottom of things. Of it all.

"Where are they? The others below?" She swallowed. "Are they safe?"

He looked at her like she'd grown a third eye. "Your tower's empty." He tested the reach of his injured arm as he spoke. "The king and his men have surrounded the base, however. They are prepared to shoot."

"At?"

"You," he said. "Or me, if I don't emerge with proof of killing you." He cocked his head at her.

Penrose stared back at him. He was either a lunatic or ...

And even if he was, she couldn't get out of the tower by herself. Her traitor lungs had seen to that by now.

Silence stretched between them as she considered her options. *Talking with him doesn't mean believing what he's saying. And short of falling out a window, there's only one way out of this place.*

"Then let's hear your plan," she said. "*Mercenary.*"

Chapter Thirteen

Mongrel

Malik's body was sore from the journey down the endless steps to the tower's base. His legs ached from the strain, but he couldn't stop now.

As he came through the entry doors at the very bottom of the tower, he felt every ache and bruise and cut in his body.

You shouldn't have done that. Idiot, he bade himself.

But it was too late to change what he'd done now.

Clicks filled the night air. He was reminded for one ridiculous second of the beetles that had attacked him on his ride here.

No. This was the sound of too many weapons training themselves on him. The barrels of revolvers watched him back. Moonlight glinted on steel.

"Drop that and keep your hands open," commanded King Cassiel.

Malik did as he was told, and the stained burlap sack thudded too solidly against the ground. His teeth grinded in his skull.

"Is this the welcome of a hero? I've done what you asked, your Majesty. She's dead," Malik announced.

The Alostran king ignored him, instead gesturing at his guards.

The king's men rushed forward to grab the sack, but Malik side-stepped them. He'd intended to grab the pistol at the waist of the closest one, but his wounded arm had failed him at the last moment.

Instead, the guard held the cold metal barrel under Malik's chin. He looked the man in the eyes.

"Are you going to tell your children about this when you get home? How you blew up the head of Malik Ezar?" He smiled. "Something tells me you're the gloating type."

He could feel the man's grip on the gun shake, even if his dark eyes hardened at Malik's words. Malik wondered if it was fear or anger there but then decided it didn't matter.

"Your command, my sire?" the guard said through his teeth.

"Hold him," said the king, "until we verify it."

Malik felt the heat rise in his veins. "I need proof of our agreement. Now."

A sharp pain erupted across his shins as another guard kicked at him. Malik grunted and held himself back from collapsing.

"And I need proof that you've made good on your side of the deal," the king said. He nodded for his guards to open the sack.

A rattling cacophony broke the silence as her clothes and pieces of bones tumbled out of it. Her dress had been torn in spots, such as the long gash across the stomach. Blood had since dried to a mottled brown there, but plenty of it was fresh. It formed fat dribbles that fell slowly to the ground.

King Cassiel stared without a word. The amount of blood on the bones and clothes was too much for any one person to have lost and remained whole. At least, for long.

The guard informally assigned to Malik pressed the gun harder into his skin. "Is this a joke? His Majesty knows that's not the witch," he said.

Malik couldn't talk. There was too much pressure underneath his chin to do so. Malik stared at the night sky above him, waiting for the deafening sound that would ring in his ears and signal his death.

"It's her," said the king.

Malik chanced a slight twist of his head, and to his surprise, the guard eased his hold on him. It looked like the king had sampled some of her blood and decided that it tasted like her.

King Cassiel stared at the smear on his hands.

Malik shrugged out of the hold of the soldier, aiming a glare at him. "There was some spell on her. That happened when she died."

"Your Majesty?" The guard at his back looked to Cassiel.

A boy who looked like he attended to the horses had appeared at the king's side with a cloth. The bastard king wiped his hands on the rag as he spoke to Malik.

"You've done exactly as I anticipated the son of Raphael Ezar would. Truly, you are as bloodthirsty as they say," he said.

Malik noticed how his words danced the line between praise and insult. But he didn't care about that. He massaged his skin where the barrel of the gun had dug into.

"Drop of moonlight, I believe your words were," Malik said, this time cracking his neck. He was going to have to get one of his father's women to get that kink out of his shoulders. Everything else aside, they were pretty good with their hands.

If he allows you to speak to him again. Malik ignored that thought, though.

But King Cassiel was silent as tremors came from him. Malik didn't realize why until he heard the laughter.

He abruptly stopped and said, "The only way through the barrier was if her true love match walked through it and woke her up. And to believe that it was none other than this filth."

King Cassiel looked at him the way he'd looked at him during his fight at Belnya prisons. Like he was his prized attack mongrel. "I knew the one fated to her would be a monster. It's why I picked from among the worst to do this. Something that could be bribed so easily into attacking her."

The buzzing of the corpseflies droned in the back of his skull again. The bastard's words didn't make sense. His thoughts became flies, too. Dull. Incessant.

He tricked me.

No. Malik had allowed the bastard to trick him.

He just hadn't cared enough to resist it.

"No, you have done exactly as I'd hoped. Better," the king said, "than I had reason to. Better than the dozens before you."

Heat gathered at Malik's neck. This was how he got before a fight. He jerked to grab the revolver, but it found the back of his head before he could find it.

The buzzing in his head hadn't stopped. To the contrary, the thoughts had grown louder and louder.

True love. Barrier.

Fated.

"We had a deal." The words were grinded through Malik's teeth. He clung to that which should've made sense.

But you always knew the king was planning something else, didn't you? That he was keeping secrets?

But it hadn't mattered if he died in the tower before. Or if he killed the girl at the top of it. Why did it matter now?

"Unfortunately," said King Cassiel, "your usefulness has come to an end. Or rather, you are more useful to me dead than alive now. Dead, and you're much less a problem after you know all this."

Malik waited for the blast. Would he feel the carnage rip him apart?

In his last moments, he wondered if his father would even look at his mangled body. Or if he'd have one of his men dispose of him with the others his father had killed.

After Malik's failing, would he even claim him in death?

He didn't close his eyes. He wanted the bastard king to see his eyes and be haunted by them when he was dead.

Keeping them open was the only thing that tipped him off to what was about to happen. And Malik still didn't believe it when he saw it.

Chapter Fourteen

Black Metal

"You're not him. You're not the king of Aloster."

Penrose's voice was like a wind chime in a storm. It shouldn't have carried, but it did.

She didn't have a plan. This wasn't what the two of them had agreed on. Penrose wasn't sure why she had stopped and turned to look one last time at the strange Karsian boy who had carried her in his arms down all the stairs in the tower.

The same one who had claimed to have been hired to kill her.

She'd been careful. She had waited for the moment when this clearly unstable and violent criminal had demanded something of her. Or tried to take her against her will.

And yet, none of that had happened.

She'd listened to his clearly wrong version of events. She wasn't quite sure if he was a pathological liar or truly believed in what he was saying. Her father would have never ordered her death.

But she had turned around. And watched.

Penrose should have been running. Malik—that was the mercenary's name—had told her to.

After they'd found the skeletons in the tower, Penrose wasn't sure what to think had happened during her wedding. But she'd agreed to his plan on the condition that he helped free her.

She'd even bled some for the ploy and changed out of her dress. It had all seemed the ravings of a boy going through mental trauma—that was Penrose's working diagnosis—but she saw now she had been wrong.

It was real. The king had wanted her dead.

But this wasn't the Alostran king. This man was not her father or any of her kin. He was a stranger to her.

And he was going to kill Malik.

He was truly hired to murder me. And they're going to kill him for it.

Time seemed to slow for her. Their heads whipped to where she stood among the forest's edge in the shadow of the tower.

Her freedom had been steps away. All she'd had to do was run. Run and not look back.

She hadn't even been able to do that.

The man that the others regarded as the king stared at her then. Penrose felt she couldn't breathe.

It wasn't that she knew him. But he looked at her with features so twisted that it would have been impossible not to think otherwise.

No one could be so enraged at someone they didn't know.

None of them seemed to know what to do at the sight of her. Somehow, they'd all been convinced that that bag of bones had been her. Malik had seemed unhinged before he'd suggested it, but she'd gone along with his plan in absence of a better one.

What is going on?

Her eyes went to where Malik was. Something was held against his head, and he'd been forced to his knees.

"Run," she shouted at him.

It was that second when the others seemed to come out of their collective trance.

The man claiming to be the Alostran king ordered his men to fire on her, and while some of them took swords from their sheaths, others aimed at her with black metal contraptions that had been slung across their backs.

Penrose didn't wait to find out what they were. Her heart hammered inside her chest as she dashed back for the woods where she'd been heading. She hoped Sorrowtail was well away from her then. She'd urged him to fly to safety when Malik had helped them out of a relatively low window on the other side of the tower.

She wasn't sure if she could live with herself if something happened to her bird companion.

A series of noises louder than she'd ever heard pierced the air in rapid succession. Penrose ran harder, but her lungs protested, and she started to wheeze for air.

Not now. Please, just not now.

The trees around her shuddered as something hit their bark. A ringing started in her eardrums, beating down into them, and she could hear no longer.

But she couldn't go on. Dizziness assaulted her, and she wasn't pulling air inside her anymore.

I can't stop. I can't let them catch me here.

A strong grip found her arm, and her heart shoved into her throat. These people had demonstrated their willingness to kill. She was going to die here.

Malik's face appeared before her. He was saying something to her, but she could only hear ringing.

"Get us out of here," Penrose gasped between wheezing. "I don't care how. I'll pay you what he owed you. Just get us away."

In the blur of movement and shadow, she saw something in his hand. It was the machine that had been held against his head by the guard earlier.

With one arm, he took her by his waist so that his body half-hid hers. In his other hand, he aimed the black metal machine at something just behind her.

Burnt smoke filled her nostrils. Heat rose from the earth, and she realized.

They're burning the forest down.

Words were streaming from Malik's mouth. His finger pulled the machine's trigger, and another explosion of noise erupted near her.

This time, it brought a true silence.

Chapter Fifteen

Better this Way

All of Penrose's body ached. She felt as if she'd been sleeping on rocks.

When she opened her eyes, she found that the truth wasn't so far from that. It was dark, and a light breeze tickled her exposed skin among her bandages.

The memories of how she'd escaped the tower hit her like a rock to the head then. She twisted where she'd been on the ground near a soggy fire pit and saw *him*. Her would-be assassin.

She froze. That wasn't all.

Malik's eyes were shut, and his breathing was slow and laborious. His breaths sounded like hers during one of her attacks.

She saw his face then. His golden skin had turned strange and pallid. Sweat droplets had coated his hairline.

Penrose rushed to his side. Whoever he was, he had saved her when it would have been infinitely easier to let her die. Even if he believed in odd delusions.

And maybe—she had the beginnings of a plan. Or at least a step forward.

She pressed the back of her hand to his forehead. His skin was too hot. Her pulse pounded in her veins.

He's sick from one of his wounds. It must have gotten in his bloodstream.

She was no healer. She hadn't even completed her studies in the area. But she had to try.

Penrose had no belongings of her own with her, so she dove into his pack. It was limited—in fact, she suspected that these things hadn't been his at all and that, during his escape, he'd stolen the items from those men and the false king.

The bag contained a few waterskins, a compass, a rolled map, small parcels of bread, and the cold, metal device he'd used to get them away from their pursuers. Her touch lingered just a moment before she slipped the small machine into the pocket of her trousers, careful to keep from touching the trigger point she'd seen him use to fire it.

Somehow, these people had technology that her father could have only dreamed of in his laboratories. She pushed the thought away. As soon as she got back to her parents, she would get to the bottom of who these people were.

And what Prince Cassius had done.

Don't you mean your husband, she thought, but it made her queasy to think on it. She couldn't linger on that yet.

Penrose came to her feet again. There had been nothing resembling medicine in their supplies, but she had to do something.

After uncapping one of the skins, she dribbled some water on a rag. It wasn't that cold, but it would be colder than his forehead. She placed it there as he gave a shuddering breath.

With a light touch, she tilted his head back and parted his lips. His breath blew into her face, and she swallowed. Unbidden, the memory of her first kiss sprang to mind.

Faster than she could blink, a fist encircled her wrist holding the container of water. His eyes flew open. The force exerted on her wrist made her drop the water, and it splashed all over him. He didn't seem to notice or care.

"What are you doing?" he demanded.

"You're sick," she said, pulling back from his grasp. "You have an infection."

"That doesn't answer my question," Malik said, but his hand sagged to the ground. He closed his eyes and let his head rest against the earth once more. "If you're going to kill me with magic, do me the decency of not dragging it out."

Penrose stared at him. *It must be the fever.*

"It's not magic. I'm trying to treat you, but we don't have any medicine. Where are we?"

Malik opened his eyes to squint at her. "Hm. Not a witch, then."

Delirious. He needs some water. It's all I can do right now.

She grabbed another of the full containers in one hand, but instead of trying to help him down it, she held it out for him to take it this time.

It worked. After a glance at her, he grabbed it and guzzled its contents.

"What do you want?" he said between gulps. "Why are you doing this?"

Because you helped me first.

But the unspoken words stopped on her tongue. She couldn't be so naïve anymore and assume other people's intentions were so golden. Doing so had almost cost her her life—and more importantly, her country.

Maybe it already has, she thought.

Instead, she said, "Because I'm hiring you."

***

Malik felt like his head was going to explode. A new wave of the fever washed over him.

This girl didn't know what she was getting herself into.

In his silence, she continued. "Your skills are for purchase, isn't that right? That man had already hired you." She angled a look at him. "I'll pay for your services. I'll need a guard to get where I'm going."

Malik was pretty sure the girl—what was her name again? Penrose?—was right. Something hadn't gone right from his wounds. It could have been from his fight at the prisons. It could have been from the magicked vines. It could have been from the glass shards he'd used his body to break apart or the king's men.

It didn't matter. He was in the grip of an infection.

But Malik had enough energy and awareness to realize how ludicrous it was. He laughed where he lay on the ground with enough force to make his abdomen hurt.

"You have no idea how expensive I am," he said to the girl. He had the pleasure of watching her reaction to that.

Redness sprang to her cheeks, filling them in nicely.

Despite the blush, she didn't flinch. "I happen to have a lot of resources. Including funds to pay your fees. However high they may be."

Malik jerked upright a few degrees. The haze had cleared from his brain just enough for some coherent thinking.

The girl was valuable to the king. *That* was worth a lot of money in itself.

The infection crouched on his brain, trying to muddy his thinking. But he could see the beginnings of a plan even through the smog inside him.

King Cassiel was untrustworthy and a bastard in more than one sense. He was going to pay for trying to make a fool of Malik and House Ezar.

No. He wasn't going to make a trade with the bastard king for some kind of clemency or payoff. Any hope of a deal between them had been long shot.

No one made a fool of him twice.

And something told Malik it wasn't just her desperation talking. That, perhaps, there was money here, too.

He looked at her. How much of what Cassiel had said was a lie and how much of it truth? The bastard king had said much, but scarecrows did like to talk.

"I'm not in the habit of making deals with unknown parties," Malik finally settled on. Even wracked with infection and fever, he had to keep his wits about him. There was no sense in losing his head over a girl when he'd only recently kept it attached to his neck.

Everyone in this life had a motive.

Malik rested against the dirt and closed his eyes. Sweat made his clothes cling to him. He focused on his words and the effect he needed to create with them. It was the only way to get them out at all.

"The horse I stole from them is just past the bushes concealing us. You're right—there is no medicine with us. When we ride, you will explain to me who you are." He opened one eye to look at her. "And we will talk of your down payment."

For perhaps the first time since they'd crossed paths, Penrose looked … pissed. Malik smiled at her expression.

The fair maiden casts aside her airs of amiability.

"If that's how you want to play it. Agreed," she managed through her teeth.

Malik rolled to his side as the headache bored further into his skull. It was better this way. Better that the girl start to understand just who she was dealing with.

Better that he prove more of Cassiel's lies rather than allow them to fester in his brain into truths.

Better.

Chapter Sixteen

The Forgotten Princess

Penrose stared at the map, waiting for it to rearrange itself into the correct boundary lines of the three kingdoms.

This is the product of a madman.

It was all wrong for a multitude of reasons. First and most obvious, Karsia didn't exist on it. The boundaries of the kingdom had been removed from this map and renamed south Aloster. Most of the identifying features and towns had been scrubbed from it, too. The only places that were named within its borders were a couple outposts and a *Belnya prisons* near what was supposed to be the border.

Second, the kingdom of Cavana—her husband's kingdom—had been reduced to the *province* of Cavana. But really, even Cavana was a part of Aloster on this map.

It was ridiculous.

Penrose sucked in a breath. A defective map was far from their worst problem now. Her hired help was before her on the horse, slumped against the horse's neck as they rode.

Another day had passed without medicine. And it showed on him.

They were about to lose the cover of night, but by her estimations, they should soon be within bounds of Aloster's crown city, Alsra. Her heart hammered faster at the thought.

It was a large city, but as soon as she got to the castle and her family therein, Penrose would be safe again.

Securing Malik's help had been insurance to get her there, although his state had deteriorated since she'd made the deal with him. He'd saved her life, though, and she owed him at least for that.

"When we ride, you will explain to me who you are. And we will talk of your down payment."

What an ass.

Penrose snuck a glance at him then. His eyes were shut, and his entire body felt like it vibrated with heat. He hadn't gotten the chance to interrogate her yet, and she didn't see it happening before they got to Alsra.

She shifted on the horse. It was hard not to ride pressed so close to him. His muscles heaved with every breath, showing exactly how defined they were. She reminded herself of his attitude again, and the distracting thought went away.

She watched the landscape flee around them while they rode near the river, and something stole her attention. Dawn had started to break along the horizon, and the first strands of daylight had begun to glance off the water.

While she'd noticed the ship in the distance earlier in the night, she hadn't seen it properly until then. She stared until the sight made more sense.

Heavy black smoke was rising from the bow. The ship was aflame.

Penrose urged their horse into a brisk gallop.

They're not too far from the shore, but the crew will need help. I have to check.

No matter that someone was trying to kill her. She glanced again at Malik and bit into her lip. It was harder to bargain away his time, but there was the chance that someone on that ship could use her help.

Their horse huffed, and she hated to ride him so hard. But they were close now.

Penrose stared some more. It didn't make sense.

The smoke appeared to be coming from a chimney built into the boat itself. Penrose allowed the horse to slacken their pace some. The dawn light illuminated the workers on the ship's stern. They appeared to be going to and from their assigned duties. Not one ounce of panic.

Penrose's hand went to the mechanical weapon shoved in the pocket of the trousers which she'd taken from Prince Cassius's rooms in the tower. She was careful not to jostle it overmuch and risk triggering it.

Her eyes went to the horizon before them. They were travelling off the path, but she could see what they were headed for. Out of the darkness emerged the shapes of buildings much larger than the ones Alsra had.

When she spoke, her voice was surprisingly even.

"Malik. What year is it?"

When he didn't answer for many minutes, Penrose was left to the horror of her own thoughts in the meantime.

He broke the silence with a croak. "It's been one hundred and thirty-five years since the sleeping disease began to spread." Though they were ringed with exhaustion lines, he opened his eyes.

Penrose kept her eyes on the river. And tried not to think.

And failed.

One hundred and thirty-five years since the curse started. Father fought in the first wars over it in his youth.

When the curse had been known for only a few years past.

I slept ... for a century.

Cassius caused this.

My husband.

She should have been forming a plan. She should have been trying to piece together the puzzle before her. She should have been breathing, at least.

My parents. There's ... they're gone.

It was why she hadn't recognized the king of Aloster.

Her fists were shaking. She shoved them in her lap. Her gaze shot to Malik's, and she saw he was still looking at her.

"Who is the king now? What happened to King Barinus and Queen Laurel?" Her parents. Penrose didn't recognize her own voice. It sounded hollow.

"I never cared to understand the politics of a people long turned to ash," he said. Penrose felt as if an arrow had pierced her chest at his words.

He closed his eyes before he spoke again. She wondered if she'd imagined the change in his tone or if it was wishful thinking. "They lived long lives. Likely due to the fact that they abdicated the throne to the prince."

"The prince?" Her throat felt tight around the words.

No. He can't be here. That can't be him.

"Cassius. The uniter." Even though Malik's eyes were closed again and his voice hoarse, she imagined a note of derision in his words.

She felt sickly. Penrose clenched her fists with enough effort to hurt.

But even though a rage powerful enough to make her dizzy filled her, something else hid behind it. It was the feeling of looking into the darkness.

And seeing something look back.

And hearing it scrape along the walls.

And feeling something breathe on her neck.

"How did he die?" she asked.

He had to be dead. He had to be gone.

Reduced to ash. Like everyone she'd once loved.

Malik didn't answer. In her preoccupation, their horse had stopped.

In the light of the dawn, she saw the soldiers watching. A group of them had been waiting for them outside the walls of Alsra.

The closest one pulled out the metal weapon that had been slung across his back and angled it before him. And aimed straight at them.

Chapter Seventeen

Monsters

Everything was hot.

Malik wished he could peel his skin off like lizards did.

You've lost it.

His stomach clenched. Someone was talking. Someone other than the girl.

It was his first indication that everything had gone to hell since he'd opened his eyes last. It was also his last chance to let the girl die and be on his way.

Malik opened his eyes in the same moment that he kicked the horse forward. The king's soldiers were already aiming their guns at them.

Everything was a weapon.

Penrose was yelling at him, but he didn't hear her. He shouted back at her, "Tuck your head and roll. *Now!*"

The ground pummeled his body, but it was still preferable to death. Penrose landed halfway on Malik, but he was on his feet again in a matter of seconds and her behind him. The horse had charged on the soldiers, but they wouldn't be distracted by that for long.

Bullets flew past, and one of the soldiers shouted over them.

"The girl is to be taken alive. Kill Ezar if he resists."

His body protested, but Malik didn't care. If they got their metal in him, he wouldn't be moving at all once he bled out.

Malik was on the one nearest to him, the soldier who had tried to fire on them. His fingers went for his eyes in a double jab. They came away bloody.

"You bastard," he shrieked at Malik, his other hand going for the trigger on his rifle despite the fact that Malik had at least temporarily blinded him.

But he needed to do more than that. Malik twisted the rifle in the soldier's grasp so that the stock hit squarely against his right temple. The soldier fell forward, but before Malik could wrestle the rifle from him, his body stopped working altogether.

Malik fell to the ground next to his downed opponent. His palms hit dirt, and he heaved.

When the barrel found his forehead, Malik still tasted the bile on his tongue.

***

Penrose's eyes couldn't stop swiveling. This was not her Alsra.

She found she couldn't focus on any one thing for long enough. The soldiers' horses were going too fast, but she caught peeks at massive buildings. Warehouses. Lantern posts dotted the street regularly, and strange, twitching light wavered from within them.

The air was harder to breathe in this Alsra, too. Even though the day had dawned over an hour ago, a dull grayness clung to the sky and obscured the new day.

They'd tied her wrists together behind her back. Short of trying to fall off the horse they'd tied her to, she couldn't do anything. Her eyes flicked to Malik, but they hadn't even bothered tying him down. He hadn't risen after he'd vomited and the soldiers had knocked him out.

At least, she hoped they'd knocked him out instead of the alternative. Each breath came tighter in her chest.

They were taking her to *him*. There could be no mistake.

No one was going to rescue her. No one was going to intervene.

No one even knew her in this world—except her controlling, manipulative husband. And he was about to get her back on a silver platter.

After a few moments, she became aware that two of the soldiers riding ahead of them were conversing and stealing glances back at their prisoners. She willed her mind to focus on their words. Anything was better than the thoughts left her now.

"He confessed to killing them all. All the healers in Alsra trying to cure somnus. And he was going to die for it. But the king made a deal with him instead."

The soldier's gaze left Malik's unmoving form. He'd caught her staring and listening. Penrose's heart shot into her throat.

The other soldier looked at his partner. His voice barely carried, but Penrose made out the words. "How long have you had it? How long do you have?"

He has the sleeping curse, Penrose realized. *But how is he awake? That's not how the curse works.*

The soldier stared into her face despite the fact that he was still speaking to the other man. "Not long enough to live with the consequences. You?"

The other soldier didn't even look back at them. "Bring her, too. I'll tell Arnoff he's resisting."

As it turned out, Penrose couldn't force herself to think of a plan when her brain wanted nothing more than to stop thinking.

The two soldiers splintered from their group and brought her and Malik to an alleyway between warehouses. Malik had remained unconscious, so they'd led the horse carrying him here. When they stopped, one of the men shoved Malik off the horse. His body thudded against the cobblestone ground.

Penrose darted forward to help him, but the other soldier grabbed her by her waist before she could make it to him.

"Let me go," she said between her teeth.

"He's not worth it," he whispered along her neck. She wanted to bite him for being so close to her.

But the knowledge of what he'd done sat inside her, stirring nausea in her belly. She'd known he was a mercenary and hired killer.

But this? Killing the healers trying to cure the sleeping curse?

Maybe it was time to face the person who Malik really was, after all. He'd tried to tell her, but she hadn't listened.

I can't believe it hasn't been cured in a hundred years. Her stomach flipped. There wasn't enough time to consider what had happened while she slept.

Gods, I lost what should have been my life.

This was not where she belonged at all.

The other soldier pulled Malik against the wall of the building next to them. He slapped him into wakefulness.

He wasn't doing well. His body shook under his weight as he opened his eyes. He opened his mouth and showed his teeth to his captor in a snarl.

The soldier spat in his face. "I want you to beg for your life. Now."

"Make me do it," Malik hissed.

Before he'd finished saying the words, the soldier pulled back his fist and punched Malik's stomach. Malik doubled over, spitting saliva mixed with blood on the stones.

Penrose's breath froze in her throat. No one deserved this.

He crouched near Malik. "No one will know you died here, Ezar."

Malik tried to stand, but the soldier kicked his side when he started to move again. The soldier continued, "Even the kingsguard hears the scuttering of rats. They say on the streets that your father disowned you. They suggest that he wouldn't even take revenge for you if you died."

"Stop it!" Penrose's words felt like they were ripped from her throat. "He's done."

There was only one way out of this for them. She had to save them both. She would.

The soldier attacking Malik looked at his comrade. "You're supposed to keep her in line."

Her captor tightened his hold on her, shoving her closer to him where he'd pinned her to him by the waist. His other hand went to her face. He traced the outline of her lips.

If only she could get her hands free, then she could save their lives. Even if she had to break herself a little to get there.

"Please," she whispered. "Tell him to stop. I'll do what you want."

The words tasted like poison on her tongue. She had a plan now, but what would be the cost of it?

"Is that right?" The soldier's breath was in her face again. He turned them so that she was shoved between him and the other wall. "Be careful what you promise for the sake of a monster, girl."

All she had to do was inch her bound wrists to the right a few degrees and she'd be able to pull out the weapon they hadn't bothered to check her for. The black metal machine that was shoved into her pocket.

But as soon as she started to move her wrists, his palm smacked them against the wall beside her. His other palm found her throat.

She couldn't even gasp, let alone call for help.

She was going to die here.

Dizziness consumed her thoughts as he pressed harder. But somewhere in the fog of her mind, she heard a voice.

"Get your hands off her."

Chapter Eighteen

Those that Crawl

"*O*r I'll remove them myself."

But Malik was already moving. The one who had sucker punched him was on the ground, unmoving.

He didn't concern himself with that one any longer. He didn't concern himself with anything but the *thing* between him and her.

Malik took the soldier attacking Penrose by his throat and lifted him into the air with both hands. Gasping sounds like futile attempts to breathe or perhaps plead for his life sputtered from the soldier's mouth.

Sweat soaked through his clothes, and he felt as if he were going to hit the ground at any moment. But he had enough energy for *this*.

He cocked his head at the bastard. "Is this how you like it? Rough?"

Malik lifted him higher until his feet dangled off the ground. But it wouldn't be enough until he watched the life drain from his eyes. Until he heard the last of his pathetic attempts to beg for mercy.

Malik wasn't quite sure what had happened. One moment, the other soldier had been kicking the guts out of him.

But then he'd seen her and what this piss-poor excuse of a man was doing to her.

It wasn't as if he'd owed her that. Rather, it was as if something had burst in his brain at the sight.

Well, he *was* broken. So, there was that.

Malik blinked the sweat out of his eyes. She was staring at him. He was doing this wrong.

"By rights, his ass is yours," he said over the man's gasps. Malik's chest heaved, but he didn't drop him. He raised one eyebrow at her. "Do you permit me to take his life?"

Penrose didn't move except for her eyes. They flicked from his face to the soldier he was suffocating. "No. No," she repeated. "Put him down."

Malik did as she said. He shrugged to himself. He'd dealt with the other soldier in his own way. But this one belonged to her, and he wasn't about to take that choice away from her.

It was an insult to take the blood of someone whose death was already spoken for by someone else.

His father had taught him that. Malik's back hit the other wall of the alley, and sweat poured like rivers down his body.

They had to move.

The man was face-down on the stones, broken enough that he wasn't moving except for shuddering breaths that made quiet gasping sounds.

Malik wanted nothing more than to join him on the ground. But he had to go on. They had to move. The other soldiers weren't going to leave them alone for much longer.

And if he was going to spend the money that he was making from her, he first needed to live long enough to do so.

With one shoulder still pushed into the wall, Malik gestured his chin in the direction they needed to go. "C'mon. I have a place."

Penrose came to her feet at last, and Malik turned to lead them out of the accursed alley. His legs were weak, but he pushed them to move. *Just a little farther.*

There was a sudden racket behind him. As he spun, he realized the stupid mistake he'd made. One of their rifles was within a few paces of the man he'd nearly choked to death.

The soldier's hand was already on the stock of the gun. It was too late. A bullet was always faster than a man, and Malik had been slowed and weakened from the beating and his sickness.

"That's enough." It was Penrose's voice.

Malik's gaze jerked to where she stood behind the man crawling on the ground. A revolver was in her hand, and she'd shoved it against the back of his head. The man who had attacked her froze and stared straight ahead at Malik.

He could see it in her eyes. This would break her. Even if she had the right to do it.

He locked away the newfound pride he had for her and stepped forward. If she was really from a different era, she couldn't have been familiar with firearms. But she'd already picked up how to threaten a man with one.

Good girl.

He kept that thought wisely to himself, too.

Sweat poured down his back, and his legs shook with the effort of holding him upright. He swallowed back the bile wanting to rise in his throat. There would be a time for that.

Malik held out one hand where he stood beside her. "Allow me to show you something."

She wasn't going to do it. She didn't trust him not to blow out the man's brains. After seeing that, she didn't trust him not to act as the monster that he was.

When she relented and gave Malik the gun, Malik couldn't decide if she'd changed her mind about him or the man.

The bastard remained still on the ground, but Malik could sense his eyes flicker to the rifle just out of his reach. Faster than a blink, Malik smacked the revolver against the back of his head.

This time, the bastard stayed down.

Chapter Nineteen

A Good Man

P enrose couldn't stop shaking. Perhaps it helped that they couldn't stop moving or else they'd be hunted like rabbits. If it weren't for that, she wasn't sure if she would have been able to take another step forward after what had happened in the alley where they'd left the soldiers.

Malik was silent except where he directed them forward. She knew he didn't intend for her to see how his body tremored when they stopped in the shadows or how he had to support himself against light posts and brick walls.

She'd hired a murderer to protect her. She supposed she shouldn't have been surprised at that since he should have killed her in the tower.

Why didn't he?

Clearly, he had no qualms with violence. Even ill as he was, his body moved with the grace of someone more accustomed to shadows and daggers than daylight.

Daylight had started to infiltrate the gray hanging above the city. Penrose couldn't stop staring at the foreign world around her.

Nothing was as it should have been. Her head spun. She was barely able to keep track of where they were inside Alsra. A few streets past, she recognized a bookshop that had opened inside the city when she was a girl.

Her parents had allowed her and Lesabeth to visit it before the owners had officially opened it to the Alostran public. The family that owned it had served the princesses baked rolls of swirled cinnamon drizzled with hot icing.

Now, its exterior was worn and faded. The bright yellow pigment in the paint had been bleached to an off-white, and the glass was smudged and foggy where it had once been crystalline clear and new. She wouldn't have recognized it at all if it weren't for its familiar name.

The reminder of her family made her stomach flip over and over.

She'd only had sixteen years with them. It didn't seem fair.

Fifteen with Lesabeth, she remembered.

Malik pulled her by the arm around the corner of a building. Her heart fell into her stomach. She hadn't been vigilant enough. They'd found them.

Her eyes scoured the alley for them. "Where are they?" she hissed. She hated the thing in her pocket, but she wasn't going to die today.

Malik's teeth were gritted. His shirt was dark with old sweat, but more of it streamed along his forehead. He shook his head and slumped against a shut set of doors.

Penrose rushed forward to hold him upright. She wasn't sure what bade her do it. He felt weak to her, near the point of passing out. She suspected it was the only reason he didn't shrug away from her touch.

Malik raised his head. He didn't even seem to notice he'd nearly fallen to the ground or that she was holding him upright. His knuckles clanged against the metal with too much sound.

"Open up, you dirty bastard," he called out against the closed doors.

Seconds of silence passed.

"By definition, only one of us is Father's bastard," came a voice. "So, it's not much an insult."

When the doors opened, Penrose wasn't sure what to expect. But it wasn't this.

Her eyes were like diamonds in the night, bright but sharp. Most of her ebony skin was visible in a dress the likes of which she'd never seen. It was made of what looked to be an impossibly soft fabric, and the front of it plunged low.

Fabric had been cut from the skirt of her dress, as well, and a single leg was visible all the way to the thigh. A dagger was strapped to her leg there. Penrose suspected there were more other places.

She was gorgeous and dangerous. She had to be Malik's sister.

His sister looked at Malik and then to her. Her expression froze to iciness.

"What the hell happened?" she said between her teeth.

Light from inside the building leaked into the doorway where they stood. After the darkness of the new dawn and the dim streets, it made her eyes ache.

"We'll talk inside, Aisha," Malik managed to say. Malik side-stepped Penrose's help and moved into the building fully.

Penrose didn't have time to deliberate. Right then, she trusted the unknown more than she did the known horrors roaming the streets of this Alsra.

Apparently, Aisha hadn't missed the fact that she'd followed them inside the building. "The mouse is coming?"

Penrose heard the music and the low hum of voices before she saw anything. Strange muted purple and blue lights illuminated a wide room outfitted with crevices, velvet seats, a platform, and a long bar.

Malik didn't look back at Penrose as he walked forward. "She's with me."

Penrose saw that there were people hidden in the corners of the room, though she tried not to draw attention to herself. She suspected that, as day had recently dawned, this was the remnants of their business from last night. Incense and heavier, unidentified scents tickled her throat, and she tried to avoid coughing as well as she could.

Ahead of her, the two led her deeper inside the building.

"Get Henrik," Malik said under his breath.

"Malik," Aisha said, "what the hell happened? You were supposed to be doing a deal with Mars's men. When you didn't come back, and no one knew shit about where you were, what was I supposed to think?" She didn't stop for a breath. "I thought Mars killed you."

"This wasn't him," Malik said forcefully. "I'm fine."

Aisha gave a short sarcastic laugh. Her eyes flicked back to Penrose for barely a second and then went back to his face.

"I need to speak with you," she said. "Alone."

Penrose considered tuning out their conversation, but she'd never been much good at ignoring potentially valuable information. As she listened, her eyes went to every corner of the wide space, and she made a map of its crevices should she need to make a quick escape from these people.

"We'll speak after Henrik." Malik's voice was almost too low to hear. After a moment, he added, "Is *he* here?"

When Malik spoke, his eyes had gone to what seemed to be a balcony above the bar that was separated from the room by thick, darkened glass. Bumps dotted her skin.

They were leaving the main room behind with its showy blue and violet lights and smoke, but Penrose couldn't shake the feeling that eyes watched them go. They descended stairs down a hall.

Aisha said in an equally low voice, "Father's out. He hasn't returned from last night, though it's early for him yet."

"Have them alert me when he returns," Malik said, his gaze moving forward again. "There's information I need to discuss with him."

Aisha's words weren't meant to carry to her, she knew. "Information about a mouse?" Aisha asked.

But if Malik had a response to that, she didn't hear it. They had reached what seemed to be the basement floor of the bar above.

Only, it wasn't anything like a basement she'd ever seen. The room was wide with long, metal tables on either side of it. Strange metal instruments stood on some. On others, liquids in glasses steamed into the air. In one far corner of the room looked to be a small library of books, and in another corner, a furnace emanated heat.

She knew what this was.

A laboratory. Or a production facility.

Perhaps both, she realized as she thought of what went on above them and the strange perfume in the air.

"Henrik," Aisha called out.

Aisha stepped forward as a man was dragged to her by two other bulky ones.

The man being dragged didn't make eye contact with Malik's sister, though he spoke immediately. "As I told him yesterday, I don't have any solutions yet."

"Henrik," Aisha repeated in a softer voice. Her hand moved quickly, and Henrik flinched from the suddenness.

But all she did was cup his chin and move it until he faced her. "My brother is unwell. Until he is so, it is your new job to make him well. Our father will forgive the delay. Do you understand?"

It was clear that Henrik was about to nod, but he seemed to think better of it with Aisha's hand where it was. "Yes."

She nodded at him as she stepped back. "Good man."

Penrose watched the interaction as a realization came to her. *This man is being held against his will.*

Her eyes cast about the room for any hints as to what they were forcing him to do. But before she could try to piece it together, Malik had stepped forward and called to someone outside the room.

The woman came inside the lab area, her eyes only on Malik. Her hair was drawn up into an elaborate style, revealing gems studded into her ears like stars.

"I thought you'd never ask, Malik," she said. It was a moment before she seemed to witness the clear air of malaise to him. "You're—"

He smiled, revealing his teeth to her, though it felt more like a threat. "Back," he supplied for her. He stepped to the side, revealing Penrose. "You owe me a favor. I'll make sure the others know you're off for the rest of the day. Make sure our guest has everything she wants."

Malik finally turned and stared down at her. "Put her in the suite next to mine."

Chapter Twenty

Awake

Penrose knew it was silly.

What was falling asleep when she'd endured much worse within the last few hours alone? But even before she'd been put under a cursed sleep, there had always been reason to fear sleep in her kingdom.

Before she could help it, she remembered what the soldiers had said to each other.

"How long have you had it? How long do you have?"

"Not long enough to live with the consequences."

What had changed in a century? When Lesabeth had surrendered to it, it had been after days of slumber. Her body had deteriorated, though, well before that.

First had been her color—the tinge of her cheeks and mouth. Then it had been her hair and the fullness of her face.

Snap. Out. Of. It.

Penrose blinked. It was over. Her sister wasn't suffering anymore. Hell, she wasn't even dust anymore, maybe. She bit into her tongue to refocus herself.

The rooms she'd been given were nothing short of lavish. The bathtub alone was big enough for four people. Penrose wondered if four people had ever been inside it at once and stopped that train of thought before it went somewhere.

The windows were dark enough to filter the sunlight before it got hot but not so dark that the room was dimly lit. A sprawling, unfamiliar city waited below, but Penrose ignored looking at it for too long. The view reminded her too much of her time in Cassius's tower. Cushions lined every surface imaginable, even outside the wide bedroom.

She'd told the woman, Eleris, to have a proper day off after she'd brought her to her rooms. Although, Penrose had allowed Eleris to bring her food before she'd left.

But she hadn't expected it to be a veritable feast. Roasted duck, bowls of creamy broth and rice, a platter of spring greens drizzled in a honey dressing, and glazed fruits of every kind were only the beginning. And yet, she'd left only crumbs on the plates.

She forbade herself from the bedroom. It was too tempting to sleep when she was in there. Even if her body craved it.

What if I don't wake up this time? What if I somehow still have the curse on me?

What if another age passes while I'm asleep?

Time seemed more fleeting than it ever had before. Before the tower, it was something to pass. Something to trade for an event on the horizon like Lessa's visits with illicit novels smuggled inside the castle or time with her father while he tinkered in his study.

Now, she couldn't afford to lose more of it.

What if I don't wake up at all this time?

She knew the fear was silly. But knowing something is illogical doesn't always help in not believing it.

Instead of giving in to sleep, Penrose sat against the cushioned lounge in the sitting room and considered all that she knew, her present options, and what she needed to do next.

First, Prince Cassius had done something to her.

He'd tricked her, and she'd fallen ill with the sleeping curse as a result. Except she hadn't died after a short bout with it but woken after a hundred years.

Second, he was still after her. Somehow, he yet lived. There was little doubt in her mind that he'd sent those men after her. This was his plot, and she had played right into it on their wedding day.

Stupid. Stupid. Why didn't I see the signs earlier?

You did, answered another voice. *You just didn't do anything about them.*

Penrose's entire body shook as the feeling overtook her. She wanted to be angry at Cassius. At the soldiers who had captured and then attacked her like she was nothing.

At her parents, who had traded her to a kingdom for the greater good.

Even at Malik.

But she knew, at the root of it all, she was mad at herself.

She'd thought she could save her people by giving him what he wanted. In reality, she had likely doomed them. A hundred years had passed, and the curse had spread and even worsened.

And in her absence, he'd stolen her throne.

Third, Cassius was connected to the sleeping curse in some way. The memories of her wedding night were muddy in her mind after her long sleep, but a betrayal was a hard thing to forget entirely.

He has some control over it. He cured those people and then threatened to reverse it.

Penrose frowned. None of the pieces made sense together. The sleeping curse, or *somnus* as Malik called it, had first appeared over one hundred and thirty-some-odd years ago.

Already, it had spread for decades before the night she'd been lost to her time.

Back then, Prince Cassius hadn't been more than eighteen years old. If he'd been the cause of it all along, somehow weaving it and spreading it himself, then why had it started well before he'd even been born?

Penrose knuckled her forehead. She didn't know enough yet.

Suddenly, the world blurred around her. With several blinks, it straightened itself again.

Sleep was waiting for her, stalking in the shadows like a cat, but she couldn't allow herself to fall prey to it. Penrose's vision blurred again, but this time, the teardrops hitting her knuckles told her it wasn't from impending sleep.

The wide seat she was on was angled to encourage lounging, but she refused to do so. She brought her legs to her chest. It kept her from trembling.

Penrose willed her mind to go blank, but it refused to cooperate.

If I don't sleep, then I'll end up thinking.

And *thinking* was almost worse than sleeping at the moment.

As she stared forward, she froze. Across from her was the window that spanned almost an entire wall of the room. Something had drawn her eyes there, but this suite was on the second floor, above the bar and smoking den Malik had brought her to.

Penrose rushed to the window and jerked it open as a flutter of blue feathers assaulted her. Her laugh bounced off the walls of the room. They were big, throaty ones that made her dizzy for air, but she didn't care.

Sorrowtail chirped and flew around her head, his black eyes bright. The two of them slid to the floor together, his taloned feet planted in her palm as he nuzzled her face. She didn't stop laughing even after the tears began to stream down her cheeks.

He cocked his head at her as if to say, *it's almost an insult how surprised you are.*

"I didn't think I'd see you again. Not after ..." Penrose swallowed the words. It was too much.

Ignoring the dizziness that rushed her when she sprang to her feet, Penrose grabbed a plate left from her meal. Sorrowtail huffed, his chest feathers puffing so that he looked bigger than he was.

"Too proud to eat scraps, huh?" she asked him. "It's a shame. These people really know their food," Penrose said, flicking into her mouth one of the few berries she hadn't devoured.

Sorrowtail watched her chew, though he acted like he wasn't. When she moved to grab another one, his beak darted for it before she could.

Penrose laughed behind her hand, trying in vain to hide her amusement at the expense of his pride. He didn't look at her as he ate another red berry.

In an attempt at an apology, Penrose found a few pieces of spring greens that hadn't been coated in the sweet dressing and passed them to where he stood on the plate.

He gave a high chirp, and she relaxed against the lounge chair and smiled. "I am relieved you forgive me, my friend."

Against her permission, Penrose's mind drifted like a stone gliding to the bottom of the ocean and her eyes closed. Suddenly, she drew in a sharp breath as she woke herself. Sorrowtail looked at her with his head askance.

Her eyes went to the bedroom.

She brought Sorrowtail close to her chest, and he pressed himself against her in a nuzzle that she returned.

Her voice was barely loud enough to carry.

"You'll fall asleep with me, won't you?"

When he pushed against her chin in answer, she rose to her feet. After cleaning up the plates and putting them away, she walked both of them to the bed.

In the bedroom, Penrose carefully put the mechanical weapon in a drawer beside the bed. Sorrowtail took flight from her finger to rest on top of the wardrobe.

When she realized what she was wearing, Penrose nearly ripped from her skin the clothes that had belonged to Cassius.

She wanted to burn them.

Instead, she opened the wardrobe and shoved them in the back of it, past hangers of black and white cuff shirts and various trousers.

These must have belonged to whoever they kept here last, she considered. Her thoughts jumped to the man they kept prisoner in the lab two floors below her, Henrik.

How long had they kept him here? What would happen to him if he didn't give them what they wanted soon enough?

Penrose shut the thoughts out and grabbed a shirt haphazardly. If she woke up again, there would be plans to make.

And if she didn't, then she wouldn't have anything left to worry about.

Sleep claimed her at once, and she drifted.

In the darkness, someone unlocked the door to her rooms.

Chapter Twenty-One

The Diviner

The king of Aloster watched as the Karsian woman entered his throne room. Her family's features were strong about her face, but he swept that thought aside for the moment.

This wasn't about what had happened, but what was to happen.

Sarina had been in his service for many years now and was well aware of what he could do. Once, he'd saved her life.

But her loyalty had been proven beyond that.

He'd felt the change coming, the bond between him and the witch weakening, and he'd found this woman after learning that her father's divine-touched gift had been passed to her.

The king almost snorted at that.

Divine-touched.

It was another of the gods' little jokes.

"Something's changed," the king said without preamble. It was an accusation, and the diviner knew it.

Sarina seemed to think some before speaking. This was wise. "Your Highness, may I remind you that my dreams often don't reveal a certain future, but a possible one?"

"She was supposed to be weaker. Almost drained of life, I believe your words were."

"She lives," she muttered. Her eyebrows pushed together. For a moment, Sarina's eyes wandered from the king's. Though he couldn't read minds, he could see it on her face clearly enough.

The diviner was most surprised at this.

"So, that's what that meant." Sarina was still speaking to herself. Her gaze bolted to his face suddenly.

"What is it?" he demanded. "Enough of this half-speak."

A smile crept up her face, bit by bit.

"Then I will tell you in plain language. She will be the key, Your Highness. This will solve it," she said.

"You will show me." The king of Aloster rose. "Tonight."

The diviner was right. Her futures weren't always certain. But they always revealed truths.

No matter what, he had business with Aloster's forgotten princess. It was time to lay a trap because this princess would be worth the trouble.

Especially if it lifted this curse from him.

***

Malik opened the door to his rooms with a shove and the force of his body, even though it still ached. This was despite the heavy doses of medicine that the healer had administered. The stitches in his arm begged to be scratched, but he suppressed the feeling.

His head pressed against the glass of his windows. The medicine turned his stomach, but it was preferable to being dead.

How long?

He opened one eye to look down into the rat's nest that was the crown city of Aloster. Somewhere, someone was slipping the information to Raphael Ezar that his son had survived the execution he'd helped orchestrate.

He wasn't naïve. His spies had surely seen Malik enter Jackal's Hide.

Aisha didn't know. Or, more accurately perhaps, she didn't wish to see the obvious.

Even if it hadn't been for the damned mistake he'd made, his father would have blamed it on something else.

Malik's failing hadn't been *one* thing. It had been everything.

Raphael had chosen Aisha to succeed him.

And absolute power never shared.

While his sister might not have seen him as competition as head of business for House Ezar, their father most certainly would have. Kings and queens had their heir and then a spare.

But spares stopped being useful when heirs rose to power.

In fact, they became threats.

Malik forced himself to move. If he didn't bathe now, he wasn't going to before ruining his sheets with grime. He pulled the bloodied shirt off his body and stepped away from his windows. The scarred figure reflected in them moved his eyes away, too. He didn't need a reminder of the injuries mapped across his body.

As he walked into his bedroom, Malik started to unbutton his rough leather pants. He stopped, his eyes glued to a sight that didn't make sense.

On top of his wardrobe was a sleeping bird.

Instinct took over in the seconds it took him to process the sight, and Malik reached for a revolver that wasn't at his waist.

The answer to where the stolen gun was, of course, was that it was with the girl. Penrose.

And this was *her* bird.

Malik spun on his feet to find a slumbering girl in his bed already.

Eleris, you absolute conniving witch. *You knew whose rooms these were.*

He and Eleris were most certainly going to have a talk. Perhaps more than a talk.

His forefinger and thumb pressed tight against his temples. It helped keep his fist from finding the walls, which was a good thing when there was a sleeping girl only paces away.

His head darted up to confirm. Her form rose and fell in regular increments. *Good. She's still asleep.*

Malik re-buttoned his trousers when he realized he hadn't yet.

On top of everything else, there was her. *She'd better be filthy rich,* he told himself as he turned around.

"You going to let me in or ...?"

Aisha's voice came from the other side of the door to his suite. Malik gnashed his teeth. This was something not even Aisha would let him live down.

No, especially not Aisha.

When Malik opened the door, he made sure to shove himself inside the entryway to block her path.

Before he could open his mouth, she was talking.

"Some men are here asking about your mouse." Aisha leaned closer. "Who the hell is she for kingsguard to come after her?"

Malik's blood pumped through his veins. "Where?" His teeth clenched around the word.

"In the den."

"We'll talk below." He closed his door and ensured it was locked behind him.

***

Penrose's heart felt as if it had stopped in her chest.

She'd nearly gone for the weapon in the drawer next to the bed. It had been *him.*

Anger had risen inside her initially, but from what she'd peeked, he'd been surprised to find her there. And perhaps angry.

And undressing.

She resolved not to tell him she'd seen that. Heat washed over her features as she thought of the novels that she and Lesabeth had read.

Penrose pushed those distracting thoughts elsewhere in her mind. She flung open his wardrobe to find the least-worn yet most-fitted trousers she could find and claimed them for herself.

She'd add it to the bill she was paying him.

And how are you going to pay him if you're no longer a princess?

Whatever was in the treasury at her parents' castle was hers by right, she reminded herself. Even if she had no way of getting to it.

This was another distracting thought she ignored.

She pulled out the mechanical weapon from the drawer and carefully nestled it inside a belt that looked customized to hold it in a sheath. The belt had the added benefit of keeping his pants attached to her.

Penrose swallowed. She'd heard their conversation clearly enough.

Her *husband* wasn't giving up. The word curdled the contents of her stomach.

And she wasn't going to barricade herself inside here, trembling at every noise outside Malik's rooms. This was her fault that they'd come sniffing around here.

Besides, she had more than a few questions that needed answering which she was certain Malik wouldn't just let slip. Certain questions like *who these people were* and *what they were doing downstairs*.

Before she could get to the door, a weight landed on her head and a high chirp pierced the air.

"This is too dangerous for you," she admonished. But he hopped out of her hands again and again as she tried to pry him from her hair.

She sighed. "How can such a small body contain so much stubbornness?" she asked the emptiness around her.

Penrose blinked. The more she stared at the ceiling, the more she realized what she was staring at. She'd seen something like it before in the privies in her parents' castle but never would have thought to see one outside such a room.

Just above the windows was a metal grate with a thin, swirling design that she'd assumed was decorative. It was angled under the eaves so that rain wouldn't get in.

Ventilation, she realized.

Her thoughts went to the space below. It was not only a bar but a smoking den. It stood to reason that a place such as that would require at least a modicum of ventilation.

That was how she was going to find them and even listen without being discovered.

"I'll bring you," she announced to the bird on her head, "on the condition that you'll help me."

When he chirped his agreement, Penrose held out a finger for him and brought him inside the collar of her shirt.

She kept the weapon at her waist. Even though the thought froze her heart inside her ribs, Penrose almost hoped that the soldier who had nearly choked her had come back for her.

Chapter Twenty-Two

The Spy in the Hold

Penrose hovered at the end of the vent, waiting for the chirp that was their signal before she moved forward.

When his chirp bounced off the walls of the vent this time, it was even smaller and the sound tinnier. She'd moved farther from him this time.

"Not close enough yet," she said through the vents. Penrose moved through the halls like a ghost, but it seemed more and more like this plan wasn't going to work like she'd hoped it would.

And the closer she got to the smoking den below, the more her options narrowed.

What if they take you like they did Henrik? What if you become their captive, too?

And then there were the king's men. Her hand hovered over the weapon she didn't quite know how to use yet.

No. I'm going to hold my own this time.

As she snuck down the halls between rooms that she assumed were for the others who worked here, Penrose stopped and closed her eyes.

If she wanted to navigate his world, she'd have to think like one of them.

The bar below is a front. At most, it's a meeting place between them. What they rely on is what happens below it.

So, it's not as if they want to smoke and drink the night away themselves. But if those who meet with them have looser tongues, perhaps that's even better.

Penrose opened her eyes. The vents for the bar below wouldn't be connected to the rooms on the second floor.

She slumped against the wall of the narrow hallway.

What now?

She couldn't go back and hide. If this was about her, then she needed to know what was going on. If she needed to run again.

Maybe the vents aren't connected to the bedrooms. But that doesn't mean there's nowhere to overhear them.

As she conjured the mental map she'd made of the area downstairs upon her arrival, she picked her spot.

When she found the next metal plate covering a vent and heard Sorrowtail's chirp, she called him back to her. They were going to infiltrate the snake's den.

And maybe find a few cracked eggs.

After a few minutes, Penrose froze on the other side of the stairs until she heard Sorrowtail's quiet signal indicating that the way was clear. By the map inside her head, the entrance to the enclosed balcony that looked over the bar should have been somewhere along this wall.

Penrose frowned. Nowhere along the wall was anything resembling a doorway.

This was impossible.

Steps echoed from below. Someone was coming up the stairwell to the rooms above.

Her heart jerked in her chest. What if it was one of the king's men come for her? What if it was one of her so-called allies, looking to trade her away for the trouble?

Neither was safe, she decided. Penrose did the only thing she could and shoved her body in an alcove along the stairwell that was built into the wall.

Inside the narrow cavity was an ivory pedestal that seemed out of place for a criminal's operations center. Her eyes traveled to what was on top of it and held back a gasp.

The footsteps were close to her. She remained utterly still while hiding herself behind the object. It was a sculpture that her parents had commissioned by her mother's favorite artist who had still been alive at the time. The sculpted nude woman held two daggers with her arms crossed before her chest.

She'd always looked to Penrose like she was on the verge of dancing or killing someone. She'd never decided which.

Her heart hurt in her chest. The footsteps had long passed her hiding place.

How had these people ended up with such a priceless artifact? Penrose's eyebrows pushed together.

She was staring at yet another thing that didn't make sense.

The trim along the floor ended abruptly along one corner of the alcove's floor. Penrose looked at the wall directly above the space where the trim was missing.

Nothing else seemed out of the ordinary.

Penrose frowned to herself. There was a smoke and drinking den downstairs. And a hidden laboratory below that. Everything here was extraordinary.

So, therefore, the ordinary is out of place.

She rose to her feet and, before she could convince herself that her logic was flawed and that this was a ridiculous idea, she pushed against the wall.

The wall didn't give. It rotated.

The floor inside the room that wasn't supposed to be was surprisingly soft, which was a good thing because Penrose hit it with the full force of her body.

Her heart fluttered in her chest as she checked the collar of the shirt she'd stolen.

"Sorrowtail?" Her voice was too loud, but he wasn't where he was supposed to have been.

A moment later, a feathered weight landed on top of her head. She sank back to the floor in relief.

"Don't scare me," she breathed. He chirped back as if in to chuckle.

As she saw the space around her, she sucked the breath back in.

Could it be?

It was a small room, but it didn't lack for comforts. Soft carpet had cushioned her fall, and a velvet-covered chaise and two chairs filled the space. They surrounded a low glass table that Penrose would bet her life usually held drinks.

Blessedly, it was empty but for the two of them.

Penrose walked to the wall where the hidden door was. On this side of it, it was much more obvious, seeing as the wood was a different color from that which surrounded it.

And there was a *lock*.

She couldn't believe her luck, and she quickly toggled the metal mechanism. She didn't need any unexpected visitors.

As she turned to the wall that the three chairs faced, she knew where she was. There could be no doubt. Penrose walked to the wide glass set into the wall.

It was a window overlooking the entire bar area. There was hardly a corner that she couldn't clearly see from this angle.

They can't see in, either. At least not without a light on in here, she realized as she remembered seeing the built-in gallery from the other side when they'd entered this place.

It was the perfect spot to spy on them from.

Her eyes caught on movement below, and her chest tightened. It was hard to tell for certain from this distance, but ...

She saw three people sitting together in one of the most secluded corners of the bar. Two of them were Malik and Aisha. She wasn't sure of the third.

"It would be perfect." Penrose frowned. There was no vent along the walls, here.

I was wrong even when I was right. She allowed herself to collapse against one of the chairs. Somehow, it was even more comfortable than it had looked.

A tapping noise sounded from the other side of the room. "I know, Sorrowtail. You miss the food from the rooms." She sighed. "We'll be back soon enough."

He gave a sound somewhere between a huff and a chirp. Penrose's gaze darted to him. And to what he was standing on.

"You beautiful bird! Smart, handsome boy," she cooed, scooping him up in her hands.

Somehow, his breast feathers puffed up even more, and his eyes shone.

I should have known. His pride is bigger than his belly. She laughed, though not too loudly.

They were standing on a vent, and if the position of this hidden room was any indication as to its purpose, this vent led to somewhere very important.

Possibly to the most hidden corner of the first floor, she considered. *Somewhere where the business happens.*

There was only one way to find out if she could hear them from here. Crouching low to the floor, she gingerly lifted the small, decorative metal grating. Even if she couldn't fit through it, she didn't need to.

With any luck, sufficient sound would travel.

And, based on the construction and the intention behind this hidden room, she thought that it would.

She pressed her ear close and listened.

Chapter Twenty-Three

The Messenger and the Message

"She's worth more traded to the king than she's paying you."

Malik leaned back as he considered the man's words. Aisha sat next to him, silent, but he could hear the questions in her head.

Soon, he bade her as if she could hear. Heat prickled at the base of his neck as he looked at the man across from him.

"Even if that's true, there's something else you haven't thought of," Malik said. "I don't like you." He leaned forward even more so only the man could hear his words. "I would have done it. Don't ever forget that."

A black and purple bloom was forming under the soldier's left eye. Osric had given him that when he'd shown up, demanding things in the name of the king. Malik envied Os for having done it.

I should have killed him in the alley with the other, Malik thought.

This was the other soldier who had attacked them and hurt Penrose. If his death didn't belong to her, he would have been dead by now.

Unwisely, the soldier wasn't fazed.

"You don't know yet, then. You don't know what she is." The Alostran soldier revealed his teeth in a smile that was more like a threat. "She's a smart girl for that."

Malik felt like he was back in the arena above Belnya prisons and the corpseflies were buzzing around his head. His blood thundered through him, though he didn't give the man any indication that it affected him.

He's bluffing.

The king had already lied to him about who she was once.

"I think it's time we brought our guest somewhere where he can talk more freely," Aisha said to Malik. "One of Father's machines should do, don't you think?"

"We were talking, girl," snapped the soldier. "I'll speak freely enough with him."

A whoosh pierced the air beside Malik, followed by a ripping noise. Aisha's dagger had landed in the chair's upholstery that was exposed between the soldier's legs.

"Good aim this time," Malik said to her.

Aisha narrowed her eyes. "Actually, I missed."

The soldier's lips were thin. To his credit, he didn't cower or piss himself like other men did when Aisha scared them. Since it was one of her favorite things to do, Malik was used to their reactions by now.

"I'm here only to deliver information, so you'll get your answers without all that," the soldier said. He met their gazes. "Under the king's orders himself. Unless you wish more of my kind here, then you'll hear out the information. It's to your benefit, regardless."

Malik itched to drag him downstairs for the fun of it, but a war with the crown was not something any of them needed.

It was then that something occurred to him. Something he should have considered before.

The idea soothed him at once. He could get through a conversation with this bastard if he paid attention to that thought enough.

Soon.

"Just speak," he said out loud.

"On the condition of no more surprises," the soldier said, watching the two of them.

Malik licked his lower lip. It turned into a smile when he saw the man watching even that. "No more surprises," he echoed.

This should be good.

Despite finding himself in a bed of jackals, the soldier accepted one of the drinks that the barmaid offered them. He leaned back and spoke when she left.

"She was sealed in that tower for all those years for a reason. In her time, the sleeping curse was different. It was less torture and more of a mercy, but much more fatal than it is now," he said. He met Malik's glare. "By unleashing her, you've unleashed a deadlier version of somnus. The curse will become worse than what it was even then."

Malik allowed the tension to hover on the air before he said it. He used it as a weapon like he'd used his chains to kill the other prisoner at Belnya prisons.

"We don't give a damn about that here," Malik announced at last.

The man just stared at him. His knuckles grew white as they held tight to the glass in his hand. He leaned forward.

"The prince of grime is what they call you. But they call you that because even though you talk and walk like you're something big, you're a child. You've no idea the horrors of this godsdamned disease. How could you? You've no idea of anything but your own constructed world."

Malik stared back.

The hand holding his drink trembled. The soldier continued, "They say it passes in the water. The man that you killed in the street. His name was Aren." A bead of sweat appeared at the man's temple. "He didn't tell me he had it, but I heard it when it started. The nightmares. We were bunk mates. The king's military doesn't provide for very spacious barracks." He smiled at them, showing his teeth. "When he woke up, he threw up over the side of his bed. The next night was when it started for me. Even if you killed me tonight, I wouldn't have enough days left for it to matter."

Sweat gathered at the back of Malik's neck.

"Say the rest of it," Malik said at last. He could tell the man was holding back. "Before we change our minds."

"She's the princess—the one from the old dynasty," he said in answer. "The one that was supposed to have died from somnus a hundred years ago. The one whose marriage to King Cassius united the kingdoms of Aloster and Cavana."

"What are you talking about?" Aisha said. "The somnus has gone to your head."

But all Malik could think of was what he'd found in the tower in the rooms below the one where he'd found Penrose. They had been decorated for the wedding.

"Deny. It." The soldier stared only at Malik.

Malik couldn't breathe. But he had to do something. He had to cover up this weakness this cursed bastard had found in him and plied to his liking.

In the furor of his thoughts, one of his own came back to him.

Spares stopped being useful when heirs rose to power.

King Cassiel wanted the first wife of his father killed. She was a threat to his claim on the throne. That was why he'd been desperate enough to hire a condemned murderer to kill a girl cursed to sleep.

Married. The stupid word echoed in his head. He needed to straighten himself out.

"Malik," Aisha murmured.

His father would be back at Jackal's Hide soon. Malik needed to clean house. Fast.

"You're leaving. We have other business to attend to," Malik said. His head tilted back to catch the gaze of one of their men posted near the entrance.

"Not yet I'm not," the soldier said. "That's not the end of the king's message."

Malik gave a quick shake of his head to an approaching Osric. He stopped well away from their booth. Malik was almost certain he wanted to hear this part of the message as much as he'd liked hearing the rest of it.

Which was to say, not very much.

"What else could you have to spout?" he said to him.

This time, the soldier didn't fake-smile at him. He didn't threaten them, either. In fact, Malik saw something in his eyes that very much resembled hate.

Malik held his breath. The cursed bastard didn't want to tell him this part, but he'd been compelled to make sure they received it. And, whatever it was, the man absolutely loathed them for it.

"In exchange for the girl, the king is offering blanket immunity from the law for the members of your family. Consider it a blind eye."

Malik felt like he'd taken a punch to his intestines. It was exactly what he'd demanded of King Cassiel in exchange for the job to begin with. Right before the bastard king had betrayed him.

His head buzzed. *Liar,* the voice inside him chanted.

But maybe the king was desperate enough now that they held all the cards.

Beside him, he felt Aisha tense. They needed to talk, though not in front of this rat.

Malik rose, and Osric took his cue. He felt as if he were still feverish from the infection, and dribbles of sweat stuck his clean shirt to his back.

"No need," he told Os. "My sister and I will escort our guest out."

He needed to keep Aisha by him. Until he talked to her, he couldn't be sure of what she would do after hearing that.

They needed to *go.* His only consolation was that Eleris had tried to mess with him by putting Penrose in his rooms.

It was likely the only safe place in this building for her, now. If there was such a thing anymore.

Under normal circumstances, he wouldn't be this pissed. In fact, he probably would have been happy at what was coming next. Now, it was only a chore. There were too many things trying to slip through his control at the moment, so he had to make it quick.

Aisha followed silently. She trusted him, spectacularly.

When the three of them stood before the metal doors leading out of Jackal Hide, the soldier looked to Malik.

"He'll be expecting a response in three days' time," he said. "The king will—"

The rest of what he said turned to an airless gasp. Malik had pinned him against the wall with his hand on his throat.

Exactly as this man had done to Penrose.

Malik was careful to not touch him more than was necessary even though the man wasn't even able to manage a spit at the moment.

He brought his mouth to one of his ears. "I know you were lying," he said. "Not about any of that other shit. About how there would be others looking for you if you didn't come back."

The soldier tried to speak but only managed another airless gasp.

"I know what this is. This was a chance for you to fix your mistake," Malik said. He cocked his head to the side. "This was a punishment for failing to bring us to him before. You are, in fact, expendable."

The man's eyes widened by a hairline, but it was proof enough.

This time, he whispered so that only he would hear Malik. "But your ass is hers. Until you die trapped in your own nightmares, don't you dare forget that."

Malik released his hold on the king's man. As he fought to regain his breath, Malik added, "Don't come back here. Ever."

Throughout their stunted conversation, Aisha was silent. It wasn't until after the king's man had left that she turned to him.

She didn't say anything then, either. She didn't have to.

"I'm not going to ask you for a bargain. Or a deal. Or a favor. Or whatever I would ask or demand of you were you someone else," he started. He closed his eyes.

The two of them were better than that. Better than business connections or criminal associates or whatever the hell else.

"But he can't know," Malik said. "Our father can't find out about this."

"Everything, Malik," she said finally. "No holding back like this anymore. I need to know everything this time."

Malik would have laughed if he had it in him after this day. Bargains and deals were the only way they knew how to speak, after all.

Chapter Twenty-Four

The Guest

P enrose felt like she couldn't breathe.

The soldier who had captured them at the gates of Alsra had come here to look for her.

And the king was trying to make a deal with them. Immunity for their crimes in exchange for her.

Her stomach twisted in knots. This place wasn't safe for her anymore. If it ever had been.

Where do I go now? I know no one here. I have nothing in this time.

It didn't matter. She'd survived up until now, hadn't she? Aches burrowed into her body from crouching against the floor in one position for so long. But as soon as she righted herself, she realized she wasn't alone.

He was standing with one arm on the curving back of one of the chairs. He was wearing a velvet blood-red tailcoat that hit the back of his knees. The front was open to his chest, exposing a silken black shirt that shifted over his sun-blessed skin as he moved.

His dark eyes held her in place like a trance. There could be no question. Malik often had the same look to his eyes.

This was his father.

He gestured to the chair opposite him and the one nearest her. She noticed then that a silver tray rested on the low table. On it was a carafe of dark liquid next to a single glass.

"Please. As your host, I invite you to sit."

Penrose didn't move. How much had he heard? Did he know the offer that the king's man proposed? Her throat felt tight.

As the head of House Ezar and a dangerous crime lord, the proposal that the king's soldier had made to Malik would only make perfect sense.

"In exchange for the girl, the king is offering blanket immunity from the law for the members of your family."

A blind eye.

She swallowed.

"My son has fine taste. But I'm afraid I will steal his prize for the moment."

"Prize?" Penrose took a step away. "I'm no one's prize."

"Not his yet, then. All the better. Have some refreshments."

"No, I think I'd best be going, actually," Penrose said. She didn't like how he said *yet*. In fact, she didn't like anything about this.

"I would drink with the one who discovered my hidden nest. I have kept the entrance to this room secret for decades. All it took you was some sniffing around. I would know you."

Sweat lined the back of her neck.

She bit her lip, hoping she looked like a confused girl who stumbled into rooms rather than a spy and a sneak. "I got lost, in truth."

The head of House Ezar produced another glass from a cabinet near him. Penrose watched as he poured the jewel-red liquid into the glasses before them.

"You're smarter than you let on," he said.

It ... sounded like an accusation.

Penrose's heart raged in her chest. Either he knew about the king's offer, or didn't. Though her instincts screamed for her to run for the hidden door, she hovered near the chair opposite him.

How can I turn this to my advantage? What do I need?

A tentative answer came to her. But it was better than what she had so far.

"If I sit with you, I would ask some questions of my own," Penrose replied, still unmoved.

He smiled at her, and his teeth gleamed in the low light. "It's a deal."

When Penrose sat, she considered that it shouldn't be this luxurious inside the maw of a monster. New beads of sweat lined her forehead where strands of her hair clung to her skin.

How was she going to get from him everything that she needed to know without showing her own hand?

From what she'd heard about this man, Penrose considered it was quite possible that Ezar already knew all the cards in play.

Or was this just a prelude to her capture and a trip to the castle that Cassius had stolen from her? Penrose clenched her teeth. She wasn't ready to be bound at the wrists and ankles again so soon.

It was then that she recalled the metal machinery stuffed in the waistband of her pants, hiding under the oversized shirt that belonged to his son.

Maybe she could get what she wanted, after all.

After she settled in the chair opposite him, he gave a single command.

"Drink."

Penrose took a sip of the scarlet-colored liquor. Across from her, Ezar mirrored the action.

Like all spirits, it seared her throat going down. But not like it should have.

The problem was, she knew how little it took for the room to spin around her. She'd had a glass of wine at feasts with her parents before.

And those were on occasions when she'd already had a bellyful of food to sop it up.

"More than that," he said, swirling his drink around. "If this deal is going to work."

"Fine, then." The words dragged across her tongue. They both drank more of the liquor.

This was to be her toll, and she would pay it while she could like golden coin. She shifted under his gaze. She had to disguise her unfamiliarity with this world.

How would any normal person here react?

"You're him," she said. She considered all she knew about him. He seemed used to making an impression. "Ezar."

"To my guests, Raphael," he said. "I would know the name of mine in return." He tilted his head to consider her. "It's only polite."

How much does he know about who I am? Is he simply toying with me until more of the king's men arrive?

"Rose," she settled on. Though she disliked this diminutive of her name, it was close enough to work without revealing too much about her.

As if he didn't already know. Penrose bit into her tongue. It was time to do some work.

"If you're gracious enough to share pleasantries, then perhaps you'll clear up some things for me." She watched him for his reaction. "Who is that man downstairs? Henrik."

Ezar's jeweled hand was twisted around his glass. He tapped one of his fingers against it, making the glass chime.

"Ah, ah. Our deal," he said.

Again, he joined her when she sipped the liquor. Though it easy to miss, the taste of dark cherries lingered in the back of her throat.

She considered spitting it back into her glass when he looked away to keep her clear head, but he never looked away.

He leaned into his chair. "He is my prisoner. You know who I am, so by default, you're familiar with my methods. He is working on something for me."

Penrose's mouth went dry. She tried to keep Swallowtail sleeping and calm inside the collar of her shirt, but it was hard to keep herself so still.

It couldn't be, but the signs were there.

"The curse will become worse than what it was even then."

"We don't give a damn about that here."

And then there was what Henrik had let slip. *"As I told him yesterday, I don't have any solutions yet."*

Henrik was a healer. He'd treated Malik's infection. But he was also a researcher, judging by the laboratory he'd been imprisoned in.

"You're trying to formulate a cure," she said.

It was small, but something changed in his face. "I don't generally discuss business secrets with strangers. I think it's time you pay up." But his hand didn't go to his drink. He stared her down. "This time, you'll answer *my* questions. What are you doing in my house?"

This was a different kind of toll, and one even more dangerous than the blood-red drink before her. She tried to clear her face of the storm that threatened to overwhelm her inside.

"I've hired Malik as my bodyguard," she said.

Just for something else to distract him with—a reason to break their gaze—she brought her lips to the glass. This time, it swam through her.

She forcefully put down the glass. What liquid remained inside it tremored.

Raphael Ezar watched her and spoke finally. "I assume you have the funds for something as expensive as him, then. Nothing under my name comes cheap."

"I have enough for him, trust me," Penrose said between her teeth, thinking of the piece of stolen art outside this room that had once belonged to her family. The drink had begun to loosen her, though she wasn't sure that was a good thing.

He considered this and said, "I have never seen you in this city before. And I don't forget faces. Even dead ones."

Penrose resisted a shudder. Her jaws locked. She believed him.

"So." He seemed to taste the word like it was a piece of food. "Do you want to tell me who you are, Rose?"

Her stomach flipped. Could it be?

Did this mean that he didn't know of the king's deal with House Ezar yet?

Or was this bait?

Penrose's hand twitched infinitesimally. The black metal mechanical weapon was like a silent, resting beast hidden at her side.

But she knew she'd be a fool to assume he didn't have tricks of his own to pull, even in this confined space. She'd seen them fire the weapons at her enough to know how to use it. Penrose fought her climbing heartrate.

Instead of doing all that, she drained what little was left in her glass and smiled at the man who had almost certainly killed more people than she could ever meet.

There was no one left in this world who remembered who she was, save perhaps the man who had imprisoned her in a slumber of magic in the first place.

No one to remember her name. No one to care, except perhaps Cassius, if he was truly still alive.

To history, she was the girl who had helped her kingdom most by dying. Only, she hadn't died.

But she'd been forgotten. Left behind.

Which was worse?

"I'm no one," she said at last, focusing on the words to make them clear through her teeth. "Not like you people here."

Penrose stood, staunchly ignoring the room that moved around her. He'd had his time to trap her.

"Speaking of which, I'm not paying him for nothing," she said. "I'll be going now."

The words were a challenge that hung in the air between them. She was too aware of the weight in her waistband.

Raphael Ezar leaned into the luxe chair and drained the rest of his own glass.

Before she moved through the hidden door to the other side, she heard him speak from his chair.

"Come find me when you tire of my son."

Chapter Twenty-Five

To Come Willingly

As Malik and Aisha walked the stairs, he could feel his sister's gaze penetrating his skull. It was as if she could see the corpseflies he felt like were in his head. Buzzing around, bumping into each other.

Threatening the bastard had put him in a better mood certainly, but there was still too much he had to make sure of. Os had informed them that their father had arrived in the Jackal's Hide from his business the previous night.

Before the king of Alsra's underworld got wind of things, he needed to have a word with this *princess*.

Things could never be easy. Malik was sure that it all would have been easier had the executioner freed him of his head at Belnya.

"Malik," Aisha prompted as they walked. "You know I need something. Some shred of an explanation of what the hell is going on with my brother."

They were almost to his rooms where she slept. Best get it out before they were in earshot of her.

Malik was silent for a stretch of time. Then, he said, "Do you remember the team of those healers? The experts on somnus?"

"Of course. Henrik's team," Aisha said. Her eyes cut to him. "Speaking of that, I'm not sure he was the right one to leave alive, even if it was Father's plan."

Malik grinned at his sister. Sometimes, she could be even more cold-hearted than him or their father.

It was a wonder that she wasn't even blood-related to him.

"How so?" he asked, though he could guess after speaking to the man for more than five seconds.

"I've been observing him. He's not responding to the pressure like Father clearly intended. He's folding." Aisha suddenly looked at him like she'd suddenly remembered. She probably had. "Though, he's proven useful for having healed you. I should tell Father to give him more time."

"And you remember what happened to all the others?" Malik prompted.

This time, Aisha was quieter. "Yes."

Until recently, the city of Alsra had been home to a research facility dedicated to studying somnus. Though Malik hadn't seen it since Raphael Ezar had gotten there, he guessed it was a pile of smoking rubble these days.

The public thought all those healers were dead, but their father had spared one of their number at random pick, though of course, not out of a sense of mercy.

Malik's hand rested on the doorknob to his rooms. It was time to spit it out.

"I wasn't with Mars when I was gone. I was at Belnya. For the murder of no less than a dozen healers."

As he spoke, he pushed the door open but froze in the threshold when he realized.

"Belnya?" Aisha cursed. "Only the dead leave there." She seemed to register the second part of what he'd said. "Dammit, Malik. You didn't even do that."

He wasn't listening. Something was wrong.

He hadn't left the door unlocked.

Malik moved in a blur, and a knife materialized in his palm almost instantly. He didn't have to think to draw it.

To her credit, Aisha armed herself without a word passing between them. While she might not have understood what was happening, she'd been raised in the same world he had. Hesitation in danger was an easy way to die.

Malik pulled open his wardrobes, checked under his furniture, and even checked the depths of his bathtub. His gaze settled on the empty bed where she'd been maybe an hour or so before.

Aisha followed his gaze, and then her eyes went back to his face.

How the hell was he going to explain any of this? That he needed to find Penrose before something happened to her? That he wasn't taking the king's deal?

That she'd been here, in his bed?

He couldn't.

She surprised him and instead said, "There's no other way it could've happened. You let them take you to Belnya."

It was softer than an accusation but not a question, either.

As they looked to each other, Malik saw that she knew that he'd confessed to something he hadn't even done.

You know why. It's so obvious, he pled with her silently. But he could see that she still didn't want to believe what he had to tell her about that. She still didn't want to see what was going on in their *family.*

But he didn't have time for this right now.

"He can't know about her," Malik said, repeating himself from earlier. "Not yet."

He thought she was going to refuse. Perhaps she should've. But after a moment, she went to the door to his rooms.

"I'll take the den. You search this floor," Aisha said. "She can't have gotten far from Jackal Hide."

But Malik wasn't worried about *that.*

Chapter Twenty-Six

Off Limits

In the halls outside Ezar's hidden room, the liquor hit her all at once like a punch to the gut. Penrose's stomach twisted in warning.

Her palm found the wall even as it spun around her. She needed to get somewhere safe. But where that would be, she had no idea.

Malik. She needed to get to him *now*.

But what if he took the deal?

More sweat dribbled along her throat, and she sagged against the wall. Why hadn't she considered it?

Of course. All the money that Cassius had taken from her when he'd stolen her throne wasn't equal to what the king was now offering Malik.

Immunity from the law. And not just for him, either.

His family. How could she compete with *that*?

Her heart stuttered in her chest. There was no one left in this world who would look out for her like that anymore.

And perhaps there hadn't been since Lesabeth died. A dry swallow scratched her throat as she remembered how her parents had sold her to the other kingdom to make peace with them.

To join with them. To create ... this world.

And all it had cost was one princess. A trivial price for peace.

Penrose's body felt heavy, but she had to keep moving. She had to get out of here, even if the streets were dangerous, too.

Better than a jackal's den.

She'd almost made it to the front of the building when a figure appeared at the other end of the hall, blocking her way. Her hand pulled free the black metal weapon and concentrated on remembering how to hold it properly in her fists.

#

The person facing Malik was, quite possibly, the girl of his dreams.

She was wearing his shirt and pants already, and she'd just pulled a pistol on him.

Despite the fact that his mood had gone from murderous and then to frantic only minutes earlier, he felt a dark smile inch up one half of his face.

She's still here.

But his relief was quickly replaced with something else. He cocked his head at her, oozing ease even while his heart raced. There was nothing in the world like a woman who knew how to threaten him.

Those were always the best.

"Didn't anyone ever tell you that running with monsters would make you into one, too?" he murmured. He knew she'd heard him.

He started forward, his eyes never leaving her face. He couldn't resist.

That was when he noticed it.

It was in her eyes. When she swayed, he didn't care about the firearm between them. He rushed to catch her before she hit the ground, disarming her in the process.

"Malik," she whispered. "I didn't ..." Her words ran together more than they should've. She blinked, seeming as if she were trying to concentrate on him.

Malik should have been doing any number of things. Ensuring his father knew nothing of Penrose. Finding Aisha. Leaving this hornet's nest full of pickpockets and drunkards and, lately, kingsguard.

In that moment, he thought of none of those things. Only one thought was left to him.

Getting this drunk wasn't her choice.

He held her gaze. "Who did this to you?"

"I did," she said.

"Liar," he accused softly.

His mind ran. The Jackal's Hide had notoriously strong liquor, stronger than what was allowed in the taverns. Who had gotten all this drink in her? And why? She was too upright and clever to get, on her own, so mindlessly inebriated.

Or at all.

He remembered who the soldier had claimed she was. *Princess.*

She looked away from his face and pulled out of his support. "I need to go—"

Malik caught her before she stumbled down a set of stairs. "Not like this. You need to sleep this off."

He had to admit to himself, leaving was what he wanted more than anything at the moment. He wanted to throw Penrose over his shoulder and run from this place.

But the king wanted her. Bad.

Somehow, the streets were even more dangerous for her than his father's house right then. It was an impressive feat. But until he could be sure of some things—Aisha and other alliances—he needed to use his connections here.

So far, it seemed his father didn't know about the king's proposed deal. He'd arrived after Malik had escorted their guest out. He'd still need to explain himself and why the king's man had been here to see him, but there were larger concerns.

He focused on her. Penrose's eyelids fluttered against her skin as she looked away again.

Her voice was so low that he nearly didn't hear her. "No. I can't sleep. Not after what happened."

Malik realized what she meant a moment later. She was talking about the tower.

She was afraid of falling asleep.

His own voice was low and rough when he responded. "I'm not going to make you. But it's not safe to wander the halls."

At those words, her eyes shot to his face. "It's your home," she said like that countered his statement.

"Exactly," he said.

On their way to his rooms, he met Aisha. He didn't miss the way her eyes lingered on Penrose and the state she was in, though his sister consented to meet with their father now that he was back and keep him occupied for a time.

"Soon," she whispered to him as she passed.

It wasn't a promise but rather a threat.

Malik was very aware of just how much his ass had been saved by her. But what remained to be seen was if Aisha was prepared to hear the truth that Malik carried with him now.

He hadn't been. Not at first.

Malik dismissed these thoughts. Penrose was speaking to him.

"I heard you talking ... downstairs," she said.

Beside her, Malik stiffened. "How?"

The word came out rougher than a true question should've, but she didn't seem to notice.

Her lashes brushed against her skin, and a one-sided grin formed a dimple in her cheek. "I spied on you."

Uninhibited honesty. It could be useful, Malik reasoned. More questions sprang inside him from her answer, but he let them go for now.

As he considered how he could use her newfound honesty to his benefit, he unlocked the door to his rooms and stepped aside for her. "You'll be safe here." Or at least, he hoped so.

Penrose didn't walk in immediately. Instead, she closed the distance between them. "I think I'll take the same bed that I had before. It was quite comfortable." She cocked her head as she took him in more fully, a mutinous smile spreading across her face. Malik watched her mouth as she spoke. "I noticed it had the best views."

Heat gathered at the nape of his neck and other places. There was no window near his bed. It was obvious what she meant.

So, she'd seen *that*.

"You have a filthy mind for a princess," he said, tilting her head to look at him straight.

Though she tried to hide it, she shivered at his touch. Her skin was too soft. The heat under his skin built, and he thought of how she'd like it if he'd been the one to see her.

But then again, this ridiculous girl had surprised him more than once already. Maybe she *would* like that. His pulse throbbed.

When she moved, she did so faster than he could've anticipated. Her hands had almost wrapped around the grip of the firearm he'd taken from her when he stopped her.

Malik held her wrists for perhaps longer than was necessary. With their hands so close to his waist, he whispered against her ear, "Until you have more experience, I'm afraid this tool is off limits."

He observed a satisfying shade of pink flush her cheeks as he released her.

I should do this more often.

But her amusement had faded.

"I know about the deal. There's no chance you're not taking it." She looked up at him. "It's all you could have wanted," she said. "Right?"

Malik's jaw tightened as he remembered the bastard who had dared to walk inside his home and spout the king's words.

Would she remember what Malik said to her? Maybe. Maybe not.

"I don't give a damn about a thing the king says," he said, settling on a partial truth.

The other side to it involved … her … and that didn't sound believable at all. Even to his own ears. He knew Aisha already thought him a nut just for what she suspected was going on in his head.

At his words, a look passed across her face too quickly for him to decipher it. But she walked into his rooms finally, and he secured the door after himself.

Chapter Twenty-Seven

Who Did This to You?

Even if his couch was vastly less comfortable than his bed, Malik reasoned that it was a good trade.

He'd noticed earlier that her smell lingered in his sheets even from her brief time in his bed. And it wasn't his fault she'd decided to steal his clothes for her own, now was it?

Malik closed his eyes as he reclined against his lounge. Sleeping here had the added benefit of close proximity to his door. If anyone tried to pick it or break through it, he'd know at once. Along with his collection of knives, he'd taken for his own the gun that Penrose had.

He'd give it back once he taught her a few things. His thoughts drifted to silence.

Malik opened his eyes. Penrose was standing in the doorway between their rooms.

His eyebrow arched, but he held his tongue when he saw her face.

"What is it?" His hand hovered over the knife hidden along his leg.

Penrose shook her head. "It's ... nothing. It's just ... You won't lie to me about something?" she asked suddenly. A strange look came across her features then. Her eyes bounced around the room, like she couldn't settle herself.

Malik ran a hand through his hair. What the hell?

"No," he got out. "No, I won't. What is it?"

She moved to the edge of the lounge and sat. It was wide enough that they weren't touching even when he was spread out like this.

Her eyes looked straight forward and away from his. "Is he ... Does he live?" she said in a quiet voice. "Cassius?"

Her husband. A feeling rose in him that he wanted to smother. Of course. Princesses married other royals. What was so unexpected about that?

And Princesses don't sleep in the beds of criminals.

"He's dead," Malik told her. He studied her face. "He has been for years."

Her words ran together as she spoke in whispers. "Are you sure? There's no way?"

His chest hurt, but he ignored it. "He's gone."

Penrose slumped forward, her face in her hands.

Malik looked away. Of course, she was upset. They'd been *married*. He needed to get up. He needed to get out of here.

This was all wrong.

He'd been wrong. Princesses didn't even talk to street scum. To people like him, whose hands would never be clean in any sense of the word.

But before he could leave, he noticed something odd. She was shaking, but she wasn't crying. Penrose was saying something, over and over.

"He's gone. He's finally gone."

He'd misinterpreted her reaction. She'd been ... scared of the possibility that he lived.

She was *scared* of him.

Malik remembered her fear of falling asleep and King Cassiel's words.

"A century ago, my father imprisoned her there."

There was more to it. This wasn't just a single thing that had happened to her. Relief was absurdly clear in her voice.

He'd done other things, too.

Malik's blood thundered through his veins, punishing his temples and wrists and every other part of him. His jaw was already sore from clenching his teeth.

He could feel her eyes on him.

Don't scare her, he bade himself, but he couldn't suppress the anger now that it had taken on its own life inside him. He wanted to find that soldier again and fix what he hadn't done.

Don't scare her.

He made an effort to bottle it inside himself. To save it for later—and a more appropriate audience. There would be a time and place for this thing to come out of him. And when the time came, he would let it gloriously free.

He couldn't kill what was already dead, but he'd try his very hardest to find someone else just as deserving. The sick, lovely feeling of bloodlust crawled inside him.

When he finally could speak again, his voice was rough but audible. He stared straight at her.

"What did he do to you?"

***

Penrose wasn't sure why, but something inside her splintered and broke when he asked that question.

It wasn't like Cassius had hit her. He hadn't kept her chained up and locked inside a dungeon. She hadn't been starved. It wasn't ... like that.

She was shaking her head, but his hands found either side of her face. His eyes held her prisoner.

"No. Tell me what he did to you," he commanded.

The deep tenor of his voice when he spoke to her made her pulse race faster.

He shouldn't care about this. She was standing in the way of what he should want the most. To Malik, what should it matter what Cassius had done to her a hundred years ago?

It didn't make sense why he should care this much about what had happened to her.

She was just a naïve once-princess who'd been used and tossed aside once she'd been declared dead.

Forgotten by the world at large. And it had moved on without her.

"He stole everything from me. He made me thought …" Penrose couldn't even say it. She'd been so stupid. Childish.

"Say it," he said.

Penrose laughed. It was not a joyful sound.

"He fooled me into thinking something ridiculous," she said. "That he loved me."

The device she used for her breathing episodes. Sorrowtail's broken wing. His tower and servants. Her glasses. Once she started talking, it was like she couldn't stop.

When she was done, Malik was silent for too long. She clenched her teeth like she could take it all back. She'd talked too much.

It wasn't like her silly little problems should mean anything to him, after all.

But she noticed a strange thing, then. Though he was looking away from her, she saw the muscles around his jaw tense.

"So, he couldn't get what he wanted without doing that. What a piss-poor excuse for a man." His right arm tensed like it ached to pull out the weapon he'd taken from her at his waist. "Like father, like son," he spat.

Penrose released a breath. *Like father, like son.*

Her head was feeling somewhat clearer from the liquor. She spared him a glance. *Maybe it's time to get to the bottom of a few things.*

"He remarried?" she asked.

Malik leaned back against the lounge seat and closed his eyes. "He did, but there weren't any royals left to marry." He clenched his jaw at that again, and she considered something in her mind.

A united Aloster. Three kingdoms in one.

But Karsia didn't have an eligible princess to marry off.

Her stomach turned. What had happened in this version of the world? But she thought she knew already.

Malik continued in the silence. "She was the daughter of a weapons manufacturer."

"Was?" Penrose asked, though she realized this all must have happened decades ago anyway.

"She died in childbirth." His face was wiped clean of any expression as he seemed to remember something. "Married her posthumously."

Penrose just stared forward. She hadn't even been dead. She supposed she should have been thankful that he didn't just kill her and claim himself married to her corpse after the fact.

"It's why they call this one the bastard king," Malik said. "King Cassiel."

Penrose breathed and tried to consider everything she knew already. In the aftermath of the scarlet-colored drink it was a task, but she managed it.

Though Cassius had somehow imprisoned her in his tower with somnus, it was his bastard heir, King Cassiel, who had hired Malik to kill her a century later.

"He's afraid I could challenge his claim on the throne," Penrose surmised.

Malik nodded. "Yes. That's what I figured."

She leaned forward like the answer was a physical thing before her. "But why now?"

Malik's gaze shifted. He shrugged. "Hell if I know."

Penrose nodded at that, but on the inside, she didn't accept his response. There was a reason.

Why hadn't Cassius's heir had her throat slit as soon as he came to power? Or just before? The transfer of the crown from one head to the next was always when the crown's power was most in jeopardy.

She thumbed at her lower lip. What changed? What had happened now that hadn't happened back then?

What if the king's soldier was telling the truth?

"She was sealed in that tower for all those years for a reason."

What if I've unleashed another version of the sleeping curse by waking? What if this was a mistake?

And then there was how it had happened. She'd pushed the thought away for too long in the danger that they'd trudged through to get here.

Though her thoughts were still far too muddled for her liking, she couldn't stop seeing Cassius's face when she'd made her promise to him.

"Assure yourself that I will never love you."

And what had come after.

Penrose shot to her feet. "I need to speak to Henrik."

That got Malik's eyes open.

Chapter Twenty-Eight

To Sleep

"I don't think so," Malik said. He stared back at her where she stood at the end of his lounge.

"I know you're keeping him here against his will," Penrose said. "I know why, too. Let me speak to him."

Malik narrowed his eyes on her. Was that a threat?

"Or what?" he asked. When she didn't have an answer, he closed his eyes again. "Sleep first."

When she was silent even after he gave her this concession, he peeked at her when she didn't realize he was looking. She was staring into the wide windows of his room that looked beyond the city of Alsra.

He remembered what she'd said earlier.

"No. I can't sleep. Not after what happened."

He felt the smirk dissolve from his face. She was afraid of falling asleep.

"You'll be fine. It won't happen again." Malik rolled the words around in his mouth before he got them out. "You'll be safe in here."

She looked at him suddenly. "Are you so sure? You can't be."

Malik glanced away. "I'll watch you. I'll stay up." He shrugged. "I've rested enough."

What was he saying? His body barked at him like a feral dog. His *bones* were tired.

Fuck off, he told himself.

By the smallest amount, her eyes narrowed at the edges. She'd gone back to staring out the windows at Alsra. "And you promise I'm not a prisoner?"

Malik pulled free the gun he'd stowed at his waist. He made sure the safety switch was on. "Don't use it until I show you how." He placed it on a nearby table. "This could buy you your way out of here, if you waved it around at the right people."

She didn't move to take it, yet, but her eyes didn't leave it.

"Besides. Our deal still stands. Some of the fortune you're owed will be paid to me for protection services," he informed her.

Got to cover his ass, after all. If he was going to keep the king's proposed deal quiet from his father, then he'd have to have *something* to bring to the dinner table.

Maybe it wasn't blanket immunity. But a pile of gold tended to smooth over a lot of things.

Maybe even what he'd done to merit the punishment of being forced to admit to a crime he hadn't committed and take the execution that came with it.

He hadn't spoken to him since he'd arrived back at Jackal's Hide. But by now, Raphael Ezar would have heard that Malik was here. Alive.

Yeah, he needed something big to cover his ass alright.

If he was going to remain useful after his father named his adopted sister his true heir, then he would have to pull this off.

While he'd been in thought, she'd walked to the table with the small gun on it. When she grabbed it and moved so she was before him, his body tensed before he could help it. It had been trained into him when someone approached him with a weapon.

But all she did was hold out the gun, the grip facing out towards him. It was then that he noticed the look on her face.

Her lashes brushed against her cheeks as she looked down at him. "Then you work for me. I'll need your protection, Malik."

He swallowed and tried to brush off his reaction to the way she'd said his name. Instead of responding verbally and giving himself away, he nodded once and took the weapon back.

Malik stood to give her the space where he'd been about to sleep, but she shook her head. "No, don't get up. There's plenty of space on this end."

He looked at her like she was somnus-addled but didn't leave the lounge couch. Instead, he propped his feet on the low table where the gun had been to give her more room.

There was a perfectly comfortable bed in the next room, but he didn't push the subject. She'd gravitated towards the not-bed piece of furniture from the beginning, so he supposed that was the hint.

"Have it your way," he said, one of his knives already in his hands with a polishing cloth in the other. If he was going to be up all night—or day, he realized, looking at the gray sky outside his windows—then he was going to *do* something.

Penrose curled up opposite him, his clothes still engulfing her. She turned on her side, her head cushioned under one of the pillows that Aisha had shoved into his room along with the rest of her *décor*.

Malik was silent as he worked, pausing occasionally to glance over at her or through his windows at the city that dearly wished him dead.

Though her eyes were closed, he could tell by the rhythm of her breathing that she wasn't sleeping.

He cursed himself for what he was about to do. It was a stupid thing to try, and he was almost certain it wouldn't work.

Malik moved his body so that he was resting next to her on the wide lounge, though in the opposite direction.

When she stopped breathing entirely, Malik bit into his tongue. He wasn't sure what the hell any of this was—his only experience with this type of thing was with one of his father's paid women who filled up on drugs afterward—but he was fairly sure he just screwed *this* to Hell.

Suddenly, she moved so that she wasn't opposite him anymore but between him and the back of the lounge couch. She didn't say a word.

Malik stared. Before he could change his mind, he turned on his side and pulled her against him. After a moment in which he expected her to shrug out of whatever this was and curse him for touching her, instead, her body untensed by a small amount.

After another few moments, her breathing deepened. She was asleep.

He took his promises and debts seriously. She would be safe in this room, or he'd be dead.

It was what was outside the room that they had to worry about, anyway.

Chapter Twenty-Nine

The Spare

"Open up, bastard."

Malik's eyes jerked open. The first thing he understood was how, despite the racket at his door, Penrose was still asleep. And how she was curled into a perfect fit against him.

Malik extricated himself from her limbs and those thoughts, cursing under his breath.

He hadn't meant for any of that.

How the hell had it happened? *Snuggling.* He pushed the thought away. She'd been lonely and unable to sleep.

And likely as most any man would have in the same situation, he'd obliged to be used as a pillow.

Malik took a moment to allow the blood to redistribute throughout him and distracted himself with other, blander thoughts. Like thoughts of almost dying of that damned infection just a day or so ago.

It was enough to put him back in order. Malik took the gun with him when he went to his door.

Before Aisha could knock at his door again, he pulled it open with the weapon in hand.

"*Hey,*" she hissed at the sight of it, even though he hadn't even aimed it at her.

He relaxed a degree when he saw she was alone. "You'd have done the same," he muttered.

Aisha brushed past him to walk inside. "I don't think so, big brother," she said. She stared at the girl curled up on his lounge couch. Without taking her eyes off Penrose, she continued speaking to him. "Did you just wake up?"

"We're not speaking here," Malik said under his breath. "C'mon."

After she followed him into his armory room and he closed the door, she jerked to face him. "What the hell was that, Malik?"

She crossed her arms where she stood in front of another massive window set into his rooms. It was daylight outside, and it limned her silhouette in brightness. The small coils against her head became a cloud, and her dress—she was always in some impractical dress, no matter their business—shimmered slightly. Even against the glare of the light, he saw her expression. It was sharp enough to cut.

She looked like she owned this city already, Malik realized.

"I've played into this long enough," she added.

"Did you tell him?" Malik's head pounded. He felt like *he'd* been the one drinking. "Does he know?"

"Of course not," Aisha said. "But he's asked about you."

"Yeah, I'm sure he has," he said.

It was an issue he'd been trying to figure out since he'd resolved to not die.

Malik remembered the moment in his rooms when his sister had guessed that he'd turned himself in. She seemed to be remembering the same thing.

"What the hell has been going on with you, Malik? First Belnya. Now her. Your ... princess," she said through her teeth. "And now I'm lying to Father for you."

"It's not that simple," Malik countered.

"Really? Seems simple to me." she said. "Because you're acting like a dumbass. Just for some hard-to-get—"

"Aisha. It's not just her," he said between his teeth.

Heat thrummed through him, aggravating the splitting headache he'd woken with. He wasn't sure how he'd been going to tell her, but she needed to know. *Now.*

It was what he told himself as the words slipped out of his clenched jaws.

"He's going to choose you."

Aisha stared at him. From the look on her face, he saw he didn't have to clarify who they were talking about.

"No. No, he isn't," she said.

"You'd be blind not to see it by now," Malik said. His body was at odds against the hard surface of the wall. This wasn't a room intended to lounge inside.

"You're his blood." Aisha allowed a short, clipped laugh to escape her lips. "Not the girl he picked up in the slums of our people. You're his progeny. You've always been his intended heir."

"Not anymore, Aisha," he said in a dangerous voice. She wasn't the only one who could cut without a knife. "I was commanded to turn myself in for those kills. His kills. Dammit, you *know* why."

He took the steps to close the distance between them. He continued, "It's because I'm in the way of your dynasty."

Aisha's eyes kept flicking across his face as if searching for the lie she wanted to see there. Her lip pulled back slightly when she spoke, and he saw the clenched teeth beyond it.

"He wouldn't kill you—"

"Raphael Ezar cuts loose what doesn't serve him," Malik said. "Even within his own house. We both know it."

He could see it in her face that she finally understood. The silence that followed wasn't oppressive like most were. They stood across from each other, allowing what couldn't be said to fill into the space between.

When Aisha finally broke the silence, her voice was measured. Muted.

"Malik. I don't see things that way. Should he name me for succession, I wouldn't view you as competition. We'd run this together." She nodded, once, at him. "Like we were always going to."

In that moment, Malik didn't see Aisha Ezar, cutthroat princess of House Ezar and one of the women of Alsra that shouldn't be fucked with under any circumstance.

He saw the girl with hollowed-out cheeks and sharp bones that pointed against her skin. He saw her scramble for the bruised, softened fruit that the city's guards lobbed at the people in the Karsian slums when they passed through it.

Malik couldn't remember what business he and his father had been on that'd brought them to the slums, but he'd never forget the first time he saw her. It was the first time he'd ever seen his father do something solely for the benefit of someone else. Seemingly.

Without comment or objection, his father had watched the soldiers throw rotted fruit at people that looked like them. Before the sun had set entirely that night, they'd finished their business, and he'd found her in her hiding place in the slums.

She'd been scared of him at first. It was a natural reaction to his father.

But just as he'd trained Malik, he'd trained her into what she was today. Even though she'd been adopted into this family, she was as much an Ezar as he was.

Maybe more.

Malik's voice was rough. "It's different now."

Aisha looked at him. "Does it have to be?"

When he didn't respond, she crossed her arms in a mirror to him and leaned into him.

"You still haven't explained yourself. Not for everything," she accused. "Why her? Why her instead of *us*, Malik?"

Her meaning was clear. Why was he refusing to make the deal with the king—to give up a forgotten princess in exchange for immunity from the law for their family?

Malik could have said any number of things to that—explanations that made perfect sense. For one, he didn't trust the bastard king. He'd already betrayed him once. Second, he didn't like King Cassiel. Even if this king wasn't his father, he was still an ass.

Third, Malik wasn't so sure he wanted what the king offered.

None of those was precisely why he stood there, grappling for words like he was hollow-headed.

Penrose was suddenly standing in the doorway to his armory, her eyes glued to the two of them. Her face was unreadable.

All she said was, "Someone's here."

Chapter Thirty

Bait

The soldier crouched before the king of Aloster.

"I have done as you requested, Your Majesty," he said. He'd been allowed to be in the same room as the king only under the conditions that he remain on the other side of the vast throne room.

The king was well aware of the man's affliction. He was starting to sweat, and it was clear he hadn't been sleeping for the nightmares. He had perhaps another day or so.

"And you've ensured the right ears heard your performance?"

His soldier snuck a look at him from where he'd been gazing at the floor. "Ezar saw me leave. I ensured it while his son escorted me out."

The king leaned back. The ploy he'd concocted after hearing Sarina's prediction had worked.

Of course, he had wanted the Prince of Grime to know who he was dealing with. The satisfaction he gleaned from putting the brat in his place was no small amount.

That was important, certainly.

But what was coming next would be magnitudes better.

What had been more important than that was delivering his message in a way that Raphael Ezar couldn't fail to take notice of.

That had been his true aim, after all.

Nothing happened in this city without the head of Ezar's criminal dynasty knowing about it. And he intended to take full advantage of his nosiness.

Ezar had to know who the girl was under his roof—and the price her pretty little head commanded for him.

But he didn't want her dead—at least not yet.

Princess Penrose of Aloster.

He hadn't heard that name in many years.

Sarina's vision came back to him, complete in its resplendence. The princess would come to him.

And then, every last bit of terror she had for him would be used until there was nothing left. It was the only way to lift this wretched curse from him.

Just like how it had begun.

But first, he had to ensure that her fear for him was at its peak. Only then would it work.

His soldier was still kneeling half a room away. "Your Majesty, if you would." He was still looking pointedly at his polished floors.

Right. The leftover.

The king rose from his throne. "You are dismissed," he told his guards.

When they were alone, the king motioned his soldier closer. There was no pretense to maintain a safe distance anymore.

And if the man had qualms of spreading the deadly disease to his ruler, he didn't show it. The skin under his eyes had darkened so that it looked to be bruised. This was how they all got right before the end.

Likely, he hadn't slept in a week. Between the horrors in their sleep and the lack of it, somnus drove more than half its victims insane.

The king of Aloster placed his palm on his soldier's forehead. It was slicked in sweat, but he managed to hold contact with him.

"Thank you, My Liege," the man started to sputter. "Thank you for curing it. They said you might have some knowledge of how to relieve it, but I couldn't have dreamed of a cure."

He looked down at the man who claimed to be his vassal. His pledged man.

"You failed me," he corrected him. The king's voice was moderate, yet clear over his soldier's screams. "You failed to bring them straight to me the first time. And that doesn't merit a reward, does it?"

The king of Aloster breathed deeply as the man writhed beneath his palm. When the soldier didn't answer, he answered for him.

"Failure merits punishment."

The king's words were cut off by a scream. His soldier jerked out of his touch. The man's eyes were pitch black when he pulled out the long knife at his waist only to sink it into his own chest.

He died with his eyes still open, still black as the night. His blood puddled around him.

King Cassius's eyes closed and his chest heaved with the thrill of the man's nightmares. There had been something about a street rat in there. And even something about a girl with a revolver.

Fear was never more delicious than when it was fresh.

He smiled.

Cassius had been merciful to the soldier, after all. He'd sped up the inevitable.

Now he only had to wait for the dog to take the bait.

Chapter Thirty-One

The Lost Son

The words Penrose had overheard repeated in her mind on a loop.

"*You're his blood. You're his progeny. You've always been his intended heir.*"

"*Not anymore, Aisha. I was commanded to turn myself in for those kills. His kills. Dammit, you know why.*"

And then: "*Our father cuts loose what doesn't serve him.*"

To say she hadn't intended to overhear their conversation would have been a lie. After seeing that soldier come here for her, she had to be sure of Malik's intentions—that he wasn't going to sell her to the king. The knowledge she'd gotten instead was much worse.

Her heart thundered harder with every step she took. They'd been summoned to the lowest level of the building.

All *three* of them.

Malik radiated tension like the sun did warmth. Aisha walked behind them, but she could feel her staring into the back of her head.

"*Why her instead of us, Malik?*"

Penrose hadn't missed that. It was a question she'd wondered, too. Even if it stung so much worse coming from another person.

As they passed through the bar floor of the building, smoke drifted lazily to the ceiling. Penrose's chest tightened in response.

Not now. Not now.

But a cough slipped past her lips until it was an entire coughing fit. Malik spun, his jaw tightening when he saw her.

He angled his head at the stairs and spoke to Aisha. "Go ahead without us."

Penrose shook her head as her cheeks filled in with redness. "I'm fine."

It was a lie, but there wasn't much to be done other than leave the cloud of smoke hovering above them.

Not without one of her father's devices that he'd invented for her.

Penrose focused on breathing shallowly. "Let's go." She pushed ahead of them.

But as they descended the stairs, Malik was at her shoulder, whispering to her.

"This place is dangerous. Stay by me. Or Aisha."

Penrose looked at him. She kept her voice low. "She doesn't like me."

Malik's eyes were elsewhere. "She won't sell you out."

It was all the conversation they had time for. They were underground once more, and after a few turns, the laboratory stretched before her.

Steam rose from liquids, and warmth from a furnace tucked away in a corner of the room seeped into her feet, as if it were boiling her, too. Papers were piled on every surface, and a cloth covered a box on the top of one of the tables. Faintly, she heard the sounds of a high-pitched squeaking noise.

In the middle of it all was Henrik, wearing a mask with a breathing contraption that had attached goggles. He was busy enough flipping through pages of notes on his table that he didn't even acknowledge them when they entered the area.

But Penrose could ignore the other men no longer.

One was clearly his enforcer. The man had muscles rippling beneath his tailored jacket with no shirt underneath to conceal them. Various weapons were displayed openly at his hips.

Raphael Ezar stood to the right of him. Penrose tried not to stare at him and failed. When he caught her eye, something passed between them.

She hadn't told Malik that she'd already met his father, and she wasn't sure why. She'd already admitted to spying on him and Aisha when they'd spoken with the king's man.

She wondered if her omission was wise now.

Ezar settled his gaze on his son, and Penrose remembered what she knew. Malik had been ordered to turn himself in for murder—to die as a punishment for this man. All because Malik was in the way of Aisha's ascension.

He turned his gaze on his adopted daughter in question. "Good to see you've collected your lost brother."

Aisha and Malik had bowed their heads at the sight of their father so she couldn't see his daughter's face. But she thought she heard it in her response.

"Back where he belongs, Father," she said.

The words weren't quite a challenge, but Penrose knew from personal experience that they weren't the words of a grateful heir.

Raphael Ezar's gaze settled on her. Suddenly, she remembered the last words he spoke to her in the meeting they weren't supposed to have had.

"Come find me when you tire of my son."

Before she could blurt out words—anything at all to stop his staring at her like that—Malik spoke for her.

"This is my client. She's paying for protection services."

Ezar's dark eyes gleamed. "A pleasure." A second later, he gestured towards the healer and researcher he kept prisoner in this building.

"The three of you are just in time to witness the cure to somnus."

Chapter Thirty-Two

The Poison and the Cure

"Henrik. Take that off and introduce yourself. It's rude to ignore your guests," Raphael Ezar said.

Henrik was shaking when he removed his mask, and his eyes were on the floor.

Penrose's heart caught in her throat. Had he really done it? This would mean an end to so much suffering and maybe …

Just maybe it was the key to finding out what had happened to her in that tower.

And maybe even reversing it.

"Yes, sir. Of course," Henrik said. "Allow me to begin."

She didn't miss the way his gaze lingered on the three of them when he thought they weren't looking—the head of the Ezar crime dynasty and his progeny.

He has a right to hate them.

But the moment had passed. He approached the table closest to them where a box-like object had been covered with a cloth. He swiped it away to reveal a cage with a gray mouse inside it. Its eyes were closed, but it twitched every few seconds in what was likely sleep.

Penrose shared his excitement, and she hoped she didn't seem like another of his captors, but she held her tongue.

"Although somnus is primarily a human disease, mice do exhibit symptoms similar to ours. My team's—my research showed that dreams are a necessary component for the disease's viability in its host."

Henrik moved and spoke like a different man then. At his heart, Henrik looked to be a man of knowledge and learning; despite his situation, a small, almost invisible smile crossed his face when he turned to his instruments.

He continued, "We used to think dreams came from the gods as visions. But we know now that they originate from our own brains. I suggest—"

Ezar hadn't even said anything. He'd merely looked at his enforcer next to him who had produced a small vial of some liquid. Ezar's man rushed at Henrik.

He jerked away from him. "No! No," he sputtered. "Please, there's no need for that at all. I'd die of somnus before I could show you how to use the cure."

"That sounds like I'd have enough time to learn how to use it. If you're telling me the truth and you *do* have a cure," Ezar said.

"I am. Please," Henrik pleaded, his eyes still on the vial.

Ezar snapped his fingers, and his man stopped short of grabbing Henrik and forcing him to ingest the liquid.

Something in Penrose's stomach soured like old milk. He'd been about to infect Henrik with the disease—she was sure of it. She thought she was going to vomit.

Malik's father was disgusting. Her heart raced. She couldn't just stand by.

"This requires a precise hand. If I don't get the timing right ..." Henrik stopped speaking after seeing the look on Ezar's face.

Penrose stepped towards Henrik. "Let me help you."

Henrik's brows came together at the sight of her, as if seeing her for the first time among the criminals who kept him here. "This is tricky work, madam."

But she'd already donned the extra pair of gloves on the table next to the cages. The world had changed when she'd slept, but she would seek to understand it rather than be paralyzed by her fears of it.

She pointed her chin at the flask of liquid before them. "That's your base, isn't it? Is it a reactant you're using? One of the acids?"

Henrik stared at her.

Her father had been a patron of the sciences, and a student of it in his own right. She'd picked up a few things from him in his lab.

He must have decided to trust her, then, because he grabbed from his pile of instruments a metal clamp.

"Monitor the fluid levels. You're familiar with evaporative effects on liquids?" Henrik asked.

"Steam," Penrose said. One of her eyebrows rose. "Of course. Heat makes it volatile. Open and accepting to your additive." She turned to him. "This changes the ... brain?" she guessed.

"It's a stimulant," Henrik said. "So, it can alter brain activity, though not permanently." Henrik nodded at the liquid before Penrose. "Ensure that no more than three milliliters evaporate from the base, but at least a measure of one. Be careful not to directly inhale it."

In its cage, the mouse with somnus had started to squeal even though its eyes were still firmly shut. Her stomach clenched at the animal's clear signs of suffering, though she fought to concentrate on the task that Henrik had given her.

Penrose's eyes ached as she squinted at the small marks on the glass flask. The edges of it blurred, but she did as she'd been instructed. How she missed the reading spectacles her parents had commissioned for her. She bit into her lip as she dismissed the thought.

They were long gone from this world, and besides, what had she really been to them other than a peace offering to a tyrant?

She could feel Malik's eyes on her. What was he thinking now?

Penrose couldn't allow anything to show on her face, and she allowed her features to return to a careful neutrality.

But she couldn't stop her thoughts. Was she putting herself in danger by demonstrating her willingness to help their captive help find a cure for somnus?

It doesn't matter. This is far too important not to help with.

And even if Malik's father was a terrible man, how badly could he pervert the mission to cure a deadly, torturous disease?

No matter what, the world would be a better place with a treatment for somnus.

And if she had to steal this cure to release it to the world like she'd once planned to?

Well, then so be it.

Penrose called to Henrik that the base was ready. She watched as Henrik combined the substances using the tongs to lift the liquid inside the steaming glass to a new one that contained the reactant.

With held breath, she watched as he produced a small glass cylinder with measurement marks on its side. Bronzed metal gleamed in the light on either side of the object, forming a ring for his finger to hold it on one and a sharp, narrow opening on the other. When he pushed down the top of it, a plunger moved inside it, and she realized what he was doing.

The newly combined substance collected inside the tube as he drew the top of it up again. Henrik allowed a bead of the liquid to drop from the metal tip before moving again.

Penrose's mouth popped open when she put it together. "Faster and more reliable than ingestion. Miraculous. That pierces skin to deliver the medicine directly into the blood. How did I never think of that?"

Henrik looked at her. "Well, I didn't discover it. Decades of science did, dear."

"Henrik." Ezar only had to utter a single word for silence to fall again.

In her enthusiasm, Penrose had forgotten the stakes for Henrik. She stood back to give him space.

Henrik opened the cage and held the mouse's small body with one hand while the other held aloft the injection device. Although the mouse remained asleep, its squeals grew in volume. It was as if Henrik's hand was another of its tormentors in its dreams.

Henrik's eyes didn't leave the animal below him. "It's important to do this while they sleep. It should move the brain from one phase of sleeping to the next—and give the body a chance to fight back against somnus in that time."

It was done. But something wasn't right. The mouse still screeched, the sound of it drilling into her ears.

Penrose felt sick as they all watched. Quickly, Henrik removed his hands from the cage.

Suddenly, the animal was awake.

No one spoke.

The mouse rushed to its small bowl of water. Penrose breathed.

But no. Oh, no.

Among squeals and splashing water, it started to drown itself.

It can't—gods—

Suddenly, too much was happening at once. Ezar was shouting. Malik pulled her away from the sight. Aisha had stiffened next to her. Henrik was moving.

The mouse was safe in his hands, but it was too late for Henrik.

The sight of the vial flashed in Penrose's sight. Ezar's enforcer was going to infect him.

Henrik was a good man. He didn't deserve this. Raphael Ezar was already speaking, ordering his slow demise.

She had to do something.

Malik had brought her close to him, his hand on her shoulder. Securing her. Or protecting her.

It didn't really matter which.

All that mattered was the opportunity suddenly within reach.

Even if she only had the one shot.

Penrose buried herself against Malik. He was shocked, but his body soon relaxed into it, allowing the sudden close contact.

He blocked her from the sight, protecting her from the brutality of his world.

Well, she wasn't going to let an innocent man die before her. She wasn't going to pretend that *this* was something unfortunate but inevitable.

From this angle, it was easy for Penrose to pull the black metal weapon—the gun—from his waistband.

He'd shown her how to engage the safety switch—the safety was on now—as well as how to use it. She turned around.

"Henrik!" She slid the gun across the floor.

She had time only to blink before it was in Henrik's hands.

Chapter Thirty-Three

Fire

It happened too quickly for Penrose to process.

Raphael Ezar's man had gone for Henrik with the vial, but none of them had expected what she had done.

Malik shouted her name and pulled her behind him. He wasn't gentle.

"What the hell—" he growled at her.

Penrose didn't care at that moment. Let him be mad at her.

It would be worth it.

In the blur of seconds that passed after he'd taken the gun, Penrose rejoiced to see that the exit was clear. Ezar's man had faltered in the confusion. Aisha had cursed but wasn't interfering, and Malik was too preoccupied with her to do much.

He was free. All Henrik had to do was brandish the weapon a bit and run.

But he wasn't running.

"You." The word dragged across Henrik's tongue.

Penrose stared at the barrel. She didn't get it. He'd pointed the gun at her.

Not me, she realized. *Malik.*

Tears dotted Henrik's eyelids. "You killed them all, you monster. They were my friends. They only wanted to save this damned world." His teeth clenched around the words. "Well, it never deserved them."

As Henrik said the words, Malik pushed her away from him.

"Henrik!" Penrose shouted as the sound of gunfire rang through the space.

But *his* gun hadn't been the one to go off.

Penrose blinked, her brain catching up to what had happened too slowly. Henrik was shaking on the floor, his hands pressed tight against one of his calves. Red seeped from under his grip.

Malik's father had shot him.

He walked calmly to Henrik after he put away the revolver. Blood soaked underneath his black shoes when he got close enough to him.

Penrose's blood raged inside her. She hadn't realized Aisha was holding her back until she tried to rush in front of Henrik to block him from Ezar.

"Enough," she hissed in Penrose's ear. "You've done enough."

Penrose quieted. Even if her intentions had been golden, she'd caused this. Malik wasn't even responsible for their deaths, and he'd nearly been shot in retribution.

And he still had to act like he'd done it in front of Henrik and his father.

"This should suffice as motivation, then. At least for now," Ezar tacked on, looking down on a shaking and likely lightheaded Henrik. He cocked his head to the side. "Do better. Or else."

Henrik stared at the floor. "I will."

Witnessing the interaction made her felt as if she'd taken the hit meant for Malik.

Why didn't he run?

She hadn't meant for Henrik to be shot or Malik's life to be put in danger. She hadn't meant for any of this.

She turned to him. "Malik, I ..."

He didn't look at her. The skin around his eyes was tight, but other than that, his face was curiously blank.

"I didn't want this," Penrose continued.

Finally, he looked at her. She breathed.

"And why not? It would have been his right to get his shot in," he said.

Her tongue was heavy at his response, so she shut her mouth. She couldn't tell him that she knew he hadn't done it—that he'd had to take credit for their deaths as punishment. Not in front of his father.

Malik's eyes moved to look at something just past her. Penrose spun to see Raphael Ezar approaching them, leaving damp red footprints.

She hated how she could see the same expression on his father's face as she'd seen on Malik's.

But she hated more that she cared so much about the resemblance.

Her eyes were on the weapon stowed at his waist, though he didn't draw it.

"Keep your client in check."

***

"We need to talk."

Penrose was still dazed from seeing Henrik shot. Numb.

Some of the bar workers had come down to help clean the mess in the lab. She'd watched much of it in silence. Malik hadn't spoken to her again until now.

She nodded at Malik's words.

"Fine," she added.

In the halls outside Henrik's laboratory, he rounded on her.

"The hell was that?" he said.

Penrose clenched her teeth. It had been a good idea. She wasn't sure where it had all gone so wrong.

But these were criminals. She couldn't forget that. They weren't playing at war here. To them, this was war every day.

Penrose looked at him. "Why? Why does he want to cure it?"

Malik met her stare with a cold glance, and she wished she could wipe the look off his face. "Why else, Princess?"

To save this cursed world, the voice inside her answered.

But Malik answered his own question. "To make a profit."

"Of course." She echoed his words. "Why else would a cure be necessary?"

Malik actually looked ... hurt? That couldn't be right.

"Think what you may," he said, "but this is our livelihood. Not all of us were born rich."

Penrose let the comment go. She wasn't anywhere near rich right now, but that conversation wasn't one she was keen to have.

After some silence, Penrose said, "I *am* sorry."

A vein in Malik's jaw ticked. "Are you? Are you sorry you tried to free an innocent—or sorry he didn't get his hit in?"

Penrose stepped closer to him despite the warning signals he gave off. "I know who you really are. I know you didn't kill them. No matter what you say to try to scare me, I know you're not the monster here—"

His hand covered her mouth, and she froze. His mouth hovered near her ear.

"I could've. Don't forget that, Princess. The hand on you is the same that has choked many men. In this house, I'm one of them."

When he released her, they just stared.

Finally, she spoke.

"If that's what you choose."

Chapter Thirty-Four

Those who have Mercy

Penrose started helping Henrik that same day. She had no other leads as to how she'd confront King Cassiel, the most powerful man in Alsra, the son of her dead husband, and the one who so dearly wanted her dead.

Although he was long gone now, Prince Cassius had known something about somnus that the world hadn't.

And he'd weaponized it against her.

Besides, she couldn't seem to remain by Malik without getting angry again. He lurked in the edges of the room, nothing more than her silent bodyguard now.

How am I going to pay him?

In the blur of the past few days, she had forgotten about that. But recent events had demonstrated just how out of place she was here.

She couldn't forget that this was a business transaction—and that the people she was dealing with traded in both blood and money.

Henrik had been weakened by his wound, but he seemed invigorated at having her help. He'd been bandaged and stabilized, and he instructed her from where he rested on a nearby cot.

"Can you tell me what you know about the disease?" Penrose asked as she worked, gathering the supplies before her. "I'd love to know more about what you and your team discovered. I never considered how the disease affected the brain."

Henrik's eyes danced. "Well, our research indicated that when we dream, our brains are very active. We're not sure how it works, but—"

"But change the way we dream, change the disease? Cure it?" Penrose said.

"Very good." Henrik tilted his head. "Which university did you attend? Or perhaps you've been to some of my colleagues' public lectures?"

Penrose frowned. Universities? Public lectures? She'd missed so much.

"I learned from my father," she decided to say, hoping to avoid the inevitable string of questions that would follow if she divulged more of her background. "I think I was more at home in his study than in my own rooms."

Henrik's eyebrows rose. "Is that so? What's his name? Perhaps I know him."

Penrose swallowed. She kept her eyes on the cabinet full of flasks and measurement tools before her. "No, I ... He died long ago."

"I'm so sorry."

Silence stretched between them, and she allowed it. When Penrose looked up, she saw that his eyes were casting about the room. No one else was with them except for Malik, and he seemed more interested in cleaning his weapons than speaking to them.

Henrik's gaze lingered on him. She thought she saw his jaw clench, though she may have imagined it.

She wished she could tell him the truth of who killed his research team. Malik's words repeated in her skull.

"In this house, I'm one of them."

Henrik's voice plunged low, low enough that she knew it wouldn't carry past their ears. "Was it them?"

A breath rushed to leave her. Her voice was equally low. "No. No, it wasn't."

It wasn't that absurd of a question, she supposed.

"Forgive me," Henrik said, though he didn't sound like he meant it.

Penrose caught his eye. "Henrik, I'm sorry for what happened. I'd hoped for ... something else."

She swallowed and decided to ask it.

"Why didn't you try to leave?" she asked.

Henrik's brown eyes were sincere. "Maybe it seems dense. I suppose it was. Who else will cure this disease?" His voice was almost inaudible when he spoke again. "But to know they could never do this again ..."

Penrose looked to Malik who was still in the lab's corner, cleaning the revolver she'd tried to pass to Henrik. He either hadn't heard their words or didn't want to hear.

Henrik's gaze sharpened. "You should get out while you can. They're not merciful."

"I'll be fine. We have ... an agreement," she said.

Gods, she hoped so. Besides, there were few other places she could turn to as an enemy of the crown.

Henrik looked like she'd told him that the mice in the walls told her secrets.

Penrose stifled a giggle at the thought. It wouldn't do to have him think her mad.

Even if she was a little.

As Henrik instructed her, Penrose slipped the respirator device down her skull. Her fingers tightened the straps along the back of her head that held it in place.

She breathed, and clean air rushed into her lungs. She nodded to Henrik.

"Is the base ready?" he asked.

Penrose crouched near the surface of the table, bringing the flask close to her face to measure it. She squinted at the marks carved against the glass until the blurriness abated somewhat.

Now. Now it was ready. Penrose took the tongs and combined the liquids. With careful, measured steps, she brought it to Henrik.

Sitting upright on the cot, he prepared the syringe instrument and passed it back to her. She approached the cage with the sleeping, squealing mouse inside.

Penrose breathed. She'd practiced on a piece of chicken breast earlier, but a living, breathing animal was quite different to a cut of meat.

Meat didn't squirm and try to flee.

"Please," she whispered. "Let me help you."

Its squealing continued, though it stopped its thrashing. She found the spot Henrik had told her to aim for and pressed the plunger down.

After a moment, she said, "I think ... I think I did it."

Her hands shook, and she removed them from the cage. The mouse was quieting. Her heart galloped in her chest. She'd been afraid it would try to drown itself again.

This is it. It has to be.

The mouse was silent.

"What's going on?" Henrik asked. She even thought she saw a flicker in Malik's corner like he'd looked over at them.

Penrose didn't answer as she stared at the sight. Her fingers sought a heartbeat, the quick, tapping rhythm that was much faster than theirs.

It wasn't there.

She stepped away and shook her head at Henrik.

His eyes unfocused. "It can't ... No." He looked at her. "Check again."

She removed the respirator device from her face and ran a hand through her strands. "Henrik, it's gone."

"We performed this exact scenario before. It worked then! Why not now?" His gaze shot to her again. "Are you sure you measured correctly?"

"Yes. Absolutely."

Did I?

Her hands slicked with sweat. She sat down. "No. I can't—I can't always see well."

Gods, did I mess up? Was it my fault?

"It's alright." He deflated. "This mouse's time was soon. You likely spared him a prolonged death."

Penrose knuckled her forehead where she sat. How were they going to do this?

There's more to this than Henrik realizes. He should know.

She glanced at him. He was a man of knowledge and science. Would he listen?

Was it safe to tell him who she was? Would he think her unhinged?

"We used to think dreams came from the gods as visions."

What if there was something to that? In Penrose's world, the sleeping curse had been a sign of the gods' disfavor.

In this world, it seemed to be treated merely as an infectious disease.

I know what I saw in the tower.

Prince Cassius had *controlled* it. He'd somehow paralyzed her, and a blue haze had settled on her before she'd fallen prey to the curse.

"What if there's more to it than this?" Penrose stood. "What if they were right all those years ago about the gods?"

She could feel Malik's eyes on her this time. He stayed a silent sentinel at the edges of the room, though she wondered what he thought of this.

Henrik met her stare where he was propped up on his cot. "Penrose." He dragged out the last part of her name. "We've had a setback, but it's hardly impossible to cure it. It *can* be done."

He thinks I've given up.

"Right." She stared at the floor.

It was crazy, after all, what had happened. She wondered if she'd truly remembered it correctly.

Maybe she'd only been very lucky that the disease she'd caught hadn't killed her but only kept her in a dreamless slumber.

Lucky.

The word rolled around inside her head like a physical thing.

Chapter Thirty-Five

Hellaciously Stupid

It's time, Malik thought.

Though it was hard to tell on the basement floors of Jackal's Hide, the sun was finally close to rising on this damned city.

Penrose had fallen asleep with a stack of books before her and several more in her lap in one of the few chairs within the lab. Henrik was sleeping on his cot.

Malik had been planning out how to do this the entire day in which he'd guarded Penrose down here.

He strode to where the researcher was sleeping. In one motion, he slipped one of his knives free and pressed it against the man's throat as he shoved his other hand over his mouth.

His words to Penrose echoed in his head.

"In this house, I'm one of them."

It was time to prove that.

At once, the man's body rebelled against Malik's hold but not for long. Captives either fought or learned how to live.

Henrik had learned.

Malik's mouth came to his ear. "You've noticed her coughs. Her trouble breathing."

At the mention of Penrose, the skin around Henrik's eyes tightened. He was a learned captive, but he'd already turned to putty in Penrose's inquisitive hands.

He's worried for her.

A joyless chuckle came from deep within him. The air mussed some of Henrik's hair from his face. "I'm not going to hurt her."

Some of the tension in his face eased. Henrik gave a short, curt nod.

"When I release you, you'll make no sound except in direct answer to my questions. Do you understand?"

Again, he nodded. Malik withdrew his hand and his knife, and the captive was true to his word. He stayed silent.

Even if his temporary release from Malik's hold had emboldened the hate in Henrik's eyes.

Good, a voice in him cooed. So often in these situations, hate masked the bone-deep fear. And fear would make Henrik a man of his word.

And that was *very* important today.

Malik glanced over to see that Penrose was still sleeping. He returned his attention to Henrik.

"You've seen conditions like hers before," Malik said.

If Henrik was surprised at this topic of conversation, he didn't show it. "A few times. Her lungs are inflamed."

"You can cure her." Again, it wasn't a question.

"There's no cure for it," Henrik said.

Malik's pulse ran. Suddenly, his knife was on Henrik's throat again. "Say that again."

Just yesterday, he'd heard the bastard tell Penrose that they couldn't fail to produce a cure for somnus. So why not for her?

The hate grew in Henrik's eyes. "Am I supposed to cure every disease while I'm down here? I suppose you'll want me to cure death since it will take more than my lifetime for all of that."

Malik's teeth clenched hard enough in his head that it ached from the force.

Calm. If you leave him in a pool of his blood, you won't be able to explain this away to her when she wakes.

And then, of course, there was the matter that this man belonged to his father, not to Malik. He supposed he should have taken captive a healer for his own use.

Malik removed the knife from his throat. He recalled what she'd told him of her life in the past. There'd been a solution back then.

"There's medicine to treat it," he prompted.

Henrik watched him. "Yes. And she'll need to use an inhalant device." At his expression, Henrik clarified. "A pipe, more or less."

"I need them both."

Henrik's eyes narrowed like he was suspicious of Malik's intent. Like Malik could hurt her with medicine. He held himself back from rolling his eyes.

Even so, the man reached for a pen and some parchment near his cot, and he slipped Malik the piece of paper when he was done.

"I don't have the supplies for a such a thing here," Henrik said. "But I know someone who sells these things."

As he pocketed the paper, Malik rose. She was still sleeping. The day barely existed yet, and there was already too much he needed to accomplish.

But he'd ran out of time.

"I'll be gone for most of today. In my absence, Aisha will take my role as her guard. I expect you will not mention a word of our conversation to Penrose."

Henrik nodded where he rested on his cot, his bandaged leg visibly red once more.

Yes, this was a learned captive. So long as his father got what he wanted from Henrik, the man would survive.

And he always got what he wanted.

Like father, like son.

***

Today was the last of the three days he'd been given to respond to King Cassiel's proposal.

All things considered, Malik was making good time, even if he was sacrificing other things for it. He would have preferred to be there to guard her on this day in particular, but there was no other way. Aisha was reliable, even if she didn't agree with his decision, and, frankly, he didn't trust anyone else to meet with the king's man for him.

The secrets of Alsra's streets had given themselves up to him many years ago, and he well knew the fastest route to get what he wanted.

He'd bribed one of the city guards earlier that morning with a heavy sum of coins. An address had been whispered to him after he left the medicine supplier's shop.

Within a few days, Penrose's medicine and the device she'd need to inhale it would arrive at Jackal's Hide.

Even if what she'd done in the lab had been hellaciously stupid, Malik admired her fortitude for taking what she needed by whatever means necessary.

A woman after his own heart.

He knew it was daft. She was in love with the idea of justice, and he was as far from that as possible.

Of course, there was also the consideration that she was a princess. Malik didn't belong with her, but when had that stopped him from getting what *he* wanted?

You wouldn't be good for her, a voice inside him reminded him. Hell, he wasn't good for this city.

He'd meant what he'd said to her after his father had shot Henrik.

She needed to see what he was—what they all were. For her own protection.

And maybe—just maybe—there was a part of Malik that wanted her to see the worst of what he had to offer.

And to accept him anyway.

He almost laughed at that last thought, but he'd arrived at the place. It was time to become the Prince of Grime once again.

It was a bar like Jackal's Hide, though the comparison was more like a castle to a shack.

Malik scanned the crowd. Although there were more than one of the king's men here, just one was by himself.

In the corner where the soldier sat, he slipped into the cushioned bench across from him.

"Where's the other one?" Malik asked. "The messenger?"

This king's guard was older. A streak of silver ran from his temple.

He's lucky to have lived so long in a place like this, he thought.

"I know of the one you speak," he said, sizing up Malik. "The disease claimed him only a day ago."

In the end, Penrose hadn't repaid him what he'd tried to do to her. He'd have to inform her that the bastard was dead, though.

"Good." Malik tilted his head. "To business, then."

"To business," the king's guard replied. "Upon His Majesty's receipt of the girl, your family will have blanket immunity from the law. You will be allowed to carry out your business activities so long as they don't interfere with the crown's interests. In such a case, you will be notified of the conflict."

The soldier raised one eyebrow. "You will also be cleared of all previous charges in Alsra."

It was clear what the man was referring to. Malik hadn't quite forgotten his death march at Belnya.

However, Malik sat back in his seat like he hadn't. Like he was only just remembering he'd nearly had his head chopped off. He tried to seem like he was weighing the offer.

Oh, he would savor this.

Not as much as he would've if the other one was still alive, but he'd make do with what he'd been given.

"I trust that you speak with the king's authority and discretion here," Malik said.

"Yes. I am his ears and eyes in this matter," the king's guard said. "Regard me as you would him."

Malik locked eyes with the guard. "In that case, you can inform King Cassiel that he can go shove his head up his—"

Malik grinned, but it was one of vileness. They weren't alone.

"Two against one," he said in the new silence. "Honorable."

The cold barrel that had appeared against his head pressed harder. It had been a trap from the start.

But he'd planned for this. He didn't play fair, either.

The king's guard smiled back at him, his eyes flicking only momentarily to the person standing behind him. "Seems you don't have a choice in the matter after all."

Malik was going to take a mighty risk, but he'd risked his life plenty before.

Why stop now?

His head angled back while the knife in his sleeve slipped into his palm.

Malik's skull hit the skull of the man holding a gun to his head, causing the weapon to drop from where it had been holding him still. A curse filled his ears, but Malik was already flying.

He twisted around, the knife in his palm hovering just barely over his assailant's heart.

He should have carved out the heart there before a bullet found his instead, but he couldn't.

A familiar face stared back at him.

"Malik," was all she said.

Chapter Thirty-Six

Happy

Malik couldn't think straight. He could hardly *see* straight.

Aisha stood before him, and the revolver that had been pressed against his head seconds ago remained in her hand.

"What the fuck is this?" His voice came out as a whisper.

"This is for you," she said.

What the hell did that mean. Malik ignored the nonsense, which was quite a job, considering it was all around him now.

Malik gnashed his teeth together as the pieces slotted together in his mind. "Where. The hell. Is. She."

But instead of Aisha's answer, he heard another voice behind him.

"My son, you've failed the test. Again."

Another betrayer of his own blood. Though, he supposed he should have expected this one.

His father stood beside the king's man.

So, he'd known all along.

His eyes cut to Aisha. More likely was that he'd had some help figuring out who Penrose was and the deal that the king had proposed.

"A family affair," Malik said. "It'd be touching if not for the backstabbing."

Aisha was curiously silent. *Good.*

There wasn't anything she could say that could smooth over this. Gods, what a damned fool he'd been.

When blood and money exchanged hands, how easy it was to buy one for the other.

"Backstabbing?" His father shook his head. "My son, the only backstabber here is you." He approached Malik, his eyes full of the disdain he'd felt from him since Malik had figured out that he was the spare.

Raphael Ezar continued, "If you'd have come straight to me with this information, how different things could have been." The bastard had the gall to look sad. As if it wasn't his choice to do this to Malik. "What has been would have been forgiven."

Malik lurched for his father, but a hand on his chest stopped him. Aisha had wedged herself between them. "Malik, stop this."

No. He wouldn't stop this.

Malik showed his teeth at her. "Good to see your word means so little, Sister. Better to find out your rottenness now than when it *really* matters."

He didn't give a damn about the hurt that flashed across her face. Why were they acting like the ones that had been betrayed?

It had been his decision from the start. And he'd chosen what he'd chosen. And they'd chosen to get in bed with the king.

"Ah, ah," the asshole who had sired him said. "Aisha was the one who bargained for your life. She *saved* you. She gave me information on this bargain in exchange for keeping you alive."

Malik didn't reply except for a laugh that scraped his throat.

The fact that his father preferred him dead was no surprise. He ignored him and turned to Aisha.

"I never want to see your face again," he said.

"It was the only way to keep you alive." Aisha's jaw clenched. "And why choose *her* instead of *us*, Malik?"

"Why?" The word tasted bitter on his tongue. It was time. This had gone on too long.

His family surrounded him, armed to the teeth to oppose him. But deep down, did he really have a good reason for not taking the deal?

He had a reason, of course. But to say it here, in this bar of cutthroats and rogue soldiers and underhanded dealings would have been dense.

Like he had any pride left.

"Dammit, I was *happy*." The words slipped through his clenched teeth like they could barely stand to be said.

At the same time, he lunged forward, the knife that they'd forgotten about still in his palm.

Before he could use it against Aisha, the stock of a gun slammed against the back of his head.

***

Penrose looked up from the book she'd been squinting at. Someone had brought lunch for her and Henrik hours ago.

It was much too late.

Henrik was still tinkering with the levels of the base, experimenting with different rates of evaporation. They'd been at this all day, and she hadn't even noticed how much time had passed without him.

When she'd woken to find Malik gone, she'd thought little of it.

I hired him for a purpose.

Then again, after what had happened between them a day ago, perhaps it was better this way. Penrose's nails dug into her palm. Her anger had cooled somewhat, though smolders of it still lingered.

Regardless, she should find him. Even if *he* was still throwing a tantrum.

She said to Henrik, "Where is Malik? He hasn't been here all day."

Henrik didn't look up from his work. His face was blank, though she knew that his hate for him brewed under the surface. "I don't know. I haven't seen him."

Penrose frowned. Her stomach felt like it was sinking like a stone in a lake.

Maybe, after what I did, he decided to terminate our agreement after all.

She rose, putting her books aside. She'd barely scratched the surface of everything that had happened in the last century.

Steam power, advancements in medicine, a new process of scientific inquiry. And that was only what she could read in a few hours. She hadn't even dived into the changes in culture.

Her stomach twisted again, and she knew why.

Any book detailing Aloster's culture from the last hundred years couldn't fail to mention the Cavanan prince's rise as ruler of all three kingdoms. Penrose breathed.

What had happened had happened. Her parents had traded her to the prince of another country for the sake of peace. And, despite what had happened to her, it sounded as if peace had reigned for a while.

That's if you discount the conquering and removal of Karsia's people.

She was just starting to understand everything her deceased husband had accomplished after her *death*.

But why did he curse me to slumber when he could have just killed me after we wed? And how?

Of course, it was entirely possible that Cassius didn't want her parents to suspect his involvement in what had happened to her. Then they might not have ceded control of the throne to him, even in absence of any new heirs.

By the time she was at the stairs, she was grinding her teeth at the thought of it all. "I'm going to find him. Or his sister. Whoever."

At this, Henrik's head jerked up.

"Why don't you stay here? I could use the help," Henrik admitted. "They're as likely as not up to something foul."

Her eyebrows came together. "Henrik. I'll talk to Malik when I find him. I'm going to try to get more time for you. I promise that." She started up the stairs.

She was sure she'd be back before long. With nothing else to go on, the best thing for her to do was to try to cure somnus with Henrik—or at least find out more about the disease and how it had changed in her absence.

And maybe, just maybe, she'd be able to keep Ezar from hurting Henrik more. Her palms itched. Where was Malik?

Penrose slipped unnoticed through the bar of Jackal's Hide. She felt that the name was fitting as conversation and laughter floated in the air with the smoke. She thought back to her books on various animal species.

Canis aureus.

Above all, an opportunist.

Penrose kept her eyes in front of her, though she didn't dare breathe until she'd made it to the door to their suite. She knocked and called for Malik, but he didn't answer.

The door came open with ease. The hairs on the back of her neck stood up; it hadn't been locked.

Already, she'd picked up a few things from Malik. She didn't have a weapon with her, but he'd shown her where he hid one in these rooms.

But as she crept through the rooms, checking under beds and in wardrobes, she saw neither Malik or anyone else.

Suddenly, a slight weight landed on her head, and her heart shot through her throat until her fingers found feathers. Sorrowtail gave a bright chirp as she brought him to her face in her hands.

"You silly bird," she gasped. "You scared me."

He seemed unrepentant, but the truth was, Penrose was glad to have found some source of life in their rooms. She stuffed the song bird into the collar of her shirt to keep him close.

Malik's armory room was as empty as the others, but as she was about to return to his lounge room and wait for him, she heard something that staled the air in her lungs.

It was barely anything. The sound could have been the massive building creaking or rats running inside the walls—gods, she hoped she wasn't about to lose all semblance of sanity and actually start listening for them or their secrets.

She could have laughed at that, had her heart not been drumming in her chest.

Sweat stuck the shirt she'd borrowed from Malik to her back. She tried to call his name, but it got stuck in her throat.

Before they'd left for the basement and Henrik's demonstration the other day, he'd shown her a few things about shooting, aiming, and securing the mechanical weapons they called guns.

He'd also showed her where he kept one hidden in his rooms at all times.

Did he take it with him?

Henrik's words about him came back to her.

"They're as likely as not up to something foul."

Her hand met the cold barrel of the gun he'd stowed behind a framed painting of soft grasslands, and she carefully pulled it free of its hiding spot. She was being paranoid, she knew, but she was finding out that it was a useful thing to be.

Every day I'm here, I start to become more like them, she realized with a grimace.

With Malik's name on her tongue, Penrose pulled open the door to his lounge room. But her voice fled her all at once.

Someone had followed her inside and waited for her.

"It's time to come with me, Princess."

Chapter Thirty-Seven

To Command

S hadows crawled across her room like ants marching along their pre-determined paths. It was a familiar sight for Sarina.

She couldn't sleep. He was always watching her dreams because they foretold things that might happen. For that reason, this being that masqueraded as a king kept her here after he'd discovered her many years ago.

For the most part, Sarina had a comfortable life. The guards respected her. Officially, she was considered the king's advisor, and that came with many perks.

Unofficially, Sarina was his diviner.

Few knew the true nature of the services she provided, and that was preferable to her. Her father had had the same gift, and it was through her connection to him that the king had discovered her.

King. It was the wrong word to describe what Cassius was.

Sarina stopped these thoughts before she could allow them to consume her mind. Floral lavender tea steamed underneath her nose where she sat at a wide mahogany desk. Books were stacked on shelves above it.

Another perk of being the king's *advisor.*

No. Don't think on it.

But, during the darkest nights such as these, she couldn't help but think on it.

Her daughter was out there on the streets of Alsra, still alive. Sarina had told herself this line so much that she wasn't sure if she really believed it or not.

But this was the only thought keeping her all in one piece.

"Of course, your girl is still alive. And the old woman, too."

The voice had come from nothing—or so that's what a reasonable-minded person might have thought.

Sarina knew better. She spoke back to the shadows without looking at them.

"Of course," she repeated back to him.

"You always dream of her after not sleeping," Cassius said in answer to her unspoken question. After a moment, he observed, "You act as if you aren't cured from somnus."

Sarina's hand holding the ceramic cup trembled. She stopped it.

It was true that her dreams often revealed possible futures. But, like any normal person, Sarina also had nightmares. Visions that her mind constructed to scare her or live out her fears.

The trouble was discerning which was which.

For a moment, she allowed herself to remember her Rana. Her girl was a kind soul, but even at a young age, she could stand up for herself. Her mother was much the same way. She was an herbalist and always seemed to be helping people.

Sarina hadn't held her daughter in many years.

She'll be getting too old to hold soon, Sarina realized.

At least Mother is still alive to take care of her.

Unless—these were all lies and Cassius had already eliminated her family. He had many means to do so.

And then there was the life debt she owed him. The memories of when she'd had somnus still plagued her and interfered with her visions.

But none of those were the reason she couldn't sleep. Not tonight.

She had to pretend. She had to resume her work and put the mask back on if she wanted her family safe. Sarina couldn't seem like she was plotting to put an end to him.

"Are you so sure we should trust in this criminal?" Sarina said. "She must be brought here before Evestide. My visions show that the curse can only be broken on or before the longest night."

Although he wasn't corporeal at the moment, she could feel Cassius smile.

"He will bring her. They are not like us, these rats that roam Alsra. All they want is more coin. Or the head of another rat."

She felt the temperature in the room drop.

"So long as the details you've supplied are correct," Cassius added.

It was difficult to balance the truth with lies when it came to Cassius. So long as Sarina believed something enough, she could influence her own mind and possibly make herself dream of an event that countered one of her real visions.

But, in this case, what he'd said was the truth.

Sarina looked into her tea and spoke of what she'd seen.

"Her lifeforce is running thin from spreading the sleeping disease so much. You will need to act soon if you are to harvest the greatest of her fears." Sarina closed her eyes.

"But first, she has to fear you more than she wants anything else. More than she wants to live."

In her mind, she saw the vision that she'd had many nights ago.

A girl appeared before her on a polished floor. Her blond hair twisted around her still-fierce expression despite the deep red soaking into the tiles below.

In Sarina's vision, the girl's eyes went pitch-black.

***

Raphael Ezar sized her up with one look. His eyes didn't even linger on the weapon in Penrose's clammy hands. He was too busy evaluating the state of décor of his son's room.

"This was a family heirloom," he murmured, examining a saber with a jeweled hilt planted firmly in the neck of a plaster bust.

It looked like the sort of thing he would have done out of anger, though she couldn't be sure it hadn't been an intentional design element.

Penrose didn't take her eyes off him, and she held Malik's gun openly, though she barely resisted pointing it at him. "What are you talking about?"

He looked at her straight-on then, as if he'd only just remembered why he'd entered Malik's rooms. "I meant what I said, Princess. You're coming with me." He took a step towards her, in the process brushing aside his black coat to reveal the black metal machinery tucked at his waist.

Penrose gritted her teeth at the sight of it. Of course, he was most certainly armed. She was facing Alsra's biggest crimelord.

"Where is Malik?"

Ezar smiled at that, like she'd said something funny. "It's best if you don't concern yourself with him any longer."

"And why not?" She cocked her head at him. "I'm paying him for a service. Or do you renege on your word very often in this business?"

"Penrose." Suddenly, Raphael Ezar had closed the distance between them. He moved her chin so that she was looking up at him. She wanted to crawl out of her skin. "You don't belong here. I know you know it. I can see it in your eyes that you do."

Penrose couldn't speak. He was right, and she *had* known it for some time. Since the moment she'd stepped foot inside here, as a matter of fact.

But none of that answered her question.

"Where is Malik," she said through her teeth.

His hand drifted away from her face, and her eyes tracked it. She shouldn't lose sight of it. "My son took the deal offered to him by Aloster's king."

Too much happened at once. Penrose jerked back from Ezar, and she suddenly found herself pointing Malik's gun straight at his father's head.

After what she'd done during Henrik's demonstration, perhaps he was expecting it. Regardless, the gun at Ezar's waist was in his hands much too quickly for her to fire on him first.

At the same time, her brain slogged through what he'd said, sifting through the words to find the meaning. To evaluate the likelihood of them. To taste them in her mind.

"*Liar*," she said through tight lips.

But it only makes sense, said the voice of reason in her head.

Of course Malik took the deal—her in exchange for protecting his family. Why wouldn't he?

And after what she'd done in the basement lab—betraying his trust to try to free Henrik—she'd demonstrated just how misaligned they were.

As if locked in a dance with no name, they stepped after each other in a circle.

"You don't just belong here, poor princess. You don't belong anywhere anymore." Ezar smirked and said what she'd suspected already. "What gave you the impression he cared about what happened to a lost girl like you?"

Something stopped the words from coming out of Penrose's throat. She thought it might have been her heart.

What a fool thing.

It was over. And truly, it didn't matter if Malik had accepted King Cassiel's deal and turned her in to him or if Malik's father had.

Of course, it mattered very deeply to the beating organ inside her chest.

But, when it came to what would happen to her, the result was the same.

Penrose kept her eye on Ezar's movements. If she was to succeed now, she only had one chance. She swallowed. Only one of them was getting out of this.

In a blur, Penrose jerked back towards the windows. Before Ezar could shoot, she elbowed out one of the decorative metal ventilation plates and shoved her hand out it.

"Go!" She shouted at the creature in her hand. Sorrowtail had been a good boy the entire time that Malik's father had threatened her.

But she knew better than to expect that the bird would be let free in her absence rather than used as a test subject.

His black-bead eyes stared back at her. She didn't want to see what she saw there.

Abandonment. Confusion.

Only one of them was getting out of this, and it was going to be Sorrowtail.

Cold metal found the back of her head.

Moisture pricked at her eyes, blurring her vision. "Go, boy," she said through her teeth in a voice she'd never used with the songbird. "*Now.*"

Penrose had known she'd never be able to get a bullet into Ezar faster than he could've gotten one into her. When she felt the flurry of feathers brush against her hand and leave her, her other hand slid Malik's revolver to the ground.

Alsra's sky was almost the exact shade of Sorrowtail's wings so that he was lost to her immediately.

Chapter Thirty-Eight

Expected Visitors

"This is unnecessary," she said under her breath to Raphael Ezar. She jostled the chain attached to her wrist in emphasis.

"I don't know what you mean. Everything I do is necessary," he said where he marched them towards the castle.

"I'm not going anywhere. Where would I hide?" she muttered, surprised by the truth of her words.

"It's not you I'm concerned about, Princess," he replied.

Breath rushed out of her nose. Maybe he should have been.

How are you going to even try to get out of this?

They had ridden by carriage there, and while the pall of evening elongated the shadows of Alsra's streets, she couldn't shake the feeling that even now, the king of Aloster, Cassius's son, could see her approach.

Penrose ignored the stares directed at her. His men were clustered around them, and she stood out among them in a bad way.

She didn't know where he'd found the blue and white lace dress she wore, the hem swishing at her ankles as she fought to keep beside him. Her cheeks stung in anger. Ezar had forced her to wear this like they were going to a party and not a hostage exchange.

I'm going to get out of this. I must.

At least, that was the phrase she told herself to keep herself sane. She tried and failed not to think of Malik.

It was too obvious what had happened. As soon as she'd shown her true self, he'd decided that she was too great of a risk to keep around.

Even if only negative consequences had come of it, Penrose couldn't bring herself to regret trying to free Henrik and prompting Malik's decision to betray her.

What had once been her parents' castle rose before her sight like a dark specter. Her throat tightened. She hadn't seen it since leaving for Prince Cassius's hold and his tower.

The vining flowers along its façade had been allowed to wither and die—that, or someone had forcefully removed them while they still flourished. The central archway had been reconstructed, and instead of a graceful arch, they stepped under a threshold designed to look like there were spears or perhaps bars protruding from above.

It was as far as her observations got before Raphael Ezar stopped her with a jerk of his arm.

Since he'd chained them together at their wrists, she was forced to stop with him.

"You all. You'll not come closer," commanded one of the guards, his eyes scanning the group with her at its center. A line appeared between his eyebrows when he saw what Ezar had done to keep them together.

"I believe we're expected," he said.

The guard's jaw clenched, though he turned around as if to lead them inside. "Leave your men outside."

Ezar gave a nod to his hired help, and all too soon, Penrose was fighting to keep up with Malik's father once again. But this time, she couldn't help but stare at how her home had been transformed.

Her family's portraits had been removed from the halls. Her family's banners that had once proudly hung—displaying the emblem of the kingdom she'd prepared to lead, Aloster—had been torn down.

As they walked, the castle loomed around her, an unfamiliar beast that lurked and watched her. The great windows spanning the rooms and halls she'd ran down as a child were darkened now. They were covered by thick curtains. The sight of it made her inexplicably cold.

This wasn't her home at all.

It's almost like it never existed. Like none of us did.

No. She had to hold to something. Her life—that version of the world had been real.

She had to keep her wits about her if she were going to survive this. This wasn't what she did. It was Malik's forte to brawl, to attack, and to claw his way out of these situations.

But short of sawing her arm off that was chained to his father's, she saw no exit from the abbreviated future barreling for her.

But maybe I don't need an exit.

Malik was blessed by the gods in attacking and combat. Her gift was strategy of a different kind.

She was going to convince him to let her go.

Maybe they could work together. It was unlikely, even as Cassius's son, that he wanted this disease to spread. They'd work out a deal. No matter what it took. She couldn't rely on Malik any longer.

She had to make her own move in this world.

Guards opened the doors to a room she well knew. The throne room yawned before them. The chains uniting them rattled in the hollow hall.

Once, this room had been a site of great merriment. Festivals, Evestide, and her and Lesabeth's birthdays. All had been celebrated here.

Her last Evestide, Lesabeth had snuck in illicit novels to read with her after the torches had been smothered in the castle's halls. She well remembered the roasted rosemary glazed chicken the cooks had prepared specially for that night.

It was said a full belly on the darkest night—Evestide—would promise life and warmth in the coming year. But that had been Lesabeth's last Evestide.

Her attention jerked back to the sight before her. Across the hall filled with guards, rifles at the backs of their royal uniforms, was him. This was the second time she'd seen him since waking.

Cassiel, her husband's son and king of Aloster.

Except, this was someone else entirely.

He was older, certainly. Lines danced on his face. He wasn't as old as he should have been, but there was no mistaking it.

Gods above.

This was Cassius.

This was the prince she'd known.

Her husband.

Chapter Thirty-Nine

A Good Hostage

N^{o. NO.}

It was his eyes. Even though his face had been ravaged by time, there was no mistaking his eyes.

Everything in Penrose bucked at the sight. It shouldn't have been possible.

One hundred years had passed—unless everyone around her had been lying. But she'd seen the changes of a century's passing with her own eyes.

This was Cassius. The same prince who had put her under a sleeping spell. The same who'd tricked her into thinking he could care for her, and the same one who had tricked her into marrying him as a result.

No one else knows. Somehow, he's tricked them all.

Cassius stared back at her, and she saw that he knew that she knew. That same strange light in his black eyes reflected in the torchlight. Danced with it.

He was dressed how Penrose's father had always been during official king's business. An open collared shirt with silver trim clung to his frame, tucked into black pants and black boots. Atop his head was the crown of Aloster's king.

The one that belonged to *her*.

The plan she'd formulated was like dust on the wind—gone before she could breathe.

It didn't matter now. All that mattered was one thing.

She was going to expose him. Or die trying.

On one side of Cassius was a woman of middling age who looked to have some Karsian in her. She wore a dress of deepest midnight and a light smile that told her she was at ease here.

Unlike Penrose, she *belonged* here.

"Raphael. Good to see you eventually figured out my invitation," Cassius said once he moved his gaze from Penrose's face.

The others were bowing, Penrose realized belatedly as the chains keeping her connected to him rattled. Ezar was still lowered when he answered, "No one so much as shits in this city without my knowing." When he straightened, he grinned in a smile that showed his teeth. "Of course I came."

At that, Cassius stared him down. He looked at the chains at their wrists holding them together. "Fine, then. Release her, and your family will be exempt from the law so long as you don't cross me."

His kingsguard swarmed them, but, in one motion, Ezar jerked the chain attaching them until she was pressed tight into his side.

"Ah, ah, Cassiel. I need assurances of our deal. Written documentation, to be precise."

Penrose resisted the urge to gnaw through her chains connecting her to him like she was a rat. This was her chance.

Her mouth moved quickly and almost silently. "He's not who he says he is."

Ezar's breath tickled her face as he muttered just as quietly. "There's no getting out of this now, Princess."

"I'm not trying to," she bit back. "You must expose him. This is Cassius, not his son." She waited a beat before blurting, "He knows how to control somnus."

She couldn't believe she was trying to work with her captor. Every part of her wanted nothing more than to plead for him to take her out of here.

But she knew it would've been useless.

"Unfounded claims are useless in my industry." His mouth hovered against her ear. Penrose stared blankly ahead and watched as the king drew up papers. "Now be a good hostage and cooperate."

It was a quick process, and she found she could do nothing but observe as his men brought the stack of papers that was supposed to be equal to her life. Even as fear settled in her bones again.

Outrageous, uncontrolled fear.

No. No!

Her actions felt involuntary now. She twisted in her cuffed arm while weapons pointed at her head. Even as Cassius bade Ezar to control her.

She couldn't go back to him.

Gods. Please.

Even as the logical part of her brain told her it would be ineffectual, she resisted. She couldn't help it.

"Let me go," she said, her voice pitching higher with each word.

She had to breathe and become calm. This was very important.

This was her last chance. She couldn't screw it up by appearing to have lost her damned head already.

There will be a time for that later, she promised herself.

Or so she hoped.

Ezar spat the key from where he'd lodged it somewhere in his mouth. One of Cassius's guards took the key with obvious disdain, wiping it across the back of his glove before he inserted it into the cuff at his captor's wrist. The chain clattered to her side, still attached to her.

Her heart drummed faster and faster until she was dizzy from the force. She had to convince them before she was silenced.

She had to get a message to Malik.

"Princess Penrose," the man who she knew was Cassius began. "Or, as you claim to be. What you really are is a witch. My father—"

Penrose laughed.

She couldn't help herself.

They looked at her like she was crazy, including the woman in the dark dress who had watched the transfer with an air of disinterest.

Maybe she was.

"What is so funny, Witch?" Cassius—or Cassiel, as he was pretending to be—raised an eyebrow at her.

The fear had gone somewhere else—or it had become so overwhelming she couldn't process it.

Probably the latter, she considered as if she was outside herself looking in.

But if she were to die, she would at least take him down. The man who had ruined her life and future.

"You know who I am, Cassius."

The room fell silent. The king looked back at her.

"My father said your arts were strong—your power to befuddle the mind. But this is laughable."

Penrose deflated. What if she was wrong?

There was no earthly way he was still alive. But, things had happened in that tower that weren't earthly or explainable by science.

He gestured to his men to take her.

He wants to silence me.

It was a good sign. It meant there was power still in her words.

The blades were at her throat. It was now or never.

Even if she had to rely on Ezar—so be it.

Even if she had to rely on Malik.

She would tell the world who he was and what he'd done.

"You are a witch who was locked in a tower for her crimes," her aged husband declared.

Penrose's mind raced faster than she could keep up. How had he done it?

How had he tricked them *all*?

"How many of you saw him as an infant? Saw his birth? Saw a growing belly on the woman he doomed after me?" she spurted.

"Silence the witch now!"

The kick to her stomach came out of nowhere.

She wasn't like Malik. She fought with words and not weapons of steel and metal. But this time, even her words failed her.

Before the kick to her head came that blacked her vision, she heard her dear husband's voice.

"Tell them I am executing the witch in three days."

And then, there was nothing.

Chapter Forty

Two Choices

They didn't starve him.

Malik had to assume it was because his father didn't want him to die such an easy death.

There was a death worse than this.

Many, in fact.

He wondered if he regretted not getting his beheading over with at Belnya. He was still unsure when the rusted iron door to his cell squealed open.

It couldn't have been long—perhaps a day or so that he'd been thrown in his father's cell.

At one time, Malik had tortured men down here at his father's command.

And sometimes of Malik's own volition.

He knew what would come next.

The *breaking*.

His sister stood before him, and silence stretched between them before he said, "Get. Out."

"He was going to kill you."

"You should've let him."

He could feel her anger, but it was like a candle before the sun.

"I care about you, Malik. This was for *you*," she said.

"I can smell how much dung you're talking. It's quite the feat down here where it already stinks so much," he said through his teeth. "If you cared, you would have come straight to me rather than muddle in my interests."

Though it was difficult to tell in the dim of his cell, he could see something flash through her eyes. He didn't care to feel any twinge of empathy, however.

"When your interests become helping strange girls over your family, they become mine."

Malik stared her down. He'd thought they'd had something established between them. An unspoken bond of not fucking with each other's private business.

"When they don't harm you, my interests are my own, *dear sister*. Such as when you choose a backstabbing bastard of a king over your own kin." The words mixed with spittle, and he spat them out.

But he wasn't done. Not by far.

Aisha's lips pinched together like she had some things to say to that. Too bad.

Malik wasn't done yet. "Don't you think I wanted that, too? I already bargained with him for our family's benefit as payment for killing her." Malik stood. "He reneged on our deal first, and so I refused to carry out my part. But since you took the word of a *royal* over your own brother, this is where we are. Now. Get. Out."

The change came over Aisha's face too fast. She hadn't expected this. Malik drew a sick satisfaction in watching the anger die from her eyes.

"Malik, just ..." Aisha breathed and crossed her arms. When she started speaking again, she kept her eyes shut like she couldn't bear to speak on it for much longer. "Just forget her. Please. He's agreed not to kill you. He just wants to prove a point. Soon, you'll be free." She opened her eyes again. "Alive."

But Malik heard something in her words that he felt she hadn't meant to communicate. She was acting like ...

His voice was devoid of emotion when he spoke.

"What will happen to her?"

Aisha looked away. "I'll see you later, Malik. He's going to send you food soon. I'll make sure it's warm."

"*Aisha.*"

Into her name, Malik breathed all the fire inside him and all the promises they'd ever made to each other as the wards of the most dangerous man they'd ever met.

With her back turned to him, she stopped just before leaving.

"Tomorrow. You'll be let out after tomorrow."

It didn't matter how hoarse he made his voice screaming at the walls after Aisha left, but he did it anyway.

There was only one reason why he'd been given such a light sentence.

It meant that holding him in this cell for longer wouldn't mean anything.

It meant that his punishment wasn't being held in his father's dungeons. No, his punishment was something else.

His brief imprisonment was only to ensure what needed to happen happened.

And there was no doubt in his mind what was going to happen to Penrose in a day.

***

It was maybe a couple hours when the man who sired Malik came to see him.

His father—and the man who wished him dead.

No, that's not quite right. He just wishes he never brought me into this world in the first place.

"Cut the horse pile." His father hadn't even said anything yet, but Malik could feel the rottenness he'd been about to spew. Malik continued, "You're going to let me free from here. Now." The words scraped from Malik's throat.

To his surprise, Ezar responded.

"I think you're aware there's a price for that." The bastard cocked his head at him. "You'll have to be *useful* to me again."

His heart skipped several beats, though he hid his reaction. There was a chance. It was all he needed to go on.

"You wanted a pet to follow you around and take orders unquestioningly. You got one. What more could you want?" Malik said.

"A rule follower is better than a usurper." Raphael Ezar locked eyes with him. "You'd have understood that had you become my successor."

"Then name your price." The words came out of Malik's mouth like bullets. His wrists might have been in irons, but he had weapons aplenty still. "What do you want?"

"I don't particularly care about princesses. Or kings," Ezar said. "I care about our business. My legacy. My family. I care about control. I care about my image and my power."

He stopped where he was, looming before Malik.

"I care about manufacturing the most profitable product known to man and selling it." His father leaned close to his face, and Malik fought against the urge to attack him. "Hope."

Most people would have said the word with a gleam in their eyes or the ghost of a smile on their lips. This was the god that the coinless and the cold prayed to every night.

But his father said the word straight and without reverence.

Malik's stomach tightened. His father wasn't done speaking.

"But that can't happen without some sacrifice," he said.

"Name. Your. Price," Malik managed.

He said it even though already knew.

Say it. Out loud, he urged him silently.

Raphael Ezar stared down at his son. "Mice don't cut it, Malik. You've seen this. If I'm to make this cure, I need something better to work with."

His fool heart raged in his chest. He ignored it.

Become his father's test subject ... or wait for her to die while he slept on the floor of a cell for a night.

"Today," Malik said in answer. "You'll release me today."

***

Penrose was shoved through the double doors she used to run through as a child. With a look, the king dismissed his guards. They were alone.

"You've had a day now," he said, his hands behind his back as his footsteps echoed through her parents' throne room. "Are you going to behave?"

Penrose laughed. The sound was sharp. Her memory was blurry from the moments before she'd fallen unconscious, but she remembered what he'd said was to happen to her.

She was to die.

"If you're going to execute me, why ask that? You can kill a screaming witch in front of them while they cheer. It shouldn't matter if I behave or not," she said.

But she didn't believe that. There was hope of exposing him if he was demanding her to behave.

She stepped towards him.

"I will die cursing your name on my lips. Your real name. Cassius." She said it like a curse.

She wasn't sure how he'd tricked them all, but he had. And she wouldn't stop trying to tell them all before she died.

He was before her in a blink. Penrose wanted to move but couldn't.

The air shimmered around him, and a gasp caught in her throat.

It was him. His face was free of time's mark again, and his chestnut hair gleamed in the lamplight. The warm beauty in his dimples and easy gaze that had captivated so many hearts in her time stared back at her.

But his eyes hadn't changed. They never had.

"Rose." His hand grappled her jaw. "My wife. My princess."

The hand along her face held her in spot even when she tried to turn and run. His smile widened at her struggle. "There is no escape from *me*."

No. No. It's happening again.

Her body listened to the terror buried deep inside it, but she forced words from her mouth.

"Let me *go*."

"You have a choice to make tonight, Penrose," he said over her thrashing. Her hands clawed at her throat where he started to lift her off the ground. "You can die tomorrow. Or you can admit you love me and bow to me as my wife in front of my kingdom."

"I will ... never ..." she said between gasps. Her head swam, and the image of his face blurred between Prince Cassius and King Cassius.

"Don't doubt that he loved you *and even still, he betrayed you*," Cassius said. "The spell I put on you all those years ago could only be broken by someone who could love you. An impossible feat, unless it was me."

Penrose couldn't talk anymore. She wondered if she could breathe anymore. The ache in her lungs had grown unbearable, but her hands couldn't tear his off her neck.

"He yet, he did. And he still handed you over to me, Penrose." He whispered in her ear. "None of them could love you and protect you like I do."

"Never forget that," he added.

Chapter Forty-One

The Decision

Penrose was before Malik, dancing and then laughing as he held tight to her when he'd been unable to keep his hands off her.

Her gold hair framed her face, catching on a dying sun that illuminated her from the tall window behind them.

"I'm yours," she said in the hollow of his throat.

Malik's voice was a low rumble. "If not, you will be by night's end," he swore.

He felt her skin heat at his words and smiled. "Embarrassed, Princess?" he asked. His fingers hovered over the back of her dress where metal clasps held them together.

"I just need a moment," she said in a breathless whisper.

When she backed away from him, her grin was like the cat that swallowed a mouse. "Turn around. And don't peek."

He did as she bade, staring at the other wall of the bedroom. While he waited, he stepped out of his pants. His shirt was already gone.

"Penrose," he breathed. "You can't keep me from you forever." She wanted him, and they both knew it.

The sound of a scream cut his thoughts short. Malik whipped around.

Before him was only the window—nothing more. Wind brushed aside the curtains.

She'd opened it.

As he stepped towards the open window, her scream rang in his ears.

***

Malik woke with a needle still in his arm. He would have ripped it out if not for the leather straps holding him to a metal frame.

His instincts kicked in, and the muscles in his arms pushed against the straps. The leather strained to hold him, creaking as it threatened to break.

The hands at his shoulder pulled away after he nearly bit them.

He made a guttural noise as he whipped his body back and forth in his struggle to get free.

Penrose was dying.

Dead already, perhaps.

You couldn't keep her alive. You wanted her close—and kept her in the jaws of a beast.

And finally, there was what the bastard king himself had said that day.

"To believe, the only way through the barrier was if her true love match walked through it and woke her up. I should have known her true love would be something so low such as this. Something that could be bribed so easily into attacking her."

True love.

The words had haunted him nearly every night since.

And he'd killed her.

Not his father or the king. No. He'd allowed the circumstances to happen in which she'd been traded to that bastard.

He'd killed what had made him happy.

What the *hell* was wrong with him?

Henrik's face danced around him. It was pinched in exhaustion but also in disgust for having to deal with him. The sickness had been in Malik for several hours now. He could feel somnus slog through him like mud, staking his body for its own uses.

"How long?" The words came out of Malik's mouth too close together.

How long have I been here?

"Long enough." The mask covered his lips, but it was clear Henrik frowned on him.

Malik's breathing was labored. He didn't have time for this. She didn't have the time.

"I have to go."

Henrik's eyes passed over him like he was one of his rats.

Well, he supposed that's all he was now.

"You've stabilized for now," Henrik said. "And I've tested a great deal of your blood with different mixes of antidotes. But it's too early to tell if any of them are working. I need another day."

Malik lurched up. "*She. Doesn't. Have. Another. Day.*"

"I have more sedative if you continue this," Henrik said. But his hands shook.

"Don't tell me you don't care about what happens to her," Malik said. "Don't act like you don't know, either."

Henrik looked down at him. The skin around his eyes tightened. "It was your kind that did this to her."

He was angry. *Good.*

His bonds barely held as he brought himself up by a few inches.

"And you think I wanted that, too? After agreeing to what's been done to me?" Malik said through his teeth.

Henrik's jaw held tight. "I don't pretend to know the inner workings of a murderer's mind."

Panic wanted to roar through him like a beast, but he ignored it. It would destroy him to give into it now.

"That's right," Malik said as Henrik tried to go about measuring another syringe for him. "You don't know how we think." His lip lifted as he said the words. "But you will once you let this happen to her."

Henrik didn't respond, but he stopped fiddling with the sedative shaking in his hands.

"Are you ready to become one of us? To accept blood and death as a necessary price?" The words mashed out of his mouth. "Are you ready for that, Henrik?"

Suddenly, Henrik turned around, and the sedative flung across the floor as he gripped his head.

"*Gods*, what did I ever do to be stuck with the likes of you people!" Henrik sounded like he was on the verge of either stabbing Malik through the heart or sobbing.

When he turned around, Malik held his breath for the former. It didn't come.

Henrik shoved a finger at him. "If I don't produce something, he's going to kill me, you know!" He laughed. "No, I'm sure you know that. You'll probably be the one to do it."

Henrik lowered his finger. "If you're still alive by then, I suppose."

Malik didn't dare breathe. It was true.

And it was why he needed to get out of here. Now.

He'd be damned if he'd done this—made this godsawful deal with his father—only for Penrose to die regardless.

No, he was going to save her. He had to.

"Let me out," he said through a new sheen of sweat. "I'll do the rest."

Chapter Forty-Two

Fear

They left Penrose in the shell of her sister's bedroom.

The wallpaper with designs of clouds and towers had long been peeled from the high walls. Lesabeth's belongings had been removed, certainly, and some dusty furniture had been unceremoniously thrown inside it to resemble a bedroom. Not a cell—which was what it was.

The ball he'd announced on a day's notice already raged below, and the noise of the voices reverberated through the floorboards.

She was going to declare her love for him in front of them all—all of the new kingdom of Aloster.

Or rather—she was going to die at his feet when she refused to do so. If she couldn't expose him in front of his soldiers by her word alone, then she would at least expose him for his cruelty when her entire kingdom witnessed him kill her for not loving him.

If she had to die, then she would do as much damage as possible on the way there.

And perhaps they'd believe her words when she was gone. Or they'd question Cassius's rise to the throne.

Or, a voice inside her whispered, *you find the evidence you need to damn him.*

But how did he do it?

But there was nothing here to help her. She'd already turned the room inside and out, and there was little chance of escaping when her window and door were locked.

Penrose hadn't even realized she was pacing, but a sudden voice from the other side of her locked door made her stop in her tracks.

"If you want any food, face the opposite wall with your hands held high." It was a woman's voice. She sounded used to getting what she wanted.

This was one of his guards, undoubtedly. Penrose's jaws clenched together, but she did as she was ordered with as much dignity as she could muster and held her head high.

This was her castle, and she would behave as such.

When she heard the lock *click* and the footfalls of his guard, she expected her to leave the food—she hoped it was on a tray, at least—and leave.

No such luck.

After a moment, she heard the creaking of the floorboards. Penrose's hair raised, but she didn't move.

When the touch at her waist came, Penrose jerked away in instinct.

"Let's see what weapons this so-called *witch* keeps. She might be hiding them with her powers, after all," the guard said.

Penrose said through locked teeth, "I have nothing. I've been searched already."

But it was then the whisper came, almost no louder than a breeze.

"We're being watched. Don't react."

Penrose stared at the wall that had once been beautiful but was now scored and damaged from the removal of the paper. She couldn't seem to speak or move.

We're being watched.

This statement told her two things: this guard was no guard at all, and those loyal to him were watching.

But who is this?

Yet, she already knew enough. The fact that this stranger was concealing her words to Penrose meant that she had reason to hide what she wanted to say to her. And there was only one logical conclusion from there.

She was the king's enemy, too.

The woman's hands lightly passed over her legs. Penrose considered what she knew and realized this charade of searching her for weapons after she'd been searched already couldn't last forever.

She likely had one chance—one opportunity to find out what she needed. The missing piece to this puzzle. Penrose couldn't waste it.

Penrose waited until she felt the woman's touch near her again before whispering the words she'd settled on.

It came down to one question. She barely more than mouthed it.

"What is he?"

But the woman's touch left her. Suddenly, she heard her voice again as her boots scuffed against the floor. She was walking away from Penrose and nearly out of her room again.

Her blood pumped faster. She'd made a mistake.

Penrose hadn't taken the chance she'd been given. She should have asked something else. She should have pled with the woman to get her out of here.

"By the Spirits, she's clean," the woman announced to someone else.

Shortly after, she heard a tray rattle against the floor, the door swing shut, and the lock click once more. Penrose lurched around, but the stranger was gone.

And there was nothing—no hidden weapon she'd left behind. No lock she'd left unlatched.

Even if the expression she'd used was from a time older than Penrose's even, the woman's meaning was clear enough.

You're not a threat.

Though Penrose's stomach had twisted itself into knots, she forced herself to eat some of the mushroom stew that her guard had left behind.

She jerked the spoon out of her mouth. It had been salted to the point of being inedible. Though her mouth was parched from the excess of salt, she moved on to what else had been left behind on the tray.

This time, Penrose stopped herself after tearing a piece of the loaf off. But she still didn't quite believe it.

It's been sprinkled with salt as well.

Penrose squeezed the piece of bread in her fist.

Not a threat to them.

But a joke, it seems.

***

The dress he'd brought for her to wear clung to her, the cream white color a brightness at the edges of her vision when her escorts—Cassius's guards—came to collect her.

The woman's whisper still remained in her head like a phantom.

As far as she could knew, none of her escorts were the woman who had spoken so traitorously to her.

But what had it meant?

The probable answer sat in her mind, quiet but loud all at once.

She was simply toying with me.

Her time was up already. Penrose's heart jumped in her throat when she saw him.

They entered his grand hall at the same time. The room full of his soldiers and the aristocrats of Aloster quieted and lowered their drinks at the sight of their ruler.

He was back to the façade they all knew, the aged king.

How does he control it? How am I going to unmask him?

The crowd of ladies adorned in heavy jewels and men in cuffed tailcoats watched as she descended a spiral of stairs at the same time as he did. It was easy to miss that she was a prisoner.

They perhaps thought the entourage before and after her was for her protection.

Or did they believe his words? That she was a witch?

Yes, Penrose realized as she passed them. They looked at her as if she might be one.

Cassius stared out, the crown atop his head that was hers glittering gold in the lamplight around them. Pinned to his suit was a single red rose. His chestnut hair once more had streaks of silver throughout it.

When he looked at her across the distance, her heart plummeted and she remembered his words to her.

"I will kill them if you don't behave, little rose. All who show up."

They would all be killed because of her.

Gods, how was she to do this?

Her handlers moved her through the crowd as Cassius addressed them.

"You've come to witness something in my castle tonight. Tonight, Aloster will be changed—just as it was changed for the better when my father united the three warring kingdoms under one banner. A threat has turned into one no more. Witch no more ... but a tame wife instead."

He locked eyes with her. He didn't have to remind her of her part.

She turned and smiled at them.

She was dying already. She'd promised she'd die before walking back into his arms.

This is for a reason, she reminded herself.

Not if I can't do anything, the other part of her screamed in her mind.

The strange thing about fear, she realized, was that it doesn't rationalize.

It doesn't calculate.

It survives.

A part of her broke from the rest. She couldn't help it. She couldn't be silent.

Her knees slammed against the floor, and her hands raked her hair. She tried to contain the words by her clenched teeth, but they slipped through anyway.

"No! Gods, don't you see what he is—"

It was the most Penrose got out before her vision went black as night.

***

He stood over her. Penrose had been stuffed in a cage much too small, and her knees hit her chin.

"Rose," Cassius said. He was young once more. "I can put you to sleep again."

Around them was a fog. She worried she would get lost in it if she didn't get out of this cage.

And then, what he said registered in her brain.

Cassius stepped away. He'd become old again. "How do you think I endured this long?" He looked at her, sharply. "Because I spent your life for it, my dear."

He crouched in front of her, his face smooth and youthful, marred only by a one-sided dimple. But his eyes were cold as always. "Are you ready to behave?"

***

She was awake. Penrose wasn't sure why she wasn't on the floor. Instead, she was still walking towards the king. She was sure she'd fainted.

But that didn't matter.

That's how he did it, she realized.

He used me. My life force.

And then came a second realization.

When he stared at her now, he looked less aged. Fewer gray streaks. But his eyes swam with a darkness.

Perhaps it wasn't only her life that he was feeding from but also ...

Her fear.

No one feared him like she did.

And at this rate, he would live forever feeding off her life until she was drained of it.

Chapter Forty-Three

Hurt

Malik left the man gasping for air at his feet. Penrose wouldn't have wanted him to kill the man, so he left him alive.

He peeled the thin mask from his face and tied it against his skull. It was a poor disguise—especially if the king saw him—but there was no helping it. He was too recognizable otherwise.

It was easy enough to dispatch the guards at one of the entrances. Most of his Majesty's guests had already arrived, and he slipped past the unconscious bodies in his wake.

Every heartbeat raging in his ears was a dull refrain.

She's gone. She's gone. She's gone.

You're late. You're late. You're late.

But he had to see for himself. He had to be sure.

And if the gods ever cared anything for him, then she was still alive. The armory he was wearing had fit neatly into his clothes tonight. They ached to be used.

Soon, he bade them.

Malik couldn't help but see the difference in how the rabble reacted to murder. If his was the hand that carried it out, then he was a monster.

But if it was by the king, it was an event. A celebration.

He looked over a sea of heads. The castle hall was packed with Alsra's citizens who had bought their way inside the king's graces and most likely a good portion of his army. His banner hung from the walls as tapestries, the bastardization of three countries shoved together.

The king was already speaking, but Malik didn't focus on the words. He'd found her.

Her face was paler than normal—and was that a bruise forming under her jaw?

He'd put her in an off-white dress like she was some sort of sacrificial offering.

Malik's teeth grinded together until he was sure there were only nubs left. Verbal thought left his brain, and he slipped into the crowd with a practiced ease.

Henrik would never have the mind of a murderer. Such a thing took a lifetime of conditioning and practice.

But killing was what Malik did best of all.

Revolver or knife?

The choice was clear. He had too much distance to cover yet. The cold metal of his gun found his palm as if in response to his thoughts and not the other way around.

The high ground would be best, but he'd settle for what he could get. Malik leaned down as if to fix his boot as he evaluated this angle and distance. Lots of heads were between him and King Cassiel, but he thought he could make it.

It was then that he heard him.

"Witch no more ... but a tame wife instead."

It was perhaps the only word that could have stopped him. *Wife.*

Malik looked at Penrose, but she was only smiling.

His thoughts came back forcefully.

Royalty marries royalty. What's new about that?

Princesses don't sleep in the beds of criminals. Or at least, not for very long.

She'd made her own deal. It wasn't like she needed him to do that.

Bodies were pushing against him to move, but he didn't budge. They cursed at him, but they moved on soon enough.

"My intended," King Cassiel said to Penrose, "do you declare your love in front of the witnesses of Alsra?"

Malik couldn't believe how much of a damned fool he'd been. This time, he allowed the crowd to push him back, away from the spectacle at hand.

This wasn't an execution. This was to be a wedding.

Malik had thought his father had betrayed him. But the truth was, they all had.

And he'd let them.

***

Before the words could leave Penrose's mouth, the gears in her mind had started to move and grind like machinery.

There was something to what the strange woman had said to her. And she'd only started to realize it.

By the Spirits.

The woman's words hadn't been a coincidence. The phrase had gone out of fashion when she was a girl, so she knew it was an uncommon one.

And then there was what had been done to her meal. It had been salted excessively on purpose—but not for the reason she'd initially figured.

Spirits. Salt.

She saw her memories like pages of a thick tome, and she flipped from one section to the next. When had she read about spirits?

It had been many years ago, and even then, she'd regarded it as a bit of juvenile folklore. But there was one detail she'd remembered because of her father.

Penrose saw the dinner table before her. It was the night before her ninth Evestide, and the cooks had already outdone themselves. Lesabeth and her mother were due to arrive in the morning—just before the day's celebrations—so Penrose had been alone with their father.

But she never felt alone with him.

When she'd reached for a bit of apricot spread, she'd knocked over the salt cellar, and small quartz-like granules had spread to every corner of the feast table.

Instead of berating Penrose for the accident, her father had said that spilling salt on the nights preceding Evestide was a good omen.

"Don't trouble yourself. A spilling of salt will banish the spirits waiting to claim us on the darkest night tomorrow."

"That's not true. Spirits don't exist."

Despite her words, she felt her face turn ashen. He'd looked at her critically then.

"You've been reading the wrong sort of books if you believe that, my dear."

Just then, disembodied hands had found and seize her shoulders. Penrose shot out of her chair with a shriek on her lips.

As it turned out, Lesabeth and the queen had arrived home early.

Lesabeth couldn't smother her laughter, even after their father had consoled Penrose and apologized for the joint attack. It was the same night that Lesabeth had given her another of her own books—one on spirits.

The details flitted at the edges of her mind like shadows, unwilling to reveal their true forms. They teased her with their ambiguity.

All she remembered discovering in the book was that spirits existed below the dominion of the gods, just as humans did, as well as a note about salt's abilities to ward them off.

While she stared at Cassius, she knew the thought that he was something other than human shouldn't have been a surprise; after all, he'd used some spell or magic on her to trap her in her slumbers before.

But was this truly the answer? Or was she weighing too heavily a thoughtless comment?

Could it be? Is Cassius some form of a spirit?

The woman's words had quite possibly been a message about who—or rather *what*—King Cassius really was.

That was the question Penrose had asked her, after all.

"What is he?"

He certainly seemed flesh and bone at that moment. Penrose needed to gather more information.

But there was one certainty she knew: Penrose had to live, if only to expose him. And none of them were going to die for it.

It started with a rattling cough in her throat. She'd caught a whiff of pipe smoke on the air and breathed it in further. The soldiers near her eyed her, but she didn't care.

She bumped into the gentleman holding the offending pipe, and it rolled near her feet.

In a fluster of apologies, she bent to pick it up. Her loose hair covered up the action as she inhaled from it greedily.

The smell of smoke filled her lungs until she felt she was breathing it out.

With a shove, she put it back into the man's hands. His lips pulled back in fear and disgust of her having touched him and his pipe.

Her coughs grew to a full-on fit. Her throat burned, and air escaped her lungs faster than she could keep it in. Those around her backed several paces.

Cassius's words hung in the air. He could feel his eyes on her now.

He knew about her coughing fits.

But no one else did. Likely, they thought—

"Somnus," screeched a lady's voice behind her. It was all that was needed to start the uproar.

Bodies pushed against her, shoving her down and away. Cassius looked to his guards.

His command rang out over their heads. "Keep her contained. Put her away."

Cold metal found the middle of her back. They didn't wish to touch her themselves, though they would do so with their guns and blades.

Between coughs, she said, "The lavatory. I just need—"

"We'll determine what you need," said one of her handlers. But they didn't get closer to her, she noticed.

For good measure, she started shaking. The king's gathered began to push against the edges of the room, and shrieks of terror filled the air. The only thing spreading was panic, but it was more potent than somnus could ever be.

Her guards pushed her, half prodding and half retreating from her.

The limbs of the panicking crowd shoved against her, pushing against her to get out of the king's hall. She barely kept from falling on her face.

Her pulse pounded as they got closer to where she needed to be. This was going to work. All she had to do was get to the lavatory in the east wing of the castle.

It wasn't going to be glamorous, but there was a tunnel she could take out of the castle there.

Penrose remembered what Henrik had described of this version of the sleeping disease. It spread by bodily fluids, likely. She pressed one hand against her mouth. "I need the lavatory," she said against her fingers.

"Keep walking," came a rough voice. A metal barrel pressed harder into the space between her shoulder blades.

Penrose twisted to *accidentally* cough in the face of the guard holding a gun to her back, but she froze when she saw him.

The guard at her back had been replaced with one wearing a mask slipped on his face.

The words on her tongue died. There was no chance that she was wrong; Malik's face stared back at her.

When she stepped backwards, her side slammed into the threshold of the castle's eastern lavatories.

Malik stepped forward, jerking his chin towards the door.

Penrose's eyes were on the gun as she stepped inside, and he followed her in. They were alone in the small room paved in old stones. A new, crystalline mirror showed Malik's back to her. He was heavily armed.

She only had one chance.

After her coughing fit, her voice was shaky. "You got what you needed from trading me to him already, or was this part of the deal?"

Something passed through Malik's eyes when she said that. She would have sworn it was hurt.

She didn't watch his face for long enough to decipher it, however. Penrose went for the only shot she could make on him, a trained combatant and son of a crime lord used to getting dirty.

As she grabbled for the gun in his hands, she aimed her knee where it would hurt him most.

Chapter Forty-Four

Confessions

The pain burst at his crotch at once. She'd hit him square there, and somehow, he hadn't caught her before she'd already done it.

Malik grunted wordlessly as his knees hit the stone floor of the bathroom. The girl knew how to *kick*.

Well, it wasn't his first choice of how she'd touch him. A second later, he realized his gun was gone from his slack grip.

It was at his head. The hands holding it were shaking. Suddenly, the pain was a small thing compared to that.

"You ... You're here on his behalf, aren't you?" Penrose said as she held the gun to his head.

"You got what you needed from trading me to him already, or was this part of the deal?"

He didn't have to guess who she was talking about. Penrose thought that he'd been a part of the deal that his father and Aisha had orchestrated with the king.

A reasonable assumption, if he were in her shoes.

It might as well have been. I allowed it to happen under my nose.

When he spoke, Malik didn't recognize his own voice. "I'm here for you. *And only you.*"

Her lip trembled. "Bullshit," she said. He stifled a smile at her language. "You're here because of your father. Your boss."

His pulse throbbed for the girl standing above him, though he put aside his appreciation for her grit for the moment. He needed to prove to her why he was here *now*. Judging by her shaking hands, her new bruises, and the look in her eyes, it was only a matter of time before she shot that gun—whether at him or someone else.

He needed to prove he hadn't been the one to give her up.

Somehow.

"Malik ... is it true ...?"

The change in her voice made his head snap up. His body ached, but he couldn't give in to the weakness living inside it now. Not yet.

But Malik couldn't seem to say anything. Not when she looked at him like that.

"He said something to me," Penrose continued. "Something that doesn't make sense." A tear formed along one eyelid even as her lips pulled back to reveal gritted teeth.

Malik was deathly still.

Her head was shaking, and her hair flung across her shoulders as she did so. "But it's impossible. It can't—You can't—"

"Say it." The words left his lips like a sentencing.

Something inside him knew what was on her tongue, but he needed her to say the words. The awful, cursed words.

They were the same that the king had revealed to him after he'd met her. The same words that he'd smothered inside him since he'd met her.

True love.

Penrose was laughing, but it wasn't a joyful sound. It had all the bitterness of unripe fruit, clinging uselessly to the branch after the first frost. She stopped abruptly, her gaze shooting back to the gun.

His pulse climbed higher as a new thought entered his brain.

She must hate being in love with the likes of me. She can't bear the thought. It's clear.

Princesses may fall in love with criminals. But only as long as the criminals' heads remained attached.

Or rather, for as long as they could stand it in themselves.

He had to say something. He couldn't stand the thick silence between them.

He couldn't stand the way he felt at her rejection of that essential part of him.

"If loving the scum of the gutter disgusts you so much," Malik said, "then go ahead and shoot and get this over with."

***

Penrose's mouth gaped open. "Malik, that's not what I meant. You don't ..." Her hand moved so that the gun clattered against the floor. "You didn't give me up," she realized.

Gods, she'd been a dolt.

"Don't doubt that he loved you and even still, he betrayed you. The spell I put on you all those years ago could only be broken by someone who could love you."

He lied. That's what Cassius does, Penrose reminded herself. *But not about everything.* She looked at him again.

"You are not *scum*. And I've never thought that," she said. The tears came from anger now.

How could he think she thought that?

"Say it." Malik repeated the words he'd said earlier, but they were different now. His voice was still rough, but there was something else to it.

An ... urgency? A need?

"True love," she said.

***

Malik watched as Penrose's throat burned red—as if the words themselves were the profane part.

As if the place where they came from was somewhere damned instead of a place of reverence. A place he wanted to kiss even now.

The princess and the murderer. Malik was done with the sarcasm and fake laughter. Otherwise, he would've laughed at the thought.

Instead of responding verbally, Malik stood and stripped away the mask from his skin. He knew she saw his sickly pallor, the sweat clinging to him, and the unsteadiness in his limbs.

All early symptoms of somnus.

"You're ... gods, no." Penrose seemed to only be able to get out a few words at once. "Is it?" Her hand pressed to her mouth.

"It's somnus. Agreeing to Henrik's tests was the only way he'd let me out in time," he explained.

"No. No, you can't have asked for this," Penrose said, her eyes wild as they beheld him. Her hands found his skin, and she felt cold.

"Don't spread it to yourself," he said, backing out of her reach. He needed her to live, even if he'd damned himself.

"Malik," she said through her teeth. He loved the way she said his name. Her hands found his coat despite his words. "You can't do this to me. You can't give this to me with an end in sight."

"I'm going to end him. It's what I came here to do. After ensuring you were free, of course," he explained. "It's clear you won't be safe so long as the bastard king lives." Lightly so as not to hurt her bruises, he pressed his palm against her face.

"You can't," she said as she grabbed his wrist. "The king isn't human. It's Cassius—the one I knew a hundred years ago."

Malik blinked, trying to absorb this, but she wasn't done.

"I don't know how, but he can control somnus. He's lived all these years feeding off my lifeforce after he cursed me with it. It—it's insane, I know, but you *must* believe me."

Malik stared back at her. He could tell from her face that she wasn't lying. While fear had made her stop him from walking out the door after the king, she was in her right mind.

Exhaustion begged him to sit down, fall down, or whatever it took to get him to stop standing. He refused the urge.

Magic. Could it be true? It was what the tower been cloaked in when he'd tried to scale it to get to her. From the start, she'd been magic.

Or rather, there'd been magic attached to her.

It was then that his legs refused to support him any longer, and the room skewed to one side as he fell.

Chapter Forty-Five

Echoes in the Darkness

Penrose's arms ached, but she couldn't stop. Shadows flooded the sewer tunnel, and every slosh of water behind them made her heartbeat quicken. Water had long pooled inside her boots.

She didn't dare slow down, though.

Malik groaned and shifted on the metal cart she'd stuffed most of his long body on. It was a stroke of utter luck that she'd found the serving trolley so near where the lavatories were, and that she could slip out and in unnoticed in the chaos she'd caused.

Penrose still couldn't quite believe they'd both made it out of his castle alive. She was fairly certain that Malik would have been shot once he tried to kill Cassius.

After Penrose had obtained something to transport him with, she'd slid aside the grate on the floor of the lavatory and climbed down, bringing him and the cart separately. She thanked Lesabeth's soul that her sister had shown her that as a route to sneak out of the castle under their parents' watch.

As it turned out, she wouldn't use it until a hundred years later.

Her thoughts returned to what Malik had done to come get her, what he'd *sacrificed*, and her hands shook where they gripped the cart.

A fury filled her when she considered Malik's father and how he'd persuaded his only son to submit to a dangerous disease for the sake of profiting from it.

All Malik's weapons were shoved into her undergarments except the revolver she'd taken from him. She kept that near her hands on the top of the cart near Malik. Cassius's beautiful cream-white dress was covered in dirt and grime to her hips.

She was glad she could ruin something of his. Something of her husband's.

Her stomach dropped when she remembered that that's what he was. That he was *alive*.

And not only had he robbed her of her crown, her family, her *world*—if he was to be believed, he'd used the years of her life to extend his own.

Whatever he was, Cassius was a monster first.

A noise behind them that was decidedly not from their movements through the shallow water stopped her heart.

As quietly and quickly as she could, she shoved them behind one of the stone columns holding up the sewer's passages.

Seconds passed, but nothing happened. There was nothing.

Malik groaned again, and, this time, his eyes opened. "What the hell?"

Penrose shoved a hand against his lips, whispering against his ear for him to be quiet.

She'd forgotten how he could move. He slipped her hand from his mouth in the same moment that he darted upright on the cart. Noiselessly, he moved off it and automatically crouched as his eyes blinked in the darkness.

Slants of light from the sewer grates above them provided the dimmest of lighting, but there was enough of it to see the glint of metal in his hands. Sometime, he'd taken the gun from the top of the cart.

To his credit, Malik didn't waste time panicking or looking around, asking where they were or how he got there.

He's been in situations like these before, I'd bet.

Penrose was stock still next to him. She stared ahead. Even the echo of the noise she'd heard was long gone.

But silence was almost worse.

Kingsguard would have made more splashing sounds had they retreated from near them or gotten closer. Malik seemed to realize the same thing. He hadn't moved a muscle, either.

As Penrose's gaze moved back ahead of her, she saw it.

It was a flicker of shadow, interrupting the dim light that was cast on the stone wall of the tunnel. Penrose gripped Malik's hand, and they watched as the projected shadow of something passed before them.

Silence still flooded the tunnels around them.

Penrose's eyes met Malik's. Sweat appeared at his temples, but he seemed stable enough for now.

It was then, while looking into his face, that Penrose saw something out of her periphery. It was a pair of dark, gleaming eyes. Dread seized her.

She would know those eyes anywhere.

Before Penrose could shriek, Malik whirled on his feet and fired as he shoved her behind him.

No. How did Cassius follow us down here? He couldn't have ...

But when the smoke cleared, Penrose and Malik saw the truth. The dim light from the grate above revealed only the smoke wisping from the revolver in Malik's hand.

And a web of cracks in the stone wall where the bullets had planted themselves. No blood. No rippling water under them.

Nothing else.

The echoes from the revolver died after a few moments, and the quiet settled in once more.

In the utter silence, they waited.

There was no one there.

Chapter Forty-Six

The Embrace

Her first breath of air out of the castle and above Alsra's tunnels was the sweetest. Even if the smog lingering in the city's air tightened the passages of her lungs, Penrose couldn't stop from breathing the air in deeply.

What she'd seen in the tunnels under the city flashed in her mind, over and over.

Something had followed them through the murk.

The strange woman's words came back to her.

By the Spirits.

Malik was an unsteady weight against her. She was reminded uncomfortably of how they first entered Alsra, sick and captured by the king's men. But this time, Malik couldn't lead her to a hideout or safe place.

Perhaps there was none of that left in this city.

He was warm against her, and perhaps she should have worried more about catching the sleeping disease from him, but Penrose couldn't worry about that now. She'd had it once, apparently, and came through it already.

Her eyes went to Malik's face, and she knew she couldn't count on the same good fortune for him.

Good fortune, she thought sardonically. *If that's what a hundred years stolen is.*

This Alsra was unfamiliar to Penrose, and gloom dressed her streets in shadow and murk so that, even with the help of familiarity, she would have been lost.

All she knew was that they were far and away from the castle. They'd trudged through the tunnels to ensure that. They left mud and grime under their feet.

Malik's breathing came heavier and heavier, but he didn't hold them up. She wiped some of the sweat from his forehead.

"You need a healer," she whispered to him. He caught her hand and moved it back to her side with a shake of his head.

Suddenly, there was movement out of the corner of her vision. Malik already had a knife in his palm, she knew, but she forced her hand against his chest to stop him.

A child had been watching them—a girl with braided black hair and unblinking eyes.

"Who's there?" Malik said, and even those simple words sounded like a threat.

Penrose knew why he'd said it like that, of course. Any attention could lead Cassius back to them. They were certainly wanted throughout the city now. It had been a mistake to linger on the streets, even at this time of night.

The girl's eyes darted between the two of them, and Penrose could see it in her face that she was about to slip back into shadow.

"It's alright," she said to stop her from potentially fleeing to find a guard. "You just scared us. Where are your parents?"

Despite her calming words, Penrose's heart beat in her ears. *Don't let this be how it ends. Please.*

"He's sick," the girl said. It was the sort of thing children did—declare rather than ask.

Penrose nodded, though she could tell Malik hadn't relaxed next to her. He was probably wise to not do so.

The girl with watchful eyes settled her gaze on Penrose. "Come with me. My grandmother is a healer."

Before they could say another word to each other, the girl had started to run in the opposite direction they'd been heading. Penrose started after her, noticing as she did the tents and tarps that began to spread from alleyways into the streets. People lived here.

Malik's hand gripped her by the arm to stop her.

"What's wrong?"

Malik's teeth came together. "This won't work out here."

Penrose grabbed his hand back. "I'm not letting you get worse." She glanced around them once more. They were losing the girl, and she had to make her case fast. "There are no guards here. I'd hazard a guess that there are *never* any guards here." Her eyebrows came together. "Unless you think it's a trap."

Malik looked ahead of them at the street possibly filled with more eyes watching them. Dawn was perhaps an hour or so away.

"I'm not ruling it out." He caught sight of her face and then looked away again. "Fine then."

Penrose took her chance when she saw it. With Malik's hand in hers, she ran to catch up with the girl.

The more she saw of the area, the more she realized.

These are the Karsian slums.

She'd read some about them and what had happened to Karsia when she'd been absent from the world.

According to the books that Henrik had in his lab, this was all that remained of the great country she'd once known.

It can't be, though. Karsia was almost as large as Aloster.

The girl had ducked under the entrance to a canopied alley leading off the street. Penrose swallowed. Something told her that guards weren't waiting for them, but she couldn't doubt that Cassius had eyes everywhere. He'd controlled the city for a hundred years, after all.

But glancing at Malik, she knew they had little other choice.

He needed treatment. And even with Henrik's training, there were things she simply didn't know about this version of somnus.

"I'm Rana," the girl said as she held aside a tarp entrance for them. She stared as if expecting their names in return.

Penrose smiled. "That's a beautiful name, Rana. You can call me Pen."

"That's an odd name." Rana squinted at her as if her odd name was her fault. Penrose almost laughed.

Lesabath had used to say the same thing. Actually, she'd said that their parents had never planned to have two daughters and that she, the first daughter, had gotten the name they both should have had.

Her hands trembled at the memory, and she covered it up by shoving them against her body.

It was a surprisingly large space to be covered by tarps. Rugs spread across the floor, arranged near a pit of smoldering coals that gave off comforting, radiative heat. Barrels lined the edges of the area, likely acting as both storage and walls.

Rana spread out a quilt with interlocking designs of diamonds on it. "Bring him here," she commanded.

Malik crossed his arms. "I can still walk."

Rana raised an eyebrow. "For now."

After he got on the quilt, Penrose helped Rana bunch another blanket into a pillow for his head.

"Grab a rag." The girl nodded to a pile, and Penrose helped her make a cooling compress for Malik's forehead.

After that, Rana climbed atop a small barrel before a table. She grabbed a mortar and pestle and a handful of roots stored at her feet.

Penrose approached her. "Allow me to help you. I have some experience."

Rana looked at her doubtfully. "It's a one-person job. You make sure the coals don't cool." She glanced over at Malik who was fighting to keep all his body on the quilt. "And make sure he doesn't destroy things."

Rana caught sight of Penrose's face suddenly. She stared down into the root she was crushing up. Her voice was barely audible. "My grandmother will be here in the morning. She'll see to him then."

Penrose did as she was told and tried to quiet the clamor of thoughts in her head.

He's going to die just like Lesabeth did. He's going to die in front of me. But this time, it's my fault.

A force stopped Penrose from once more burning the stick she was prodding the coals with. It was his hand around her arm.

Malik locked eyes with her. "This was my decision."

It was as if he'd read her mind.

She shook her head, pressing her fists against her ribs to keep them from shaking. Penrose bit into her lips to keep them from making a sound—to keep what was bubbling up inside her from coming out.

After a few moments of silence, Rana stopped what she was doing and slipped out of the tented room they shared.

A few more seconds passed before Malik spoke. His voice was rough and low. "Would ... would you like me to hold you?"

Penrose couldn't speak. She managed a nod.

Suddenly, strong arms pulled her nearer to his chest. He kept his face away from hers out of caution for spreading the sleeping disease, but Penrose was on the verge of allowing it to take her, too—if only for the moment that would come with the contact of their lips together.

Malik had already sacrificed everything to save her life. It was coming time to repay the favor. She had to believe she could.

She made the vow then.

She would cure him—no matter what it took.

She would claw the cure from her husband's cold chest if she had to.

Chapter Forty-Seven

The Enemy Most Dangerous

There was a yank, and the metal cuff around Malik's neck dug into his skin at his resistance. A kick in the back, and he was forced ahead anyway.

He was on a polished floor somewhere. A man held the other end of his metal chain that connected to the cuff at his neck. Malik lunged for him, wrapping the chains around his fist to use them as deadlier weapons.

Another kick downed him before he got close. He held his stomach where the pain had burst inside him. A rib, maybe.

A familiar voice called behind him.

"Oh, brother?" Her voice sounded like a song as she called to him. "Haven't you learned your lesson yet?"

He jerked around to face his sister and demand what the hell was going on.

The words died in his throat. She was lounging on the king's throne. Gold dripped from her fingers and ears, and a necklace of jewels glittered at her throat. At her head was Aloster's crown.

"Malik? Did you hear me?"

He spit in her direction. "You are no blood of mine," he said through his teeth. "I hope you die for this."

Aisha's lips pulled back as she showed her teeth. "Patient. Perhaps one of us will get our wish sooner than you think." She gave a sharp look at the man holding his chain. "Take him back. He hasn't learned his lesson yet."

Another kick was about to come—he could feel it—but he was ready. He pulled his chain near him to strangle his keeper. His sister would be next.

He could feel the air leaving the man's throat, but Aisha's smile only widened.

"That's it."

She slid off the throne like a cat and came to him. She looked down at him where he was on the floor.

"Maybe now Father will forgive you. So long as you punish yourself enough," Aisha said.

Malik couldn't breathe. Every time he opened his mouth to shout, a gasp came out.

***

Malik's eyes opened, and he heard a sound like a paper bag being filled with air. He realized a second later it had come from him. His eyes ricocheted around the area for the man who had been choking him when he realized he'd done it to himself.

His body trembled, and he shoved his palms to his forehead.

He didn't notice until a moment later that small fists were trying to cover his mouth to quiet him.

Rana. That was the girl's name.

Her Karsian eyes were large as she looked at him, pleading with him to be quiet. He waved away her attempts to touch and shush him physically.

"I'm fine. It was just a dream," he said, though his wellbeing had clearly not been her primary concern in that moment—or at least more than getting him to shut up.

A yowling dog in the slums tended to attract more.

"A somnus nightmare," she corrected. "How long?"

How long have you had it?

Malik shrugged. "This is about the third day."

Rana's lips pressed together. "Here." She shoved something at him in a cup.

"The hell is this?" He shoved it back at her.

"Oh, just take it." She rolled her eyes.

He didn't like how easily she bossed around people more grown than her.

Little brat.

"It's no cure, of course," Rana said. "But it will help some of your symptoms."

He decided to trust her. The powdered medicine gave him a coughing fit in return. When he was done, it was his turn to ask it.

"How long?" he said.

How long do I have left?

"You already know." Rana got up. He noticed belatedly that they were alone. Where the hell was Penrose?

"Typically, it takes a week to go insane from it. Or just to die. Maybe you'll have an extra day," she said.

Malik pushed his knuckles against his head again. "Where is she?"

"Getting water. All of us here share a well nearby," the girl said. She frowned at him. "Don't make that face. Even though she isn't Karsian, we don't bother outsiders."

Malik shook his head. It wasn't *that* he was concerned about, but he couldn't tell this brat the real reason.

That they were both wanted fugitives by the crown.

He leaned against a barrel. "Why take us in? Why bother to help us if there's only days for me to count down?"

There was too much to do in four days. Gods.

He wouldn't be able to do it. Not all.

Protect Penrose.

She'd dragged him out of there, but he needed to get back to the castle. He needed to kill the king. Even if he couldn't live, he could do this for her. He could allow her to live.

And really, what would be the damage done once he was dead? He could hear their words already.

He was unhinged and a wanted murderer already. It would be no real stretch to explain why he'd done it after the fact to the disgusted citizens of Alsra.

Criminals did crime for fun and profit. Sometimes, that involved killing. Often, that involved killing those in power.

And if Penrose could live freely because of that one act?

It would be worth it.

His one regret was that he wouldn't have time to kill his father, too.

Rana spoke. He'd nearly forgotten that he was waiting for an answer from her.

"Because," the girl said. "There is a cure."

Chapter Forty-Eight

Exodus

At Rana's words, Malik's head snapped up.

"If you can live long enough. If you can get inside the king's castle," Rana explained. "He has a cure there."

She was a child. Not yet a dozen or perhaps even ten years old.

But he wanted to dispel that for her. Not her hope—but her reliance on *saviors* and kings and the like.

Or rather, conquerors. Had she been older, she wouldn't have said such a thing. Those older who still shared Karsian blood knew and remembered what the king's father had done—what the present king had done, if it was all true and Cassius was still alive after all these years.

Cassius the uniter.

"You shouldn't blindly rely on authority like that. On the king," Malik said.

Rana's lips pressed tight together. Somehow, she had nothing to say about that.

She's been told that before.

After a few moments of quiet, she said, "I know she would have lived if she could have gotten to see the king."

Malik didn't want to continue down this path. He'd said his piece.

And besides, a nagging feeling told him that there was a reason this girl didn't live with her parents.

"I should have had that girl restrain you before you fell asleep. Those infected ... get like that," Rana said when he didn't respond.

"Every night?" he asked.

What a fool thing to ask. There was a reason it was called the *sleeping disease*.

"Yes. When they dream, they get violent. Belts are what we use," Rana said.

How many people has your grandmother treated for somnus? he wondered.

How many cured?

He didn't want to hear the former and already knew the latter. Too many and none at all.

Voices on the other side of their tented room stole his attention. Malik grabbed the knife he'd stashed under the quilt. People were approaching from the outside.

His arm relaxed when he saw.

It was Penrose. She was carrying a bucket of water. Her grimy, fake wedding dress was gone, and she was wearing a cornflower blue cotton blouse that made her look radiant with a long linen skirt.

Next to her was an old woman of Karsian descent. She held open the tent entrance for Penrose.

The resemblance to Rana was unmistakable. This was her grandmother.

"Rana, you've made another mess—"

Her words stopped like they were a stream cut off from a spigot. She froze when she beheld Malik.

"You're going to leave now," the old woman said.

"Gran—"

"Quiet, you foolish child," she said, interrupting Rana. "You know not the evil you've invited inside our home."

Malik stood. He already had everything on him that he needed.

"Gladly." He showed his teeth to her.

Finally, someone with the sense enough to be afraid of him.

Penrose's face was white. He could see she was holding her words in. Good. There was no negotiation to be had here.

But that was when Rana sprinted to put her body in front of his.

"No! He's staying," she said. "He's sick, and we can help him."

The sound of the slap filled the dead quiet—though only for a second or so.

"Ignorant girl!" After she slapped her granddaughter, the old woman pulled Rana close to her body, likely to protect her from Malik. As if he'd been the one going to hurt her and not the other way around. "He is not our blood. That's the spawn of a demon." She shot a glare at him. "Leave or there'll be trouble."

Malik held the knife as his waist in case she tried something stupid—either one of them. The two of them were gone from the tent like the wind.

Outside, he still had a job to do. He needed to get him and Penrose out of the slums.

The sun was up, a racket had been made, and even worse, they'd been recognized. It was only a matter of time before they were caught.

She was silent next to him as they weaved through the streets of the Karsian slums. Stalls and tents sprawled across the street. The smell of roasting meat was heavy on the air, but his stomach couldn't help but turn.

The people who looked like him and lived here were out on their morning business. Their eyes followed them from behind their stalls and from within their tented homes. Conversations quieted as awareness of their presence spread, though they didn't do any more than watch.

Until the first of them spit.

Soon thereafter, the rotten fruit came.

It smacked him in the back of the head and bounced on the stones below their feet behind them. They started running.

It was a learned behavior. As a young boy, he'd seen the king's guards stroll into these slums and lob at the people who lived here old and molded food from the king's stores. It harkened back to a promise that King Cassius had made to his people when he'd made his ancestors' home a wasteland and forced them here.

"You will eat from the king's plate. You will have your own place in the heart of Aloster. And your country will not be forgotten in the unified future."

Malik brought Penrose before him to try to keep her from the worst of it.

"Malik, I'm sorry," she gasped. "I'm so—"

She slipped in some rotted fruit that had missed them. He stopped to help her and got hit with something that had once been some kind of melon. It was much softer than it should have been, but it still hurt.

Malik turned. The others he could ignore, but he was going to fight *this* bastard.

An arm pulled Penrose into an alley next to them.

His blood thundered. He was going to enjoy cutting someone today.

And it seemed he'd found his lucky winner.

Chapter Forty-Nine

An Unlikely Alliance

"Put that away, Malik."

Her words didn't want to make him put it away.

In fact, he thought he needed about ten more knives for this bitch.

His sister stood before him. She'd pulled Penrose to the side street likely to ensure he came after her. Beside Aisha in the narrow alley was Henrik.

"Looks like our father's low on pawns if this is the best he can do," Malik spat.

Penrose had been grabbed and promptly ignored once Malik had come after her. Her eyebrows came together as she assessed the situation. "What's going on?"

"We're not here on Father's account," Aisha claimed. "I've split from him, Malik."

None of it made any damned sense.

Lie, lie. All lies, a voice inside him chanted. The voice was usually right.

"Pen." He motioned for her to follow him out of here.

She didn't come. "What's going on?" she repeated. "You haven't said. Why are you here, Henrik? *How?*"

"You can't trust them," Malik reminded her.

"I kidnapped him from Father," Aisha said in response to Penrose, sidestepping him.

"Another word would be *liberated*," Henrik said to her. Malik realized then the bruises decorating his face.

"You fought them?" Penrose's mouth hung open. She looked between them.

"Yes, girl, I did. And maybe won against them, even." A lopsided grin flashed across the researcher's face, making the bruise there move.

"And your leg?" Penrose pointed at the spot where his father had shot the man.

"Healing still, but enough so that I can walk," Henrik assured her.

Malik placed himself between her and them. This was over.

He glared at Aisha. "Why. Are. You. Here." His voice was steel.

"Henrik told me, Malik." Aisha's teeth were gritted. "The *trade* our father orchestrated. I was a damned fool, but I want to help you. It's why I brought him." She stepped closer to him. Though the anger was still in her voice, a strange gleam came over her eyes like she had unshed tears. "I don't want you to die."

The buzzing of corpseflies in his brain silenced his thoughts effectively.

Malik turned his back. "Come on, Penrose."

A rat was a rat was a rat.

"Malik, we could use the help," Penrose said. "Henrik—"

"No," he said. "Not her. We're *not* with her."

But Aisha was still trying to talk to him. She'd blocked their way out with her body. "Malik, I'm so sorry. I was wrong."

Well, it was a little late for *that*.

What was more, Penrose wasn't moving.

Gods, they'd all been sent to torture him. He was about to lose it, and he didn't want Penrose to see that.

He looked at Pen. He could convince her. He just needed to remind her what they'd lost because of Aisha. "She betrayed you, too. Don't mistake it. She sold us out both."

He needed her to take his side. To understand why this wasn't going to happen.

They weren't siblings anymore.

And that, along with her actions, made them enemies.

Penrose looked at Malik as she spoke as if silently pleading with him to understand, too. "Henrik. I need access to some literature. Things that would have been around in my time. Nothing new." She closed her eyes. "Does that exist somewhere?"

Henrik was silent. Malik watched as the man who had once been his father's captive roll the question around in his head, as if weighing whether or not to go forward with this bass-ackwards situation.

Finally, he said, "It was closed shortly after Cassiel came to power. It was the library of Alsra's largest university. They said the closure was for repairs, but it never reopened. Structural issues, apparently." His eyes flicked to her face. "Your materials would be there, if they are anywhere in this city. I have been inside. They never relocated the oldest of what the library contained."

Penrose turned to the healer and researcher. "Can you lead me there or even get me in? Today?"

Malik wondered if he was having one of his nightmares.

"I could. Assuming I have protection." Henrik's eyes flashed to Aisha as he spoke.

Malik felt his blood pressure soar to the moon, but he couldn't get a word in between the three. They sounded about as sane as if they were high.

Aisha said simply, "You've seen what I can do."

"*Penrose*," Malik cut in.

She stepped close to him, and her hand hovered on his lower arm. He remembered how it felt to hold her close.

"I'm going with them, Malik. Please. Come with me."

Malik closed his eyes.

Maybe he could get what he wanted after all.

All of it.

"Okay," he said, breathing out the word. A moment later, he added, "But I'm getting her gun."

Chapter Fifty

Forever

The sun was high—directly above the clock tower connected to the library. Warmth pounded Penrose's skin. For once, she didn't taste the smog on the air.

This was going to work. She had to believe it.

She had to believe in *something*. For Malik.

With Aisha and Malik's knowledge of Alsra's backstreets, the four of them had slipped past the worst of Alsra's market crowds at high noon. She was impressed even though they must have had to do this sort of thing regularly.

Aisha had brought spare cloaks that she and Malik now wore over their heads. They'd had little choice but to blend within the throng at the intersections closest to Alsra's center.

Penrose couldn't help but stare. She hadn't forgotten that this world was different from the one she'd known for sixteen years, but to be reminded of it so forcefully on the streets she'd once called did strange things to her.

She'd passed by buildings of industry with chimneys spouting puffs of gray air into the heavens. Penrose had pulled her shirt over her throat in those areas to filter the smog from her lungs.

But the center of the city was different. She knew it was a library from the outside of it. It just looked like one.

Its windows were dark but tall and proud. Penrose imagined what the inside looked like when the light shone on it. She could tell by the arches and type of mason work that the building had been constructed around the era in which she'd been living. Dead ivy clung to its exterior like a child to its mother.

From the chill air, overgrown shrubs surrounding it had shed their leaves in the streets around the library, and the wind played with the leaves as they walked through them.

There was no other word for it. It was beautiful.

A pair of guards stood by the wide entrance at the top of a few stair steps. Her heart rose in her chest. They were close.

Henrik shifted next to Aisha where they lead her and Malik. Aisha picked up on the change in direction and casually fell back to walk in line with the two of them. As she walked, she shielded them from the guards' line of sight.

They were going to make it.

They began to loosely skirt the side of the library. From the outside, they seemed to be two couples taking a leisurely walk in a less polluted section of Aloster's crown city. But they needed to find the window that Aisha had previously scouted during the brief period of shift change for the guards.

Why guard an abandoned library?

That alone gave her hope that this place would prove to be invaluable to them.

Suddenly, something on the ground caught Penrose's eye. She stopped to better read what was written on a brass metal plate in the ground.

Her heart stopped. She read the words again.

And again.

Malik was yanking her arm, but she had to read it again.

"For my daughter, Penrose. We will forever love you."

It didn't make sense.

Well, it did. It was the type of grand gesture that only a king could make.

A gesture that one would expect a publicly grieving father to make, in fact.

Malik was tugging on her arm. But she couldn't move.

She couldn't stop reading the words.

He sold me out to a despot who took over our country. What does it matter that he did this?

Sometimes, actions were louder than words.

Malik was done calling her name. She became incrementally more aware of their situation.

One of the building's guards was talking to them—Aisha, specifically.

It was when he spat at Aisha's feet and grabbed the rifle across his back that Penrose realized just how deeply she'd damned them by stopping to read her father's dedication to her.

***

Malik didn't think. He acted. It was generally how he'd kept his head attached thus far.

Pen had suddenly stopped and stared at a plaque in the brick path around the guarded building. They'd almost made it, too.

Malik grabbed her. He had to hope that the medicine would last long enough to keep him vertical while he got her out of this situation.

Aisha had grabbed the end of the man's rifle to point it somewhere other than at her face.

He should have known. Anyone who looked like the two of them did didn't belong in this part of Alsra. He wasn't naïve.

Slum healer. Market barker. Criminal heiress.

It was all the same to them.

His father had certainly had a part in dirtying the public perception of Karsia's descendants, but Malik couldn't blame him for that.

You play the cards you get. Or you make a better game.

Aisha's voice cut through his thoughts. "Run!"

The word bounced off the old stones of the library next to them. He grabbed Penrose and Henrik and did just that.

Penrose was already talking under his arm. "We can't! We have to go back."

Air huffed out of his lungs. He was half-dragging Henrik behind him. He was heavier than Penrose, but he knew he should take them both.

His eyes scanned for cover, and thoughts left his brain except for those that would keep them alive. The wide street yawned empty before them, but a group of Alostrans was about to turn the corner and see them.

He had to assume Aisha could keep him preoccupied on her own. He didn't bother himself with what would happen to her.

"We need to go back," Penrose repeated.

He *needed* a drink, but that wasn't happening, either. He kept his mouth shut about that, though.

He threw the two into the overgrown shrubs, and he fell inside after them a second later.

This one was as large as an outhouse. Branches scraped his face as he came to the earth.

It was then that he saw. The other guard had come to investigate his partner's absence.

Aisha pulled free a knife. Her gun was in his waistband. It was too late to think about that, though.

In a second, her knife was gone—and between the ribs of one of the library guards.

Good aim, he thought.

And then the butt of a rifle found the back of her head. Aisha slumped easily to the ground. They didn't bother breaking her fall.

The guard who she'd stabbed cursed and kicked his sister. She didn't move.

His hand pressed tight against the wound, but Malik guessed from the location that it wasn't a killing shot. The man would live. He seemed to have gathered this, too.

Malik's breath came shorter and shorter.

"Malik," Penrose whispered at him. Her fingers tightened around his arm. "We can't leave her!"

Henrik was deathly quiet beside her. Pale and staring forward, he looked like he was going to vomit.

The guard who hadn't been stabbed looked out around them, but his gaze didn't linger anywhere. The group of citizens who had been about to discover the scene had diverged and gone a different way. The guard stopped looking around, and his gaze fell back to an unmoving Aisha.

As for the three of them that had fled the scene of an apparent crime, the guards either thought they weren't worth the trouble, or ...

They weren't bothering to shackle her. Another kick hit Aisha's side. And another. They would move to her head, soon.

"Malik," Penrose repeated.

He didn't need convincing.

Dammit, that was his *sister*.

Malik ran out of the bush.

Chapter Fifty-One

Those with Faces

They'd already assumed the area to be cleared. It was one reason why Malik had the upper hand.

The other was his rage.

"Fuck-face!" Malik's yell echoed against the library's wall.

They both looked up from their kicking. Malik grinned and shot them both in their fuck-faces.

Maybe he would have given them better deaths if they hadn't have responded to the epithet.

Malik doubted it.

The gunshots still rang in his ears when he picked up his little sister's unconscious body. He hoped that she was merely unconscious and not the alternative.

There was no space in his brain to consider otherwise. Actually, there was space for little else.

"Malik!" Penrose's eyes were wide. She and Henrik were running to them.

Henrik finally vomited.

"Malik, is she—" She looked to the guards on the ground at his feet. There were bits of them everywhere, and blood was beginning to pool.

To her credit, Penrose didn't vomit.

He needed to get them all out of here. Now.

Henrik had joined them at last. He glanced at Aisha and pinched his lips together. "She needs help."

"Perhaps we could regroup in the library?" Penrose's eyes pleaded with him.

Well, there was no running through the streets with Aisha like this. And he wasn't sure how much longer Rana's medicine would keep him upright. Already, he could feel his limbs tremble and the heat of his fever build behind his temples.

Dammit, he hadn't saved his sister from them so she'd catch somnus from him.

There was no choice.

"Drag them to the shrubs," Malik commanded. "It'll buy us some time if they don't find their bodies immediately."

Henrik was horrified, but Penrose had already started. In reality, hiding the bodies probably wouldn't give them extra time when there were chunks of them everywhere. But he had to try.

The gunfire would have attracted any guard in several blocks. Add that to the fact that he and Penrose were wanted by Cassius himself, and there was barely any hope.

They had to get inside the library while covering their tracks. Breaking a window was out.

Malik walked up to the doors and propped Aisha on the ground against the wall. Her head rolled to one side, but ragged breath flowed through her. Blood had hardened her clothes, and he could only hope it was from the guards he'd killed.

The doors were locked. No surprise there.

While listening to Henrik and Penrose grunting as they dragged the bodies, he took out Aisha's knife and started to pick one of them.

He had to save Penrose.

And he had to save Aisha.

She'd done what she did, and he'd never let that go. But he hadn't been going to let some big boys strapped with rifles kick around his sister.

The truth was, those kicks had been meant for Malik. But Aisha had stepped in front of all three of them. She'd engaged the guard first so that they could get away.

Malik chipped the edge of her knife with the force of his picking, but the lock acquiesced to his demands with a *click*.

"It's open," he announced.

The other two were coming up the steps after him, panting. Malik cleaned a speck of blood from Penrose's face. There wasn't time for words, but from the look in her eyes, she knew that, too.

The door he'd picked swung open easily. Inside, a library hall yawned empty before them. Desks lined either side of the entryway. Dust motes floated in the air, already disturbed from the door opening.

Malik pulled Aisha into his arms and stepped forward. And was promptly stopped.

An unseen force blocked all of them. Malik nearly fell on his face. Penrose's palms searched the open air before them for an answer.

Henrik actually fell.

"There's ... something here." Penrose's eyebrows came together.

It was then that he saw it. The light had been too dim to notice it before.

A film of transparent blue was on the air before them.

A forcefield.

"A what?" Penrose said.

He hadn't realized he'd said it out loud. When he spoke again, his voice was hollow. "The same thing was around you when you were in the tower. It was a spell."

This was the right place. Cassius had done this because there was something in here that could beat him. Penrose had been right.

"How ..." Her eyes had found his. Talking about her hundred-year sleep wasn't easy for her. "How did you get through mine?"

Because I loved you.

He shook his head. It didn't make any damn sense. He heard the king's words again.

"The only way through the barrier was if her true love match walked through it and woke her up."

"Love," he finally said.

It was a damn fool thing to say, but it was the truth.

He'd been undone by this frail, blonde girl next to him from a different time. Until the somnus claimed him, there was no reversing that in him.

But that wasn't working now.

Henrik was busy playing with it, tapping at it as if it were a thing he could study like his lab rats.

Penrose turned. People were coming. They could hear their raised voices on the other side of the doors. It would be a matter of seconds before they found them if they didn't get past this.

Malik looked down.

His sister was breathing shallowly in his arms. Her hair, a cloud of brown curls usually, was slicked with sweat and blood.

She'd betrayed him. But she'd also saved his ass—repeatedly.

Back when it was the three of them, he and Aisha had been in it together. He fully believed it was the only way he'd endured his father's training.

Nevermind that she became what he'd never achieved: the perfect heir.

He knew she hadn't wanted it like that. It had always been the two of them ruling their streets. The king and queen siblings of House Ezar, stewards of both terror and peace.

"You fool," he said under his breath. "You damned fool."

He bit his tongue and closed his eyes. He couldn't remember the last time when he'd cried.

He hadn't thought there was any of that still inside him. He thought he'd traded it for his skills, his cynicism, and his will to live in the face of his enemies.

He'd thought his father had taken that from him long ago.

Malik stepped through the barrier with his sister in his arms.

Chapter Fifty-Two

Those who do Something

Penrose breathed in the smell of books. She could tell from the smell alone that no one had been here in a long while.

This had to be it. Coming here had been the right decision.

But she was gravely aware that there had been a cost.

She and Henrik passed through the library's barrier after Malik had broken through it. Aisha's head flopped on his arm as he carried her.

"To the back," Henrik barked. "Find a table. Away from any windows!"

They obeyed him, and when they came to what had likely once been a study table, Henrik shoved what was on it to the floor. Dust puffed up in protest.

Malik didn't waste time and spread her on the table.

"What now?" Malik's words were clipped.

"Strip her," Henrik said to them both. He swung his knapsack next to Aisha's head.

Penrose went to work on her pants while Malik cut her shirt open and pulled her arms through.

She left her black leather pants in a pile on the floor.

"Check her for wounds," Henrik said. "I'll start at her head."

Penrose's hands gently probed her skin in her search.

"Bruising," Malik finally announced. "A lot. No lacerations, though."

It was what she'd found, as well. From a purple center spread yellow at their edges like flowers spread across her body. It made Penrose want to vomit.

They'd been monsters.

Even if Aisha had betrayed the two of them, she didn't deserve this. No one did.

Henrik's hands flew through his bag. He shoved several cloths at Malik and a canteen of water. "Find somewhere to pour this over these rags. She needs a compress or rather, several." He stopped as if he just remembered something.

He took the rags and water and shoved them at Penrose instead. His eyes were sharp as he turned back to Malik. "How are you well enough to stand? What are your symptoms? What's going on?"

Penrose rushed to carry out Henrik's orders, though she couldn't help but overhear Malik relate, in detail, what had happened in the Karsian slums. Rana, her grandmother, the treatment he'd received, all of it.

Henrik released a breath. "That girl saved all our lives. Without symptoms, you're not contagious."

Penrose sagged against a bookcase. *Thank the gods for that, at least.*

She couldn't blame Rana's grandmother for what she'd done. She'd only been trying to protect her granddaughter.

But the world needed a kingdom full of Ranas.

Those who looked out at the mess and cared. Who did something. Who would extend a hand even when it was infinitely easier not to.

Gods bless her.

But Malik was still going to die if they didn't figure something out.

Penrose found a decorative bowl on a table with river rocks at the bottom. Her hands trembled as she poured the water over the rags and the bowl filled up. She ran back to Henrik who then gave her another bundle. Aisha had many bruises, after all.

Water ran through her fingers. If she couldn't save him in three days, then it would be all be over.

She could find the cure to somnus, dethrone Cassius, and save the world, but it wouldn't matter for Malik.

He'd still be dead.

Her shaking hands dropped the sopping rag she'd been holding, and it splashed water everywhere.

Warm hands pulled her close. Malik smell of blood and sweat, and she was sure she did, too. But she didn't care. Malik's fingers lifted her chin to look at him.

"You're going to be fine. He won't get you here." His grip was still soft, but something crossed his face. "He'll die before he touches you again," he vowed.

He picked up the rag in the water and used it to wipe clean the grime and blood from her face.

"Malik ..." It wasn't what she was afraid of right now, but she couldn't say that.

He chuckled. "Since we met, I'd dream of how you'd say my name. Of how you'd *plead* my name." His mouth came to her ear. "It was never as good as it turned out to be."

Heat built in the bottom of her stomach. She looked away, but now it was in her head. His thumb brushed her lips. Breath caught in her throat when she looked back at his face. His lips. She wondered how soft they were and how he tasted. She wondered how firm he'd be with her when his hands were on her.

Suddenly, something caught her eye past his face. Malik twisted to see what it was. Something was in the window nearest them.

The muscles in his back bunched up as his hand went to his gun.

"Wait!" Penrose stopped him with a hand. "It can't be," she whispered to herself.

It is.

Tears blurred her vision. She ran to crack the window, and a blue song bird flew inside.

It was Sorrowtail.

Chapter Fifty-Three

Secrets

Sorrowtail pressed his head against Penrose's collarbone. She scratched the back of it, and his feathers ruffled in response.

After she'd been traded to the king by Malik's father, she'd been certain she wouldn't see him again. Moisture pricked at her eyes at the memory of letting him go.

Well, he'd survived. Thrived, even, as he looked fatter to her eyes. As if in response to her unspoken thoughts, he nipped her fingers.

"You silly, prideful bird," she said through her grinning.

He blinked at her as if to say, *Was it that hard for you to survive without me? I thought so.*

"I don't know how I did," she admitted, then laughed when she realized Malik must have thought her mad, responding to words she'd imagined a bird had said.

Malik approached them, and she held Sorrowtail in her palm for his examination.

"Where were you, you creature?" He cocked an eyebrow at the song bird.

Sorrowtail was suddenly very serious. His black-bead eye seemed to gleam with hidden knowledge of Alsra's streets.

Malik looked back at her. "Secrets of the trade," he explained in a sober voice.

Penrose stifled a laugh.

***

Aisha was going to live and recover from her injuries. Or so Henrik was fairly certain.

She'd woken briefly and been able to answer simple questions, so there likely hadn't been any permanent damage to her head, either.

Penrose was thankful for that, for at the very least, she was still Malik's sister.

It would have broken a part of him to have seen her die like that, Penrose considered. *Even if he's still angry at what she did.*

Malik hadn't slept, though darkness from the evening had started to fill the library from outside, draping it in velvet shadows. He sat on the floor, and his back was against the bookshelf nearest Aisha's table. His sister slept between some blankets that they'd found there while Henrik slept between another pile of blankets on the floor some paces away. Even Sorrowtail was sleeping in his own nest of rags.

"Are you sure you should be the one to stay up?" Penrose asked Malik with a frown. "You need rest."

"That's the last of what I need," Malik said.

He stared ahead at the lone lantern they'd found and managed to light. The light inside danced and writhed like a demon.

Rings had started to form under his eyes, but Penrose knew that exhaustion was sometimes better than sleep.

Especially when it came to somnus.

"We need to extinguish this soon," he said, his chin pointing at the lantern. "The fact that they haven't found us here yet makes me suspicious. They either can't get in after us," he said, raising an eyebrow, "or they're waiting to pick us off one by one from the outside."

Malik squinted at her when she didn't respond. "You're going to try to look for your book." It came out like an accusation.

"I'm not sure how long it will take to find it. I should have started before, but ..." *But I wanted to see you see Aisha alive.* She didn't verbalize the thought. It seemed too fresh to him still. "I'll be fine," she said instead.

He rose, and his hands found her shoulders. "Stay away from the windows. *Please.*"

She could tell how hard it was for him to let her go by herself, but they didn't have a choice. Someone needed to monitor the others and watch the front of the library in case the barrier around it allowed more people to pass through it.

The others were all exhausted, sick, and injured. Even Henrik was still getting over his gunshot wound.

Only Penrose hale and healthy still.

And there was more she hadn't been able to say out loud—like how many days he had left.

What if I don't find what I need?

What if it's all pointless?

What do I do when I do find what I need?

She hadn't realized her hands were shaking until Malik held them together in a vise-like grip. "Penrose." Her name on his lips did strange things to her insides.

She thanked the gods that Henrik had brought medicine to treat and suppress his somnus symptoms—thereby making him noncontagious. Even if it didn't cure him.

Penrose rested her head against his chest and listened to the sound his heart made.

After a few moments, she pulled away from him and looked into his chocolate brown eyes.

He moved strands from her face and asked, "What is it you expect to find here?"

"I'm trying to find literature on something I read about when I was younger."

"That's what you told Henrik," Malik said. "What's the rest of it?"

Penrose mulled over her words for a bit before speaking more. She couldn't forget how sharp Malik was, but the rest of her reasoning wasn't the most solid. She'd taken a chance coming here, and she sorely didn't want to appear like a fool for risking their lives for shaky logic.

"Cassius is ... something else. I couldn't figure out how he tricked the entire world. My parents."

Malik was patient and waited for more.

She added, "I don't have definitive proof, but ..."

"What is it?" Malik watched her.

"I think someone else is working against him, too. A female guard whispered something strange to me during a search. She told me not to react to what she was going to say."

"*What?*" Malik's hands found her shoulders. "What did she say?"

"That's the thing. I think she was speaking in code. The only other thing she said was, 'by the spirits, she's clean.'"

He arched an eyebrow. "And you have an idea of what this means?"

"*By the spirits* is a bit of an older phrase from my time." Penrose was pacing. She wasn't sure when she'd started. "But I think the meaning is twofold. She knows who I am—who I really am—and well ... I think he's ..."

Penrose shook her head before she could finish the sentence. It was unbelievable. Ridiculous.

Firm hands found either side of her face. Malik held her gaze straight so she had nowhere else to look but into his eyes.

"I know that look," he said. Before she could interrupt, he said, "And I hate it. I hate seeing you doubt yourself because of what he tried to do to you." His hands fell away. "So tell me what you think. What you *really* think."

Penrose breathed. She'd seen him transform from young to old to young again. She'd seen him control somnus with her own eyes.

But no one else had seen these things. It had always been her word against his.

And she'd always been the paranoid, unreasonable bride. And then she'd been the girl asleep in a tower for a hundred years. Insane. Hysterical.

Untrustworthy.

Unstable.

She knew Cassius's secret—and there was power in that.

He'd tried to disguise it by pretending to be his own descendant, but the truth was plainly before her, now.

He was a monster in more than one sense.

"He made them think I was a witch," she said. "Or that's what he called me in front of them all, over and over. Claiming I had powers over somnus—that I had made it worse." She licked her lips. "It made me think that he was covering up his actions and who he really was. That he was ... deflecting." She closed her eyes as she remembered something else that had been bothering her. "And then there was what we saw in the tunnels underneath Alsra. Something was there with us."

She opened her eyes. Finally, Penrose said it.

"Cassius is not human. He is pretending to be one, and he has had years to perfect his behavior, but he is no such thing." Penrose held his gaze. "He is a being made of something like magic. He is a spirit."

It was insanity.

And yet ... Malik wasn't looking at her as if she were insane.

Instead of responding right away, Malik fished something out of his pocket. He pulled one of her hands to his and slipped the object into hers.

They were a pair of reading glasses.

"Find your book," he said. "Whatever he is, find what we need to end him."

"How ... did you ..." Penrose couldn't seem to complete the thought.

"I found them here," Malik admitted. "I thought there would be some. Books ... reading glasses. It seemed to make sense." He shrugged.

He almost seemed self-conscious to her.

How ... cute. She wanted to laugh. She wanted to kiss him.

But there was something bothering her.

Penrose shook her head. "No, how did you remember that I used glasses?"

She'd only mentioned her needing glasses to read in passing—it had been when she'd revealed to him all that Cassius had done to her.

Malik crossed his arms and looked away.

"Well. If it's important to you, then it is to me, too," he muttered.

Penrose couldn't help it. He was too cute. She giggled.

He was in the middle of turning his head to shoot her a look—likely for her to cut the giggling—when she did it.

She kissed him on the mouth.

Chapter Fifty-Four

Only When it's Darkest

As hard as she tried to keep her mind on the task at hand as the night stretched on, she couldn't.

Penrose replayed their first kiss over and over in her mind.

She'd never known it could be like that. Her very first kiss—to Cassius—had been dizzying. Confusing. Wrong.

But with Malik, it had been different.

He'd been the one to pull back. The heat had spread through her, and she'd needed more, but she'd respected his wishes.

"Silly girl. Do you even know what you do to me?" She could still hear his low baritone voice in her ear. *"Next time you try something like that, I'll have to make you beg me not to stop."*

She swallowed. She needed to *focus*.

A headache built behind her eyes. Even with the gift of clearer sight and the low lantern light, this was proving a challenge. Penrose was sequestered in the section of the old library that contained books on mythology and culture.

On one side of her was the pile of books she'd already checked. She observed an inverse relationship; as the lantern's flame waned, the pile grew taller than her.

What if she couldn't find the answer in time? What were they going to do, then?

And if I find a definitive answer to what he is, will there be a solution to this all?

Penrose's fingers skimmed a passage about the gods and the celebrations they required on the page before her. This wasn't the book she was looking for.

Suddenly, she stood. The book fell to the ground with a dull *thump*. Her fingers went to her scalp.

Dammit, this was supposed to be what she was good for! She'd already read or skimmed half the books in the section that was supposed to contain the answer.

None of them so much as hinted at the story she remembered.

What was the use of having spent half her waking hours crouched over books when she couldn't find the one that could save Malik's life?

The silent, dark library watched her back. This was supposed to be where she shined. Penrose stopped herself before she hurt a book. Her back slumped against a shelf.

A swallow scratched her throat.

Had her father had this library built right after her supposed death? Or had it been years later?

What would it have been like if she'd been alive when it had been built?

She closed her eyes and imagined it. They might have spent all day here when he was still alive. Her mother might have even taken a day from her duties as ruler and joined them.

Her eyes opened.

If her father had dedicated this library to her after she was gone, then it was possible that ...

Penrose grabbed the dying lantern and perched her reading glasses on her head like a crown.

Cassius closed this place.

But he didn't remove the oldest books and materials.

As if ... he couldn't.

Pen passed the stacks faster and faster. The light of the lantern followed her like a column of light.

If he wanted no one else to find the books hidden here, wouldn't he have destroyed it instead of preserved it?

She stared ahead. *The barrier wasn't his doing.*

There's a reason no one has infiltrated it after us.

Penrose's breath came faster. She needed to slow down and catch her breath, but she couldn't. Where was it?

Where was the source of the barrier? The ... magic?

Penrose stopped. The light of the lantern fluttered, casting strange shapes on the spines of the books around her.

Suddenly, the light went out.

She blinked in the new darkness. She'd crossed the side opposite of where Malik and the others were. She could hear her own breath and heartbeat thrum through her, and her skin raised in bumps.

Is there someone there?

Penrose twisted around. She'd thought she'd heard something—a rustle—but there was only a blanket of silence and utter darkness.

Her hand hovered on her hip where she kept one of Malik's knives. "Who's there?"

But the only answer was her quickening heartbeat.

It was then that she saw it. It was so faint that she wouldn't have been able to see it except in absolute darkness. She walked forward.

A weak, blue light flickered ahead of her. Penrose sprinted past more bookshelves until she came to where it was.

It coated the book's cover like lacquer. It was the same as the barrier that had kept them from entering the library initially.

She hesitated only a moment before pulling the book from where it rested. To her surprise, there was no resistance.

The front cover stared up at her. It was familiar.

The blue light hovered above it like a lantern.

She thumbed it open to the front page and nearly sagged to the floor when she read it. Inside it had been scrawled a quick message.

"For my little sister and bookwyrm, Pen. Love, Lessa."

The blue light puffed out of existence, and she was bathed in darkness once more.

This time, she allowed her knees to weaken, and she sat on the ground. Penrose pressed the book to her chest and closed her eyes.

Somehow, her sister had helped her.

Thank you, Lesabeth.

The story she'd been looking for was inside this book. Her father must have donated the small library of books in Penrose's room to the collection here when it was built.

In the quiet of the abandoned library, she let her tears flow freely as she clasped these tokens left to her by her family.

Maybe, just maybe, beating him would be possible.

In the darkness of the library, she relit the lantern and devoured the words on the page.

***

"Penrose. It's time to wake up."

She jerked awake. Malik's touch left her shoulder. Penrose blinked against the brightness.

How long had she been sleeping?

Light streamed through the high windows of the library. Dust floated around her like an aura—like the dust itself was excited for her discovery.

"Malik!" She jolted to her feet. The book that had been in her lap slid to the floor.

Suddenly, his knives were in his hands. "What's wrong?" His eyes darted in all directions. They settled on her. He replaced his weapons at his waist, and his hands wrapped around her arms as he pulled her closer for inspection. "Are you okay?"

Penrose wanted to laugh at his hypervigilance, but she knew it was warranted.

"I'm fine. *I found it,*" she said. She saw herself in his eyes and knew her expression was wild. She didn't care. "I found the answer we needed."

It was then that she saw how dark the circles under his eyes had gotten. They looked like bruises. Her fingers touched his cheek. His hand captured her fingers and held them tight.

"You didn't sleep." Her lips pinched together. "How long since you've slept last?" she asked.

At the end of her question was another one, like a near-silent echo of the original.

How long?

He released her fingers. After a second, his expression softened. He moved her hair behind her ears.

"Tell me what you need me to do, and I'll do it," he said.

Penrose straightened. He was depending on her. And the fate of the world was depending on how well they executed what was to come next.

She breathed. This was what she'd been preparing for—even all those years ago when she'd decided to marry Cassius just to steal and spread the cure for somnus.

She was ready for this. She just had to remember that.

She remembered the tone her mother used when making her dictums. "Gather the others. Tell them about me. Tell them about Cassius. Everything, Malik." Penrose opened her eyes. "We'll reconvene in an hour. I need to be sure of some things first. And then, we'll make our plans for tomorrow."

After a moment, Malik smiled.

"I love a woman with murder in her heart."

Chapter Fifty-Five

The Origin of Nightmares

In an hour, Penrose came to them. She'd memorized the stack of tomes in her hands, though it was a small stack. She placed the books on the table that Aisha had been sleeping on.

The three of them stared back at her.

"By now, Malik has told you," she said. She stared down Henrik and Aisha. "You've both chosen to involve yourselves in this so far. For that, I'm grateful." She leaned forward, her palms on the table. "But what I'm about to tell you—well, sane people wouldn't believe it."

Aisha tilted her head at her. "Go ahead, then."

She paused. "Right. What I'm about to propose we do will be dangerous. But I know this is my fight." Penrose breathed. She needed to say it out loud. "I'm queen of this kingdom by birthright. It's my responsibility to do something about Cassius."

She leveled her gaze with each of them. "I wanted to offer the three of you the chance to back out before this goes deeper."

Her eyes went to Malik first. He crossed his arms in response to her stare. "I think you know the answer to that."

Penrose smiled, though she knew he had the most staked in this. "You could leave, you know."

"It's too late for that," he said. His eyes flashed a look at her. "Besides, I don't give up what's mine."

Heat flared through her at his words, and she averted her eyes. By doing so, she saw how Henrik was staring at her books.

The man met her eyes. "For most of my life, I've studied somnus and tried to work towards a cure. If one exists, I'll be damned if I'm not going to be part of it."

Malik actually clapped a hand on his shoulder. Henrik looked like he nearly fell in response.

"It doesn't mean I'm going to be killing anyone, however," Henrik sputtered. Penrose wanted to laugh. He seemed nervous to see that he and Malik were on the same side.

Aisha was still quiet, though Penrose could tell she was looking at her. Her stomach turned. She'd been the least sure of how she'd respond to all of this.

Aisha had proven herself and her loyalty to Malik. But that didn't mean she'd want to accompany them a mission that Penrose had brewed—all to stop a man who she claimed to be well over a hundred years old and who could transform his looks with no prompting.

"Where Malik goes, I go," she said simply.

Penrose nodded, relieved to have her help.

She wasn't sure if the four of them were all going to get through this, but she'd made her best plan to keep the others as much out of harm's way as possible.

"And now that we're all on the same page, I'll explain." Penrose continued, "Cassius—not the mask he wears, Cassiel—is not human. And I even have proof."

After a moment, Aisha said, "If he's not, then what is he?"

Penrose smiled. She'd hoped someone would ask that.

"He is *somnus*. Personified."

She let her words settle in their minds for a few minutes.

Henrik's eyes were on the book of fables and folklore she'd brought with her. It was the one that Lesabeth had given to her. With his eyes still on it, he said, "What do you mean?"

"In my time, the sleeping curse was a sign of the gods' disfavor." Her lips pinched together. "As a matter of fact, much of what we did daily and how we did it concerned what we thought the gods would think of us."

When they held their meals. What they ate. Evestide and other celebrations.

Malik's tone was dull. "That sounds damn exhausting."

Penrose cracked a smile. "It was."

She opened Lessa's book to the page she'd marked. "But not even those of us back then knew the origins of somnus. It was ... all we could rationalize it as." She looked up again. "But what if that was literal? What if the gods were simply ... mad?"

Henrik's arms crossed. "What we realized in a hundred years is that we can't blame the gods for every problem we have. We can't interpret every failing as their displeasure at us."

Penrose shook her head. "That's not quite what I mean, either. This is not a curse on *us*."

"Then who?" Malik asked in a flat voice.

She smiled at him. "On Nightmare himself."

Penrose breathed to steady herself.

Either they'll believe me or they won't.

It was time to lay out everything she'd gathered thus far.

When Penrose spoke, the fable from her childhood came to life before her eyes.

***

Once, there was a spirit born from magic who roamed between the realms of humans and the gods. Unlike other spirits, he sustained himself by feeding on the dreams of those sleeping.

One sunny day, he happened upon a beautiful maiden sleeping on an altar in the woods. He reasoned she was a priestess tasked to tend to a shrine of the gods, and while he usually chose to sustain himself on the dreams of those who led more exciting lives than she did, he was ravenous.

When he began eating her dreams, he realized they were much more plentiful and appetizing than he could have imagined. Dreams he had never seen before and ones far more powerful than any he'd encountered yet lined the inside of her thoughts.

Dreams where he was loved like no one had loved him before.

But he'd gone too far and eaten all her dreams. When he was done, he saw that the maiden had died.

At once, a bolt of light hit the altar, and it caught aflame. Before him was one of the gods, appearing as a winged man.

In his fury, the god nearly killed the spirit, but he held back.

"You haven't any idea, have you?" he demanded of the spirit. "You've killed Love."

The maiden hadn't been a priestess at all but a member of the pantheon of gods. She'd been the goddess Love, tasked with matching fated souls to one another.

Her lover, the angry god, cursed the spirit to walk the human realm without end or until he reformed. What was more, the god cursed him with a thirst for only dreams that inspired terror and dismay.

Thus, the spirit Nightmare was created.

***

"When I first heard it as a young child, I regarded it as nothing more than folklore—the type that explains otherwise unexplainable but natural things like the moon or death," Penrose said.

Malik raised his eyebrows at her. "Of course."

He seemed serious, but Penrose was suspicious of him. She ignored him.

"Then you're saying Nightmare is somnus? That the folk tale is actually explaining the origins of the sleeping disease?" Henrik said. He pressed his lips together. "But you're not suggesting this is literal?"

Penrose stared into Henrik's face. He was a man of science and logic. He was more than that to her, though. He was someone who had turned out to be a friend. But the time was gone for acting as if she weren't aware of what she was dealing with.

No one else here had as much experience as she did with Cassius. No one else knew him like she did.

Hell, no one else here was married to him.

"I respect your way of thinking, Henrik," she said. "But *normal* doesn't apply to Cassius. He isn't of this world." She leaned towards them. "I have watched him give someone somnus—and then take it away. He pretended that some other liquid had done it, but it was by his hand."

She looked at them all, pausing at each face in turn. "One hundred years ago, he held our wedding party hostage to force my hand. He threatened to curse them with somnus. He did the same a few days ago."

"The truth is I wouldn't be here today if it weren't for him and his powers." Penrose crossed her arms. "In fact, I shouldn't be here. He shouldn't either."

That got Malik's attention.

"What was his purpose in all this?" he said with narrowed eyes. "What does he want from you? He has the crown."

"Cassius told me he used my lifeforce to extend his own—but I think the truth is that he fed off my nightmares of him rather than my life." She continued, "He happened to choose me because I was in line for a throne, but any heir would have done for him. My title gave him the reach and power over others to spread the curse even further." She closed her eyes and remembered how he'd trapped her in his tower and made her think that she was overreacting. Like he hadn't took away her ability to leave and painted her as crazy in front of everyone else. "So long as he could make them fear him enough."

True to his nature, Malik asked the question she'd been waiting on him to ask.

"If it's not a man, how do we kill it?"

Her eyes opened. "The opposite of what Nightmare feeds on. And salt. Lots of it." The memory of her oversalted meal came back to her. Penrose owed quite a bit to that guard who had defected from Cassius—as well as her father for his cautionary tale on Evestide.

This was something else she'd realized. Regular bullets and weapons weren't going to hurt him. They'd proven that when they'd shot at him in the sewers. He wasn't a man, after all.

She raised an eyebrow at Malik. "You have a supplier for your munitions, correct?"

Malik's grin widened.

Chapter Fifty-Six

Chosen Family

Penrose scanned the spines for the book she knew should be there. What self-respecting library didn't have at least a few books on the history of its kingdom's conquered parts?

The victors write history, she remembered. It was one of her father's favorite sayings. She supposed he was still right, a hundred years later.

"Hey."

Penrose turned with a pile of books in her arms. It was Aisha.

Her bruises were visible beneath a lavender silken dress. She stood, her body leaning over the back of a cushioned chair.

Penrose's eyebrows came together. "What's going on?" Her eyes moved around the library. Had something happened to Malik?

We're cutting it too close. We need to get out there already.

As if she could read her mind, Aisha said, "He's fine for now. He and Henrik are cleaning our weapons and gathering together what we'll need." She looked away. "Listen. I needed to say something to you."

Penrose put down the stack. What was going on?

"I came to apologize for the shit storm I caused," Aisha said when she didn't respond.

"No, I ..." Penrose bit her lip. "I know why you did it. He told me your father would have killed him if it weren't for you. It's not what I would have wanted to happen, but ..." She started over. "I'm glad you kept him alive. I'm grateful for that."

A strange expression passed over Aisha's face. "Yeah. If only I could keep him that way."

Aisha tried to walk towards her then, but she stopped, her hand flying to her lower leg. Air hissed through her lips as pain clearly gripped her.

Penrose went to help her up, but when she did, Aisha's hand held her shoulder, keeping her near her. "Please. Please save him."

Words stopped in Penrose's throat.

Penrose managed to say, "I'm trying to."

"We'll do whatever's necessary," Aisha continued to whisper. Her dark eyes flashed. "Promise me you'll save him. Please."

Penrose stared back at her.

Had she figured out ...?

"I promise," Penrose whispered back.

As Penrose helped her back to her feet, Aisha said, "I'll do all I can, as well. And I meant what I said." She glanced sideways at her. "You're important to him. So, this is important to me. I wronged you."

Penrose shook her head. "You were justified. I forgive what you did, Aisha. Of course."

Aisha sagged into the chair she'd been hovering over. "Thank you for that." She closed her eyes. "He chose you. So, I do too." Aisha's eyelashes fluttered apart as she opened them and locked gazes with Penrose. "I hope you realize what this means."

Penrose's mouth popped open. "I ... Aisha."

"You're family, now. And *this* family makes up for its mistakes. It's that simple." Aisha leaned back, seeming as if she were seeing something beyond the abandoned library around them. "My blood gave me up and made me an orphan when I was born. In my life, family has always been a choice to be made. For better or worse." She looked at her again. "I chose him as my brother. He chose you. So, I do, too."

Something lodged in Penrose's throat. She stared at Aisha. Had she really meant it?

She didn't know what to say to that.

She hadn't had a sister since Lesabeth. Her hands started to tremble, but she made them into fists. She was going to defeat Nightmare. Somnus. Cassius.

Whatever name he was going by.

"I choose you, too, Aisha."

There must have been something about the way she said it. Aisha looked at her, though she remained quiet for several heartbeats. She wondered if she'd said the wrong thing.

Aisha suddenly came to her feet. Penrose went to help her, but she was already elbow-deep in one of the satchels she and Henrik had brought with them.

"For the record," Aisha said as she dug, "I believe you about it. About everything." Her eyes passed over Penrose.

When she pulled it out of her bag, Penrose stifled a gasp. It was the dress she'd been wearing when she first met Aisha.

The midnight black fabric moved over her hands like water.

"I want to give you this. Wear it when you want to wear something to kick ass in."

After a moment of marveling at the dress the likes of which she'd never owned, Penrose cleared her voice.

"Thank you, Aisha."

Chapter Fifty-Seven

Entangled

Penrose was crouched over the fifth book describing spirits and other magical beings that she'd found. In all of them, the only commonality to banishing them had been salt.

It had to work.

They were going to acquire the salt bullets when they left the library to infiltrate his castle. But there was a voice inside her that knew better. That knew that curses weren't reversed by salt.

Whatever necessary. Her vow to Aisha remained in her mind.

The shadows of night had fallen again. She rubbed her eyes behind her reading glasses. She had to do it if it came to it. She would save him over her own happiness.

A tear ran along the side of her cheek. She'd never meant to be in this time. Everyone who had ever cared for her had long since passed. Everyone who had known her had been dead and buried for years. And a different world had arisen in her absence.

Despite all that, she'd found a new kind of family here.

Wasn't it worth it if they could live? Even if it meant …

"Pen." Malik's fingers tilted her face to his where he stood above her. He was behind the chair she sat in.

Her voice was hoarse. "Are the others sleeping?"

Will you stay awake with me?

He nodded.

"And you've ... taken Henrik's medicine?"

His answer was quiet. "Yes."

"Distract me." Her voice was a plea.

His eyes were hard on her, but his lips parted. A second later, they were on hers.

Another second after that, Malik had slung everything on top of the table to the floor. He hauled her by the torso on top of the table, cupping her neck and the small of her back.

Malik had shed his shirt by the time her hands moved there. Her mouth was urgent on his, searching. Her other hand moved down the hard planes of his stomach, and he made noises when her hands played at the top of his pants with the ties that held them together. His skin was beautiful, even where it was marred by scars and healed injuries.

"Bad girl," he said in her ear. "Not until I make you call my name."

Her heart sped faster. She'd never done anything like this, but she wanted this with him. She wanted to have this moment with him in case ...

Her hands had wandered to his waistband again. Suddenly, he grabbed both her wrists in one hand and pinned them above her head.

Her breath came in a gasp. "No fair." She felt the blood rush to her cheeks.

"I never said I was fair." His smile was devilish.

Before she could respond, his mouth was on her chest, kissing her bare skin as he undid more of her shirt. Heat spread across her skin as he travelled lower.

Well, she wasn't going to give into him that easily and allow him to win this game he'd constructed with her. He thought her easy to seduce because of her inexperience, did he?

Well, she'd see about that. She hadn't read all those novels Lesabeth had snuck in for nothing.

He might have had her by the wrists, but the rest of her was free. Her legs hooked around his waist. She brought herself close to him so that he couldn't ignore how they felt together. Penrose swallowed, and her own desire flowed through her with a ferocity.

Okay, maybe she did need him.

"Cheat," he said, forcing her body down with his own to make her stop moving. His breath was in her ear. "Careful, Princess. You're playing with fire. You wouldn't want to make me lose control and—"

Her mouth was on his again.

He was wrong. Maybe, for once in her life, she wanted to choose to lose control.

His hand not holding hers above her head went to her pants and slipped them off. She hadn't meant to moan into his mouth, though he seemed set off by the sound. She was getting close to winning this game of theirs.

But when he touched her, she couldn't help it. She broke their kiss, and his name was on her lips like a prayer. "Malik."

His mouth went to her ear. "There's a good girl."

She chose then to strike. She slipped one hand out of his grasp and to his pants. She swallowed at what she found there.

"Ah, ah," he said, and she could hear the grin in his voice. "You first."

\#

Penrose rested her head against his chest. They were both clothed again, curled together on a cushioned chair. Her eyes were already closed, and she was about to lose consciousness when Malik said something into the silence.

"Pen, are you okay?"

She didn't answer and pretended to be asleep already. She couldn't say, anyway.

She wouldn't know the answer until after tomorrow.

Chapter Fifty-Eight

Ultimatum

Penrose was drifting on top of a black sea. She watched as its waters rippled at her hands and legs, but she felt no fear of sinking.

What had she been doing?

She wasn't sure, but she would get to land soon. She was sure of it.

Suddenly, the black water turned to shackles around her wrists, and they tugged her beneath the water.

Penrose gasped out a mouth of water, struggling against the chains trying to drown her, but they were too strong.

"No," she shouted, but it was too late.

The water had engulfed her, and she was under.

Penrose hung by her wrists to a pole somewhere. Sweat streamed down her back, and her arms felt like they would dislodge from their sockets.

Cassius was before her, and he was somewhere between the boy she'd known and the king who had stolen the throne from her. Somehow, he was both.

"What do you want from me?" she snarled.

"Your dreams are so quaint." His fingers pulled her chin up. "It's too bad I have no use for *those*."

"I know what you are. Somnus, the spirit," she said.

Cassius stared at her. All pretenses of levity and goodwill had left his face. In a blink, he was right before her face, breathing on her. She wanted to writhe from his touch, but she couldn't move. His hand held her face in place.

"You always liked to meddle, my human bride." He said the words through his teeth.

"Tell me how to break the curse," Penrose said.

Cassius took a step back from her. His face was expressionless. "You already know."

Black shadow engulfed his body in a swirling miasma, but she still heard his voice.

"A mortal must fall in love with me. One that I have also fallen in love with."

She felt a cold ripple against her cheek. The shadows moved and re-formed before her.

Cassius, made of mist and whispers and with the blackest of eyes, looked at her.

"You are my love. You must act like it. You must proclaim it in front of the world and all the gods to see. Only then will I be released from my curse." The word hissed in her ear.

The mists he was made of moved across her skin as he added, "Become my wife in deed rather than just word."

Malik.

Penrose could think only of him. She was no stranger to personal sacrifice in order to achieve a greater good. But Malik had her heart, and there was no taking that back.

The Cassius before her now was the one she had first known, the one who had been her nineteen-year-old suitor. The lines of time had dissolved from his face.

"Refuse or fail me, and he will die by sundown. I will ensure it drive him to death," he promised in a whisper at her ear.

Malik!

***

Penrose was awake again. But this time, the world was chaos.

When she recognized what it was that she saw in front of her, she'd already started screaming. When had she started?

"Malik," she screeched.

Malik's blood drenched her and the floor. His fingers were stained with it.

The red poured down his arms like small rivers from a mountain. She shouted at herself to move, to do anything at all.

Stop the bleeding first!

Penrose pulled the knife out of his hands that he'd used to cut himself. But she didn't have enough hands for everything else.

"Aisha! Henrik! Anyone," she shouted to the library ceiling. Her hands quaked as she whispered to where he was on the floor. His breathing was ragged. "Hang on, Malik. Please. Just wake up."

Suddenly, one of his hands had found her neck and started to squeeze. His eyes were still shut, and Penrose's nails dug into his hands. Her screams became an airless gasp.

Malik, stop! Please wake up, she begged in her mind, but it was no use.

Malik's hand was ripped from her throat. Aisha had kneed her brother in the chest and pinned his bloody arms to the floor next to him. Henrik was already working.

"Bandages," he barked at them.

Penrose was still gasping, so Aisha went to work helping him stem the blood leaking from the cuts along Malik's forearms.

Finally, Malik's eyelids parted. He tried to jerk out of Henrik's grasp, but Aisha kept him on the floor.

"What the—" His eyes rolled in every direction until he found Penrose sitting on the floor across from him.

"What happened? Are they here? Did the bastard touch her again?" he demanded.

"You're fine now, Malik," Aisha said. "You're going to be fine."

"I know I'm fine, but what. The hell. Happened," he said through his teeth.

And then he seemed to properly see Penrose's expression. His gaze moved from person to person until he settled on his bloodied knife thrown across the floor.

Malik stared at the floor as they stopped his cuts from bleeding him further and wrapped him in bandages.

"I'm sorry," Malik said to the floor.

Penrose wanted to tell him it was fine. But she couldn't seem to find her voice.

When she looked to the library's tall windows at the end of the rows of bookcases, she saw that the sun had just risen.

It was the cold season, close to the solstice.

She had approximately seven hours.

Chapter Fifty-Nine

Confessions in the Last Hour

Malik's head rested against a bookcase.

He was fine. He'd lost more blood than that at once before. The shaking and weakness in his knees were from somnus, and that couldn't be helped.

One way or another, this would be over by tonight.

He couldn't bear to look at her and to know what he'd done.

Even if he'd been in a somnus fit, he couldn't forgive himself for allowing it to happen at all. He'd been weak and given in to sleep.

Right next to her, even.

He might as well have been awake when he'd hurt her.

Gods, he'd messed up one of the few good things in his life. His fists tightened even harder into themselves, and his teeth ached from clenching them.

How the hell was he supposed to protect her if he was the one hurting her, too?

"It's time to go, Malik." Aisha was trimmed to the teeth in weapons.

He hated the way they all looked at him—like he was a threat to himself. Well, he wasn't going to go to sleep again. Not unless he died or was cured.

It made things easier that way.

She extended a hand to him and helped pull him to his feet. His forearms twinged with pain, though they weren't really anything but some scratches. He remembered what Rana had said to him in her tent.

"When they dream, they get violent. Belts are what we use."

I should have suggested it earlier.

They were all a little broken in some way now, but they were all they had. If they didn't stop the bastard Cassius, then no one would.

Even if Malik died, he would at least make sure Penrose would live.

As he walked with his sister to the front of the building they'd been hiding in, he considered that their father didn't matter anymore.

A few days ago, Malik had vowed to kill both Raphael Ezar and the demon known as Cassius before the disease claimed Malik's life.

But the two of them had already dealt the finishing blow to Raphael Ezar.

They'd both forsaken him—his child by blood and his child by choice.

Aisha's hand found his shoulder. They were still alone. "You have to promise me you'll live," she said.

Malik laughed. At his reaction, he could almost hear his sister grinding her teeth in her head.

"I'm serious, Malik," she said.

"I am. You realize how long I've had this, now?"

"We're going to do it." Her eyes cut to him. "I believe her."

Malik was silent as they walked to join the others.

It all seemed too easy. Attainable.

It shouldn't feel like this.

Once they were out of here, they were going to meet with Mars in the market district and get the salt-capsule bullets from him. From there, they would split up, and Aisha and Henrik would make a distraction at the front of the castle while he and Penrose were going to infiltrate it via the sewer passages they'd taken out of it before.

Then, they were going to kill the bastard with the salt bullets, or at least banish him from his human body.

It was all Pen's plan, but it felt like one he would have come up with himself.

Malik stopped. He looked up to see Henrik and Penrose waiting with their supplies.

Aisha strolled up to them and shoved the butt of a revolver at Henrik. "Time for one of these." To them all, she said with a jerk of her head, "Are we ready? Back exit?"

"Wait," Malik said. "I need to speak to Penrose. Alone." His eyes were on her, but she hadn't yet looked back at her.

Aisha shoved herself in front of him, blocking his vision. Under her breath, she said, "We don't have time for this, brother."

"No, it's okay," Penrose said. She stepped forward and finally looked back at him.

#

"Penrose."

"It's alright. It was the somnus. I know that," she said and gave Malik's hand a brief squeeze.

The two of them were alone, well out of earshot of his sister and Henrik. Malik was well aware of how short their time was, but there was something he hadn't yet been able to convince himself out of thinking.

"No," Malik said. "You know why I pulled you aside. You *know* what I'm talking about."

"I ... No." Penrose's lips came together as she seemed to process his mood. "I don't. We're wasting time."

Malik blocked her attempt to get away with his body. His hands came to either side of her face as he leaned over her.

"You know what I'm talking about," he said. He didn't care that he was being an ass. This was serious.

"I don't, Malik."

"That was plan B. What's your real plan?" he continued. He wasn't going to give it up.

Penrose stared at him. She had no answer, now. It seemed he'd hit a nerve.

She hadn't told him about it. That could only mean one thing.

"You're trying to give yourself up," he accused.

This time, Penrose just stared at the floor.

"I'm not going to let you die." The way he'd said made it sound like a threat. "Have you ever thought that maybe your death would kill me anyway?"

At that, Penrose's gaze jerked up. "He doesn't want to kill me. He wants me to become his wife. I would save you and reverse the curse." Moisture spilled over one edge of her eyelid, but her face looked like she was begging him to understand her decision.

Malik felt numb. He stared into a space of nothingness between them.

Wife. Marry.

No. NO. Not her. Not to that monster.

A lifetime chained to the monster who abused her.

"Penrose ..." He remembered when she'd been silent after they'd spent their night together.

She'd been planning it then.

"You will *never* be his. Not if I have anything to say about it," Malik vowed. He looked into the depths of her eyes, searching them.

He hated to say this last part, but he had to.

He said through his teeth, "Until the day that's what you want. What you *really* want."

Penrose held his gaze for several moments before she buried her face in his chest. Malik didn't think he'd been breathing when he released the air held prisoner in his chest.

From somewhere pressed against him, she said, "I love you. Always."

Malik couldn't breathe again. How could he respond to that?

He settled on: "I love you, too."

She looked up at him and smiled. "Are you willing to try to trick him?" She was suddenly serious. "It will be hard."

"Do you have to ask?" he said.

Chapter Sixty

Family Reunion

The four humans and Sorrowtail—nested in Penrose's hair—came to the back of the library, and it was a mirror to the entrance where they had first rushed in. After leaving behind the main hall with the bookshelves, they came to a small vestibule where the barrier ended. On the other side of it were the doors leading outside. With them were only the essentials like their weapons and some scant medical supplies.

They were close, but first, they needed to get through the shield of magic.

Penrose watched the barrier that had kept them safe and touched it. Its translucent blue surface rippled, bending light around it.

It seemed evil wasn't the only force of magic that existed in the world.

"Thank you, Lesabeth," she murmured.

At her words and touch, the barrier blinked out of existence.

Next to her, Aisha's lips parted. "How?"

She'd forgotten that Aisha had been unconscious when they'd rushed through the barrier.

"Family looks out for each other, right?" she said with a grin.

In truth, Penrose wasn't entirely sure how it worked or how she'd found the book she needed in the library. But she couldn't deny that she'd felt a connection to her family in this building that she hadn't felt in the castle where she'd lived with them her whole life.

All she was sure of was that this hadn't been Cassius's doing like the spell over her had been.

Somehow, they'd helped her. They'd been here.

Malik stepped between them. Around his mouth was a cloth mask that obscured his lower face. "Enough of the bonding. We have a demon to kill."

As they walked past the point the barrier had protected them, air whistled past her ears. Penrose didn't realize what was happening until Malik shoved her to the ground under him.

Breath rushed out of her lungs, and she saw when she craned her neck where she'd been shoved against the ground that forms moved behind the desks on either side of their exit.

Black barrels peeked over the desks. They'd been camped here, waiting on them.

It was then that Hell broke loose.

"Cover me," Malik screamed.

Suddenly, Malik pulled her to his side and ran for the brick column where Henrik was. Behind the other column was Aisha. As they ran, her bullets riddled the surface of the wall opposite them and the desk hiding their enemies.

Henrik was hyperventilating where he sat among the bags of their supplies. Aisha must have ordered him there, but Penrose hadn't heard anything but the bullets and Malik.

"Cassius was waiting on us," Penrose said through her teeth.

She should have known.

But Malik shook his head. The look on his face made her pause. What was going on?

At once, the firing from the other side stopped. He walked out in the open with his men on either side of him. He wore an onyx coat with opal buttons and a white silken shirt underneath it that exposed his throat.

Ezar stopped some paces from them and greeted his children by name.

"Aisha. Malik."

They didn't have time for this. Penrose looked at Malik, but he couldn't seem to tear his eyes from his father.

We have until sunset. That's too soon.

"We need to get past him," Penrose whispered to him.

"I know," he whispered back, but he looked like he would rather stay here and bathe in his blood.

Out loud, Malik called to him, "And what the hell do you want?"

Raphael Ezar smiled.

"What I want is my children back. *Both* my heirs."

Chapter Sixty-One

Liars and Believers

*L*iar. Liar. Liar.

Malik couldn't afford to believe his words.

It was too much like one of those games where the gold piece disappeared under a cup. Two out of three times, you pick the wrong one.

But there was always that one-in-three chance.

Except the coin stuck to the inside of the cup when it was flipped over.

A trap. Every time.

"Then why fire?" Malik said, breaking the pregnant silence.

His father walked forward, signaling to his bodyguards that they should remain where they were.

"Don't lie to me, Malik. As soon as you saw me, you would have fired. I ordered them not to hit you." He raised one eyebrow at him. "You know they would've otherwise."

Malik clenched his teeth.

Convenient. Then again, lies usually were.

He looked over to where Aisha hid behind the other pillar to mouth out a plan with her, but what he saw made him pause.

She was looking at the bastard that was their father like ...

Like she believed him.

No. She wanted what he was spouting, but that couldn't make her blind to the ploy so obviously at hand. Could it?

Their father was talking again.

"Join with me again. Join with me, Malik." He locked his eyes on him. "Come with me, and you will be cured. The king has passed to me information that he will do this." He turned to where his sister was behind cover. "And Aisha. You've only wanted to protect your brother. You will rule Alsra together. We all will."

"And you suddenly forgive me?" Malik needed to keep him talking. His father had more men with him than they did, but Penrose was right.

They didn't need to win this fight. Only side-step it.

They just needed an opening.

"My son," he said. "There was never anything to forgive. I was wrong to claim you were unworthy. You are my blood and one of my heirs. Nothing could change that."

Malik stared at him. Until very recently, that was all that he could have wanted to hear from his father.

That it came now at a time when he wanted nothing to do with him felt like a sick joke.

Raphael Ezar turned to where the others hid next to Malik. "The other two—the girl and Henrik—may do as they please. Neither of you are prisoners here."

He could feel Henrik stiffen beside him.

Yeah, right.

Human capital was one of his father's favorite products to keep and trade in.

Malik had to say it. To keep his words inside him was making him sicker than he already was. "Hell—"

But Aisha had stepped forward. Dammit, why hadn't she signaled her plan to Malik?

It was almost like she truly believed him.

"Father," she said, and her voice was laden with emotion.

"My daughter," he said, stepping towards her. "How I've missed you. Do you accept me and this plan?"

He kept his hands on his guns, the pads of his fingers tapping at them. Malik kept waiting for her signal. The explosion.

A sign that he needed to cover her ass and spray them with fire.

Instead, she started removing all her weapons to pile them beside her.

"Of course," she said when she was done. Aisha kneeled before him how they'd done as kids.

She looked up from where she was at his feet and repeated her words. "Of course I accept you, Father."

Malik couldn't believe it. This had to be a joke.

Instead of waiting and attempting a joint attack, she'd …

Given in.

He's only a liar. Doesn't she see that?

But Aisha had always been their father's daughter. The central gem in his crown.

And maybe his offer was valid for her—there'd be no punishment for straying from him.

But, for Malik, there was certainly no hope for that.

Their father offered his ringed hand. Aisha took it and kissed it like he was their king. His men had already scooped up her weapons—their weapons they needed for the siege on the castle.

And it occurred to him. Perhaps she truly believed this was the answer. That maybe they'd convince their father to storm Cassius's hold together.

Maybe it was possible.

But that didn't excuse what the hell had been done to them.

"And you, my son?" he asked.

Aisha was still kneeling at his feet.

"My answer?" Malik stepped forward, out of his cover. He could feel Penrose try to pull him back, but he gave a subtle shake of his head.

No. He had to take care of this.

Malik looked him straight in the eye and said, "You will *never* be worthy of calling yourself my father." He moved his cloth mask under his chin and spat on the floor. "Not ever again. What you've done to us in the name of your empire—I'm not going to swallow the bullshit anymore."

He took another step, and his men followed the motion, their barrels trained on his head. He knew Aisha had heard him loud and clear despite her not moving.

I will not be a part of this *family.*

But Malik wasn't done. "In fact, I was never your son. I was only ever your product. Your weapon to sharpen and throw out when I wouldn't cut for you anymore. So, my answer's no."

Malik showed his teeth and drew his gun. "Save a spot in Hell for me, Father."

That was when the explosion happened.

Chapter Sixty-Two

Father

One second, his sister was still kneeling. The next, she was a blur.

Malik was already firing. It was convenient that all their eyes were on him. The moment was ripe to take a hostage.

In the end, it was their father's fault. He had built them just like him.

Always have a way to win.

Never trust words. Only blood and coin.

Everything is your weapon.

Aisha's knife—the one Malik knew she always kept concealed and strapped to her thigh—was at their father's throat faster than Malik could blink.

"*Stop firing,*" Raphael Ezar shouted at the room.

Malik stared at Aisha and knew that this had been her plan all along. She'd simply needed to wait until Malik became the explosion to cover up her own sleight of hand attack.

Aisha was shorter than their father but tall enough to draw beads of blood by pressing her knife at his neck. Tall enough to stick the blade through it when the time came, too.

The blood drops fell and absorbed into the snow-white shirt he wore. The wetness spread to his skin, gluing the fabric against him.

Aisha jerked her head at the group of their father's men. "Malik and the others won't be touched. You're going to let them through now," she dictated.

Their father didn't say a word.

Malik helped Henrik and Penrose gather their supplies. He needed to get them *all* out of here, but he wasn't going to waste the opening Aisha had created, either.

Their enemies glared as they sprinted past them, but Malik was more concerned for the weapons in their hands.

"Aisha!" Malik looked behind him just before they'd made it to the door. "Come on," he called.

But she only shook her head.

"Malik!" Penrose's voice bounced around the small space. It was then he realized what had happened in that moment.

All of a sudden, one of his father's men had kicked the back of Aisha's knees while she'd been distracted by Malik.

"*Damn* it," Malik screamed.

Bullets whistled past them, and Malik threw Penrose towards the door. Let them hurt him, but he'd get the others out of the way if he could.

Their father held a handful of Aisha's curly hair in his fist with a gun aimed at her head. "Obey me, Malik," he snarled.

"Go! Leave me," Aisha shouted.

"Like *Hell* I will," Malik said to both of them.

Damn it, damn it, damn it! I can't do a damned thing. And I didn't even get Henrik out, either.

His fists ached. Malik had ruined it all. Penrose was at the exit, but knowing her, she'd probably throw herself into the crossfire if it had a chance of saving him.

He couldn't shoot their father when he held Aisha hostage like that. He knew that Malik wouldn't do it, even if he reviled him enough to pull the trigger.

"Drop your gun," he commanded Malik.

Malik's trigger finger twitched, but he didn't dare take the shot. From this angle, he would have possibly hit her, too.

His only options were either run or stay and drop the gun.

Neither would save Aisha.

As if she'd seen and realized this, too, Aisha said, "Just go! Now."

Their father snarled at her, "You'll shut up *or else*, girl."

"Malik is right. You're not our father."

That was it. An expression flashed through Raphael Ezar's face that no one could fail to understand. It was an expression of pure hate.

"Make no mistake—even without my blood, I made you. And I can unmake you just as easily." Their father's jaw ticked like his teeth were clenched in his skull. He jerked the revolver close against her head. An unmissable target.

The shot rang in Malik's ears.

Much too loud, yet not loud enough to smother his thoughts.

Chapter Sixty-Three

Evestide

Raphael Ezar looked down at his chest where the bullet had exited. Red was already blooming from the spot, soaking into the white shirt and then the onyx coat he wore over that.

He'd been shot from the back. Not from where his son stood before him. Or even from where his daughter knelt on the other end of his gun.

Malik watched as his father gargled blood and collapsed to the ground.

On the other side of him was Henrik and a smoking revolver.

From then on, Malik didn't think. It was his job to get them out of there alive.

But even in his death, the men that Raphael Ezar had recruited were loyal to him. Aisha grabbed a rifle that had been left on the ground and fired on his men as the three of them ran to the exit.

Penrose held the door open for them, her face pale from the spectacle of death. She clutched her quivering bird to her shoulder to shield him.

Air burned in his lungs as he breathed through his cloth mask, but he didn't dare slow down. There'd be time for that on the other side of the door.

In a blink, a spray of bullets hit the door that Penrose held for them. Glass rained as it shattered, and Sorrowtail took to the air as Penrose shielded her face.

Malik twisted to look behind him. Their father's men were gaining on them, and one had aimed his rifle straight at Malik's face.

This was it. He was going to get blasted apart.

It was then that Aisha wrestled the gun out of the man's grasp, and it skidded from them. But the others had caught up.

From where she was still behind him, Aisha gave him one look. "Go! Leave me," she shouted.

"I'm not," he said through his teeth.

Malik had made it to the exterior of the abandoned library with Penrose and Henrik. But it seemed they had attracted the attention of the city guards and the citizens of Alsra. A loose group of soldiers was beginning to run their way. Cold sun touched the back of his neck.

"I'll meet up with you," Aisha said from inside the library.

Penrose pulled Malik by the hand. "I'm sorry, Malik. But they're coming."

Soon, they would be cornered between the king's men and what remained of his father's empire.

"Do it," Aisha hissed to him while she dodged a knife from one of their father's men. Her neck craned back. "I mean it, Malik. I'll hold the soldiers off, too. Let me do this."

A stream of curses left Malik's mouth. Why was it always a choice like this?

He followed her command and ran with Henrik and Penrose towards the bustling streets of Alsra before the soldiers could follow.

\#

Henrik said what Penrose and Malik were thinking.

"We don't have the time to get your salt bullets." His eyes never rested on the crowd around them. He looked like he was constantly on edge—or desperately searching for a lavatory.

Out of all three of them, he could fake the part the least.

Penrose didn't respond. She felt as if she didn't have words left.

Malik gave a subtle nod in answer. Their salt-rubbed blades would have to do the trick.

Penrose trusted the soldiers hadn't tracked them as Malik had looped them through several blocks of the city for the past hour and a half. If they were going to catch them, they'd have done it by now. Or she hoped.

Penrose could see on Malik's face how leaving behind his sister had damaged him.

But they kept going, pushing through the crowds of vendors and citizens. It was an unusually cold day for the usually temperate crown city of Aloster, but she figured the cold season had started in earnest by now.

The more she saw of Alsra, the more she realized. Banners and wreaths of pine decorated storefronts. The people around them were dressed in hues of silver and starlight blue.

"It's Evestide," Penrose gasped.

"It explains the crowds," Malik muttered next to her. "They're here for the festival and food."

Penrose shivered, and Malik pulled her closer. On the outside, they probably looked like any other couple in the city to enjoy the end of the year festivities, along with their chaperone.

She wished that was all they were right then. Penrose rehearsed the plan in her head.

Penrose was to go through the front of the castle and act as if she were giving herself up and returning to her husband's side.

Malik and Henrik would infiltrate the castle through the sewers. They'd originally banked on Aisha and Henrik causing a distraction to cover up Malik's movements—a feigned attempt to save her—but they didn't have enough firepower for that anymore.

From there, Penrose would confess her love and act as if she accepted her role as his wife.

Then, Malik would arrive, and together, they'd behead him with a blade rubbed in salt.

If it all went according to plan, they'd reverse the curse and banish the spirit of Nightmare from this world all at once.

Her hands shook, so she shoved them against her sides. Malik blinked and seemed to noticed what she was wearing for the first time since they'd set out from the library.

"Isn't that Aisha's?" he asked.

Penrose smiled. "It's her kick-ass dress. She loaned it to me."

Her fingers threaded through his.

Under his breath, Malik said, "Can you do this? Are you sure about all this?"

Penrose stood on her toes and stole a kiss on his lips. It also served as a way to cover up her lips in case they were being watched.

"When it comes time, I want to do it."

The castle she'd been born in loomed in their sights. It was time.

Chapter Sixty-Four

Arrival

Penrose's hands were bound at once, and her blood thundered through her with an intensity that made her head want to split apart. She hadn't envisioned it like this.

The soldiers jostled her through the doors to the castle's entryway.

You have to play the part, she urged herself.

Penrose jerked away from the edge of their weapons. "I am the king's wife. I will escort myself to him."

She didn't wait for their response. She walked with her head high into the halls that were rightfully hers. Penrose thought of her mother and how she'd been raised to be a queen from the time of her birth.

Penrose needed to act the same.

She felt their eyes bore into the back of her head. One of the kingsguard opened the door for her and the other guards. Her eyes followed the rifle strapped to his back as he knelt before the figure on the throne.

Cassius rose. His hand gestured at the doors behind them. "Leave us. We must speak." His eyes settled on her. "Alone."

Please, Malik. Come soon.

She had already shed her weapons before turning herself into his guards, but she itched for something to defend herself with.

It wouldn't have worked if I'd been armed, she reminded herself.

And besides, she only had to last until his signal.

"Before sunset, I believe your words were." Penrose looked to the windows where the last remnants of daylight streamed through it.

"What a mouth you've grown to have," Cassius observed as he closed in on her, circling her like she was an exhibit in a museum.

Penrose was silent. There was no real answer to that.

Suddenly, his hand was on her face, turning it from side to side. He was colder than she'd remembered, but then again, he'd only pretended to be warm before.

It was then that his gaze caught on what she was wearing. "But first, you'll need to change clothes."

He never changed, did he? Penrose remembered how he'd insisted on changing her hairstyle before their wedding.

Before, she'd bowed to what he wanted without question. She knew better now. Even if she had to fake still being the doe-eyed bride.

She caught his hand and held it within hers. He needed to stop touching her face. "Consider it part of my dowry. It's what I come with."

Penrose pulled his face closer to hers. At this angle, he could see well past her plunging neckline.

Even as a spirit, he still acts like a man.

Cassius's eyes flicked from where he'd been leering to her face. A smile curled on his mouth. "Fine then."

He fisted her hair in his hand as he pulled her head back. His mouth was at her ear.

"In all other things, you will submit to me, my wife."

***

Malik watched her disappear from his sight where they waited on the streets of Alsra. Knowing she was unarmed and walking into the arms of her oppressor made him more than a little crazy.

Focus. There's a point to this.

Henrik helped him move aside the cover over the sewers. Penrose had confirmed with him which direction these passages ran. Following the one in this alley should take them directly to the castle.

He was about to lower the researcher down into the hole when Malik remembered something. He stiffened.

"What's wrong?" Henrik was too jumpy, and his voice was too loud. If they weren't careful, they would attract the attention of someone on the main street.

Malik stared down into the darkness.

He got to his feet. "We need to find some other way inside," he said.

Henrik stared. "It's right here. We could get inside without alerting them. It's the perfect way."

Malik turned on him, and his voice was deadly quiet. He didn't know if he was being foolish or wise.

"There's something down there," he said. "Don't ask me what or how. But we saw it when we fled through these tunnels the first time. I'll be damned if it—he—catches us down there now. We have to assume it's him."

The researcher ran a hand through his hair. "How are we getting inside the castle, then?" He paused. His voice pitched higher. "We can't. This is impossible. We can't do this. Not by ourselves."

Malik grabbed the man by the shoulders. "Impossible is what you did this morning. Impossible is killing Raphael Ezar and getting away with it."

Henrik's eyes were wide, and his teeth gritted together. "She told me, you know. She told me he did it and not you." He was shaking. "And I did it. I did it for all of my team." He laughed.

Malik needed him to be functional. He grabbed Henrik tighter and forced him to stare into his face.

"And what is the world they wanted? Did they want somnus to spread and a bastard king to feed off it?"

Henrik breathed. He shook his head.

Malik released his hold on the researcher. "If you're in, we need to go. It'll take time to figure out another way in. If you're out ..."

Then leave. But he didn't complete the thought out loud.

Finally, Henrik said, "Lead the way." His eyes narrowed in the direction of the castle. "She's waiting on us."

Chapter Sixty-Five

The Truth

Malik's breath came in puffs as they closed in on the outside of the castle. They'd slipped from the people crowding Alsra to the edges of the castle gates. But even from afar, it was clear that he'd stationed his soldiers everywhere.

Shrubbery lined the exterior of the gates, and Malik pulled Henrik with him to the other side of one. He knuckled his forehead.

They were in every window, every doorway, and he'd even sighted a pair of them patrolling the outer gates. Henrik was silent beside him.

They could try to swarm them in bullets.

They'd get a few paces before being shot.

He knew. Of course he was expecting us.

Light was receding from the sky. They didn't have time for this.

"We have to rush them. It's the only way in." Malik's gaze flicked from the castle's front to where they needed to get inside the fence. They could make a climb for it, but something told him they'd be riddled in bullets before getting to the other side.

"And this will work?" Henrik whispered, and his eyes were desperate on him. "This will get us inside?"

Malik didn't answer.

A patrol was heading along the outer perimeter of the fence—straight for them.

It was their only option. But before he could pull free his revolver, hands pulled him against the fence.

***

Penrose stood next to Cassius at the head of the feast tables. Food of all kind stretched before them: glazed ducks, rosemary stuffed fish, pear and fresh green salad, cranberry goat cheese, steaming cream and herb rice broth, and slices of roasted, spiced citrus spread throughout.

It was like the Evestide celebrations from when she was younger. Except it wasn't.

In the empty halls of her ancestors, this felt like a mockery of her family.

White roses and baby's breath overfilled vases everywhere she could see, making it look as if snow was spread all over the room. Behind the throne, a fire smoldered in the fireplace that was framed with pine garlands and more baby's breath.

The last streaks of daylight were growing weak. A veritable regiment of his guards lined either side of the feast tables.

It's all insurance so that I do what I say I'll do.

The smells of the feast tickled her nose, but she had no stomach for any of it. They were to be wed over the Evestide dinner in mere moments.

Either way, she had to end this soon.

Malik should have shown up by now.

Her gaze went to the doors on the other end of the hall. If he wasn't here by now, in the vestiges of the last hour, she had to assume she was on her own.

She had to fix this by herself.

Beside her, Cassius cleared his throat.

"On this darkest night, the two of us will be joined." His eyes cast to his regiment. "And a new light will be born from our joining."

As the others bowed, so did she. She'd noticed that there'd been no salt on the table nor knives. It was no coincidence, she was sure.

Play the part.

Cassius's fingers found hers, and she straightened herself. As he led her to his throne—hers, by rights—he whispered to her.

"We will be properly married this time, my rose. In front of the gods and all."

Penrose couldn't answer with words. They wouldn't come, so she nodded instead.

So, she had no weapons on her person, no blades or even salt. But maybe she didn't need those things. Maybe it was true.

She looked into Cassius's eyes, and she saw the prince who had swept her into his tower.

"Do you take me as your wedded husband, King Cassiel of the united Aloster?" His thumb brushed her jaw, and he held her face towards his. "Do you vow to love me entirely and renounce any other?"

Renounce any other. He hadn't mentioned that in her nightmare.

Penrose thought of Malik. How could she not?

True love.

Those words had changed her forever. She hadn't known what it meant to love and be loved in that way. Despite a difference in the worlds that they'd been raised in and in the people they'd both been before they'd met one another—they'd been made for each other.

Penrose's hands shook. What was the answer? What was right?

Renounce her love for Malik to save him? Or remain true to their love and allow him to die by Cassius's wrath?

The choice was clear for her. She wouldn't allow Malik to die.

I'm sorry, Malik.

"I …" She swallowed. "Yes. I love you."

Before she could say anymore, Cassius snapped his fingers. "Now!"

Suddenly, soldiers appeared on either side of her, one with his rifle's barrel pressed against her head.

"What are you doing?" Penrose said between her teeth at him. The pretense of her love for him was gone. "You need me for this, spirit."

"To what? Break the spell on me?" He laughed before she could respond to him.

If his guards were confused by his words or the name she'd called him, they didn't show it. *Perhaps he's ensorcelled them, too.*

His hand shot out to grip the bottom of her face and force her gaze at him. "No. My poor, stupid rose. That is never what I wanted." His smile straightened, and his expression became all angles. "Do you understand now?"

Penrose jerked out of his grip. "You don't want to cure yourself of it."

"All I need to be cured of is this fragile body's lifespan." He smiled, and smoke rose around him like he was standing on a fire. "Because, my rose, no one fears me as much as you do."

Penrose's eyes widened. She remembered what he'd said to her before.

"How do you think I endured this long?" He looked at her, sharply. "Because I spent your life for it, my dear."

And then there was the folk tale.

When the spirit began eating the maiden's dreams, he realized they were much more plentiful and appetizing than he could have imagined.

But he'd gone too far and eaten all her dreams. When he was done, he saw that the maiden had died.

It had all been for this. Keeping her in a tower. Putting her under an enchanted slumber for years. Hunting her down in a kingdom that was no longer hers.

It had all been to ensure he got the worst nightmares from her. To feed himself off her life and fears.

"You need my dreams to live," she breathed.

Nightmare smiled down at her. An unnatural darkness began to fill the edges of the room.

"Only for a few minutes longer."

Chapter Sixty-Six

Nightmare

Penrose ran through the halls of the castle, out of breath but unable to stop.

She had to warn her parents about him.

Cassius. Nightmare. Somnus.

Just before she entered the throne room, she heard their voices. Her father's laughter filled the high ceilings in the next room.

Despite herself and the urgency that the situation required, Penrose's hands stopped before she swung open the doors.

Was it all an illusion? Were her parents really alive again?

That was when she heard her.

Lesabeth.

Penrose's heart felt as if it were jumping out of her throat.

Lesabeth!

She didn't care how this was possible anymore. Penrose had never been able to say goodbye to her sister. Her hands formed into fists as the tears spilled over her lids.

Even if this was a dream, she wasn't going to give it up. Not without seeing her older sister for one last time.

Penrose slipped through the doors to the throne room, and a gasp stuck in her throat.

They were all there, sitting at the feast table. A fire roared behind the three of them despite the frost clinging to the high windows.

"And you've made arrangements, then? Are you sure?" Lesabeth leaned forward over her slice of roasted and seasoned poultry.

"Lessa," their mother said, a line creasing between her eyebrows. "Of course I am sure. He will keep her in that tower for the rest of her days. A little trust from you, please."

"I made all the preparations myself." Their father's wide cheeks filled with a grin. "There's no chance she'll get out of it."

Penrose stood still. They hadn't looked over to see her yet. She couldn't move.

Her sister relaxed into her seat, nodding. "That's good. His kingdom will think they've gotten something quite valuable from us out of the trade."

They were ... happy that she was gone.

More than happy.

Their father's lips curled in a sly, half smile. "Two birds, one stone, my dear." He laughed suddenly. "And to read the letters she's written us. She thinks there's a way to wiggle out of this."

Their mother gave a shake of her head. "What a frail, senseless child. I'm not sure what went wrong with her," she admitted. "It'll be a relief when he rids us of her fully."

So quietly that not even a mouse would have heard her, Penrose backed up. She passed back into the hall without so much as a whisper of noise.

It couldn't be true. They didn't ... They weren't ...

But it made too much sense. It was why they'd never written back to her. It was why the arrangement had happened in the first place.

It was why the prince had been allowed to do to her as he wished.

It was because they didn't care. Or rather, this was what they'd wanted for her.

To get her out of the way finally.

Penrose hadn't so much as breathed since she'd exited the throne room. She didn't think she could anymore.

All this time, she'd blamed Cassius for what he'd done to her. And yet, her family had allowed it. Encouraged it, in fact. They'd sold her to him.

Penrose was aware that she couldn't stay in those hollow halls forever, lingering just outside a room with a family dining within it.

Not a family that she belonged to, though. It was clear from how they spoke of her.

Penrose started running. She wasn't sure where she was going, but she couldn't stay here. The halls remained empty, and her footsteps became a deafening drumbeat to her ears.

The feeling of her heart twisting in her chest stole her breath, but she didn't stop running. Where was her inhalant device?

When it came, her breath was reduced to shallow gasping. Her head swam as a result, but these feelings were better than dealing with those that remained on the other side of that door.

Penrose stopped. She'd gotten to the end of this hall, and a twisting staircase unfurled before her. Next to it was a metal railing that overlooked the cavernous main hall.

Her hands gripped the metal, and the cold bit into her fingers. As she stared down, she calculated the distance between the top of the railing to the entryway's floor.

The distance was farther than from one floor to the one above it. Even so, it wouldn't be a surefire thing. But it was enough to try.

If even the people she'd called family wanted her gone, then ...

Penrose stopped herself from climbing to the top of the railing.

The word *family* bothered her. But why was that?

There was something else that came to mind, but it was shrouded in a cloud of mist and fog.

Family.

She froze.

This isn't real. This isn't real.

It was then that she remembered. The people in that room were gone. Lesabeth had died before she'd been married off to the prince.

They were all gone. She didn't even live in this era anymore.

Family.

That's right.

Penrose sank to her feet. Aisha. She had a sister who lived still. How could she have forgotten?

She pulled her legs close to her chest as she savored the memory.

"In my life, family has always been a choice to be made. For better or worse. I chose him as my brother. He chose you. So, I do, too."

It was then that she remembered all of it. Malik. Aisha. Henrik. Sorrow-tail.

They were her family. They were the ones she chose—and the ones who had chosen her.

Penrose came to her feet and stared at the ceiling. She knew he could hear him.

"Enough of this," she shouted.

It was time to wake from this illusion.

She closed her eyes and called him by his real name to summon him. "Your games are over, Nightmare."

Chapter Sixty-Seven

Defiant

Penrose opened her eyes.

Just before the knife plunged into her chest, someone pulled Penrose out of the way.

She pushed against the arms that had pulled on her and came to her feet, still panting from the nightmare.

It was all fake. None of it really happened.

They didn't think that.

Her brain was sluggish to process the new reality around her. His guards had pinned her to the floor.

And there was someone else in the room, too—the Karsian woman who had been beside Cassius before. Penrose realized a moment later that she was the one who had pulled her from the knife.

Nightmare hadn't anticipated her waking before the deed was done. He stood behind them, and loose coils of smoke rose from his mouth when he spoke. Clearly, he'd been feeding on her during her nightmare.

"You fools. Get them!"

The room was nearly dark, and even the fireplace was barely a wisp.

Penrose ducked out of the reach of the guard who had nearly stabbed her, kicking at his shins in the process. Her heart outpaced her feet, but she pushed the dizziness down.

One of his guards grabbed her fast, but the other woman shoved him roughly from her. She looked past the guard's face at her. "Don't let him get you," she said across the room to her.

"It's you!" Penrose gasped. "You were the one who told me about him." *She was the one who searched me in Lesabeth's room.*

"Penrose, you have to do it," she shouted.

"Oh Sarina, that girl of yours will die for this treachery," Nightmare said to the woman. His guard had apprehended her and held a knife to her throat. "I knew never to trust in you. Just as your father betrayed me."

A dark, cold pit formed in Penrose's stomach. She stopped dodging them and held her hands away from her body.

"Don't hurt her," she said to the spirit of Nightmare. This woman had saved Penrose. She couldn't stand there and just let her throat be spilled open.

Even if Penrose had no plan and no weapon.

Penrose walked forward, but he was too fast. He dissolved before she could get to him. It was then that the woman acted.

From a hidden pocket within her deep blue dress, she freed a knife the length of her finger. And she planted it deep inside one of the men holding her.

Instead of running from there, she turned to Penrose. "You must end this all tonight. If you don't, he will end the world. If he kills you and takes the power of your fears, his influence will grow until there is no one unafflicted by self-destructive nightmares. I have seen it."

Penrose stared and shivered.

There was something to her words—some truth that she felt was inherent in them.

This was somnus personified. If she didn't stop it here, she realized no one would. Before Penrose could do anything, Sarina's eyes rolled back, and she slumped forward in a heap.

"What did you do to her?" Penrose demanded. But he was gone again.

Suddenly, a coldness gripped her. Nightmare-Cassius twisted her arm behind her back as she cried out in pain.

She tried and failed not to stare at Sarina's body on the floor.

Please be alive. Please.

"Let go out of me," she hissed at him.

His eyes were blacker than the night sky. "Only when I feel the last of your life drain from your body," he promised. His other arm formed into a dagger made of smoke.

Penrose only saw it because she was looking up. A blur of blue feathers descended from the rafters.

It was the fastest she'd ever seen Sorrowtail move before. A war screech ripped from his tiny lungs.

"Someone grab it," Nightmare-Cassius hissed.

But he'd already found his target. Sorrowtail hovered before him, pecking at his face and eyes in rapid intervals.

Penrose jerked out of his grip. "Sorrowtail," she gasped. "Get out of here!"

He must have snuck in after me and kept to the rafters.

Nightmare-Cassius cursed and reverted to a form entirely made of smoke. Penrose took her chance and grabbed her songbird friend out of the air as gently as possible.

"Get her or you all die," Nightmare-Cassius hissed at his guards.

"You have to get out of here," she huffed to Sorrowtail as she dodged his men. "Even if I don't."

The bird's eyes were glossy and black as he stared back at her. Defiant. She'd have to force him to fly from here.

Before she could make it to the door, a raucous, bitter pain snapped at the back of her legs. Penrose was down instantly.

One of his men stood over her, the fireplace poker he'd used to hit her from behind in his hands. His eyes were as black as Cassius's.

When she fell, she'd released Sorrowtail. Before he could fly away, Nightmare-Cassius grabbed him. Penrose's stomach dropped like a stone.

He stepped forward. Blood ripped from his eyes like tears where they'd been pecked. Although his eyes were still black as night, she could tell that the nightmare spirit was staring down at her.

"It's a pity he didn't blind you," Penrose said between her teeth.

Suddenly, Sorrowtail started to squeal in pain. He was squeezing him.

Penrose jumped to her feet. "Stop it! Release him," she shouted.

But in her heart, she knew he wouldn't. Not even if she threw herself at his feet and begged him for forgiveness.

He was much too vengeful for that. No.

She had to kill him for this and everything else he'd done.

Her mind blanked. Penrose launched herself at him with nothing but her hands as weapons.

***

A familiar voice whispered to Malik.

"Your friend will draw him out. Then, let me handle the rest."

Malik stared at the other man's face. The shock of hair on top of his head exposed from his undercut was swept to one side. He well remembered the scar on his temple—Malik had been there for that one—as well as the one alongside his sharp nose.

Mars, Malik's preferred supplier of arms and munitions and one of the few men he cared enough about to call a friend, stared back at him with his cocky ass smile.

Malik didn't bother to question him about how he'd gotten wind of their little adventure. Instead, he stood behind the shrubbery and let Mars do what he did best.

Henrik stared into the bush where Malik had disappeared, likely considering diving in after him, when the patrol guard further long the fence yelled at Henrik.

"Hey!"

Henrik fumbled for the gun Aisha had forced him to take, but the guard was already there. Behind their backs, Mars moved like a ghost. He brought the rifle in his hands squarely against the guard's head with an audible *crack*.

The man fell like a stone. Malik stepped out after him.

Henrik stared at the unconscious guard and then at Malik and Mars. At the latter, he said, "Who are you?"

Mars ignored his question. Instead, he turned to Malik. "Heard you killed a rooster."

"Heard he had it coming," Malik responded, evaluating the other man carefully.

He might have called Mars a friend, but lately, backstabbing had gotten contagious.

"I'll say. There's no sales like the sales in a power vacuum." Mars cracked a smile. "I should thank you."

Of course, that's all the bastard can think about. He resisted the urge to roll his eyes. Yep, that was Mars.

Malik was about to direct his attention to Henrik—the man who had actually killed Raphael Ezar—when the air left his lungs entirely.

Someone had tackled him.

Chapter Sixty-Eight

Infected

"You didn't think I was that easy to kill, did you?" Aisha snickered in Malik's ear.

"Of course not," he said in response, but that wasn't the truth. In truth, he'd thought his little sister dead.

She'd gotten a surprise attack on him, but nothing could rival his bear hug.

She's alive. Aisha's alive.

He squeezed her harder just to make sure she was solid, but perhaps that was a mistake.

In a gasp of air, she said, "Or are you trying to do the job now?"

Malik laughed and let her go. "How the hell—" He stopped and shook his head. He knew better.

Survival was what they did.

"You could have run from this, you know. Laid low until it blew over. You'd have had an empire to yourself even if the rest of this blew up," Malik pointed out to her.

"Like hell," she responded. She jerked her head in Mars's direction. "And I knew we'd need some backup, so I dragged him into this."

"For a reasonable fee, of course." Malik could only imagine what *reasonable* meant to Mars.

Mars stroked his rifle as he said it. He hadn't noticed before, but it looked awful, like some sort of monster cobbled together from the parts of different things.

"The hell is all that?" Malik glared at the thing.

"I modded it myself." Mars pouted at him. "Don't you like it?" His pout turned into a frown. "I'm revoking your discount."

His head felt like ten tons of pressure was coming down on it. As much as he wanted to stay out here and catch up with Mars and revel in the fact that his sister was alive, they had a king to kill.

"Put it on my tab." Malik jerked his head at the castle. "We have places to be *yesterday*."

Aisha drew her knives. Cuts dressed her exposed skin. As his eyes wandered to Henrik, he noticed that the man's limp had returned.

"As long as I get my cut." One of his eyebrows raised. Mars added, "And a fair share of the blood."

But Malik knew that at least some of the blood shed was to be theirs. It had been part of the plan from the beginning.

How many close cuts does Aisha have left? Or Henrik?

The bag of supplies that Mars had brought with him caught Malik's eye. It was filled with weapons and the capsule bullets full of salt he knew Aisha had asked Mars for, but there was something else within it, too.

Malik pulled free one of the respirators and looked at his friend.

Mars was suddenly too serious. "She told me." It was all he needed to say.

Malik tore off the cloth he'd tied to his face to keep himself from spreading somnus to them and replaced it with the respirator. He wasn't offended. In fact, he had a new idea.

"How about we save our bullets?" Malik asked through the filter. "I have another way inside."

***

Malik, Henrik, and Aisha rushed past the front doors with little resistance. They all wore respirator masks, and though they were armed to the teeth, they hadn't yet fired a bullet.

In Henrik's hands were syringes full of water, but the guards didn't know that. Cassius's soldiers ran to meet them at the front.

It was time to sink or swim, Malik considered. And he was going to swim.

"Stop! Drop your weapons," shouted the guard in front.

Aisha was first to confront them. She didn't falter. "This area is to be quarantined, soldier," she said through the filter. "We received an alert that somnus is spreading through the castle. The king's life is in danger. Secure the exits!"

He put his body in front of her. "You don't have the authorization—"

Henrik stepped between them, pulling an identification card from his coat. "Henrik Renard, head of the somnus research group of Alsra University. Infectious disease expert and intermediate-level healer."

Henrik didn't even pause to breathe. The man was a legend. "Has the king been checked for somnus symptoms in the last twenty-four hours?"

When the guard looked at the men behind him, Henrik raised his voice. "Has the king been checked, *yes or no?*"

The guard's eyes bounced around the room, as if searching for an answer on the walls themselves, when another voice called from across the hall.

"Let them through!" The guard already had a respirator mask on. He pointed at the three of them. "The king has ordered all extraneous personnel evacuate the castle. Their team is waiting outside to test for somnus."

One of the guards wised up and stepped away from the others who'd been bickering among themselves. "All below the rank of captain, establish a perimeter around the castle. The rest, follow me in assisting with evacuation."

The guard who had spoken up for them volunteered to guide Malik, Henrik, and Aisha through the castle to the king. But Malik didn't miss the wonky-looking rifle strapped to his back as they marched through the castle's halls to its heart.

Mods. What a load, Malik thought.

Though, if Mars could improve the cooldown on his small guns ... He shook off the thought. He needed to focus.

Their team of four flew through the hallways. Malik could hardly believe their ploy worked.

But then again, some of what he'd seen in the eyes of the guards had been fear. A slow death was always worse than a quick one.

Just a little longer. I'm coming for you, Penrose.

Chapter Sixty-Nine

The Attack

Penrose's hands had found his neck, but Nightmare-Cassius turned to smoke in her fingers before she could do anything.

"Sorrowtail!" She looked up at the bird flying above her head. "Go! Leave me!"

That was when a boot shoved into her back. Nightmare-Cassius pinned her to the floor. As she struggled to get loose, blue strands of light danced in his hand. He shoved it at her.

Penrose's hands shook. Suddenly, she couldn't budge her lower half.

"What did you do?" she said, twisting to look up at him.

He whispered in her ear. "I want you to feel the agony of a slow death. I want to taste the despair and fear in your last breath."

Above her, his arm turned into a deadly sharp sword bathed in shadow.

He'd ensured she couldn't flee by paralyzing her lower half, but she would still feel every drop of blood that he managed to drain from her. Penrose's heart raced with fear and malice.

He reared back and aimed for where her heart was.

Malik. I'm sorry. I can't stop him this time.

Penrose closed her eyes and thought of her family, both the old and the new. He wouldn't have this part of her—the cold fear. She refused it.

It was then that a series of blasts rang out around her.

And then, she heard Malik's voice. "He's got her! Aim for him."

Penrose opened her eyes. Another boom resounded through the space, and a cloud of white dust puffed up before her eyes. Shards of salt rained down on her.

Nightmare-Cassius screamed, and the sound was like nothing she'd ever heard before. She wasn't sure when his paralysis spell had ended. Penrose slipped out from underneath him in the confusion.

The salt bullet had hit him. And it was *working*.

He held his chest like it was bleeding, but Penrose saw no such thing leaking from him. Not even the shadow-mist he seemed to be made of.

It's anchoring and *hurting him.*

She looked up and saw him. He was wearing a respirator mask, but there could be no mistake. It was Malik.

Penrose knew from their clothes that Aisha and Henrik were here, too. They and another soldier wearing a respirator were fighting Cassius's men.

She locked eyes with Malik.

It was time to end things.

At first, she wasn't sure if he would do it—if he would honor her demand that she be the one to end the spirit known as Cassius. But then he bent down and slid the knife rubbed with salt across the floor.

The heel of her boot caught it, and she quickly plucked it off the ground before Nightmare-Cassius saw.

He had staggered back several paces. "Salt. Human pests," he muttered. He'd reverted back to his youthful self. His face was still strikingly beautiful despite the black pits he had for eyes and the malefic shadows wafting from him. It was an odd sight.

Penrose knew better. It was all a shell.

The real Cassius was a pitiful spirit that gorged itself on terror and despair.

Penrose slipped the knife inside the thigh strap that Aisha had lent her and ran for Nightmare-Cassius, dodging his men as the shrapnel from the salt bullets sailed around her.

"Enough of this." Nightmare-Cassius cracked his neck.

In the same instant, several things happened.

The flame in the fireplace died a sudden death. Thick shadows engulfed the room.

And Malik collapsed to the ground.

Penrose screamed his name, and she feared for his death. But she saw she was wrong.

He wasn't dead. He and the others had shed their respirators, and she could see his face twist in agony. He bucked where he was sprawled on the ground and blood started to run from the corners of his mouth, nose, and eyes. Blood gurgled through his mouth when he tried to speak.

This was worse.

Nightmare was killing him, but he was doing it slowly.

His bespelled guards held Aisha, Malik, and their other companion at gunpoint. Aisha elbowed the guard holding her in the stomach and ran to Malik.

"Malik! Malik, please," she pleaded with him.

Penrose started for him, too, but a tendril of shadow stretched in front of her. A piece of salt dropped from somewhere on the ground below Nightmare, and he reformed before her, shaking his head.

He spoke before he was entirely solid again. "My stupid rose. You never learn, do you?"

His shadow-hand found her throat. Penrose could barely breathe, but he spoke over her gasps.

"You are lucky that watching him die will make ripping the terror from you more delicious," Nightmare-Cassius said between his teeth. "You absolute slug."

She wanted to spit on his face. She wanted to beg for Malik's life.

But, as she noticed something beyond his shoulder as he lifted her into the air, she did neither.

Aisha was too busy trying to stem the blood evacuating Malik's body. Their companion, the stranger to her, had been knocked to the ground by a soldier.

He didn't get up. She hoped he was alive, but she didn't count on it.

No, there was only one who met her eyes. There was only one who saw her voiceless appeal.

Henrik pretended to faint. The guard holding him at the end of his gun startled at the response. It was the opening Henrik needed.

He ran. With one motion, he plucked one of their guns from the floor that had been loaded with the special salt bullets.

Henrik brought the rifle up to his face to aim. He never got his shot in.

While holding Penrose's throat with one hand, Nightmare-Cassius twisted his ethereal body halfway and shot a spark of blue light at Henrik's chest.

Penrose couldn't lose time to watch, but she heard his body hit the ground unceremoniously.

She channeled her rage and sorrow into one force and pulled the knife from her thigh holster.

And planted it deep into the heart of Nightmare.

Chapter Seventy

Better

A cyclone of damp mist, screams that sounded as if they came from inside a tin can, and wind rose where Cassius's body had been.

Penrose's body slammed against the ground. The knife fell a pace away some seconds after her.

She watched as the blue sparks faded from where his body had been. The screams sounded multilayered, as if they came from multiple people who spoke at once.

The cyclone of screams and wind tore through the room, sending anything lighter than a dinner plate flying. The food slammed against the walls, and the roses filling the vases shot to the ceiling like spears.

Penrose could barely stand in the wind. She tried to yell to Aisha, who still held onto Malik, but her voice was swallowed by it, too.

In a blink, the cyclone of shadows shot into the fireplace.

At the same time, his bespelled soldiers collapsed to the ground as one. It was an unnerving sight.

Penrose's knees nearly gave, but she forced herself to stay upright.

The throne room was large enough to house an army. But the only of them left standing were her and Aisha.

The rest littered the ground like leaves on a fall day.

Her voice croaked when she could finally speak again. "Aisha ..."

Aisha's eyes flickered from Malik to Henrik. They filled with moisture. "I don't ... I ..."

Penrose hated the silence that pounded into her ears. It was then that her knees gave.

She was a coward. She didn't want to see them or even Sarina dead. She didn't want to feel the warmth fleeing their bodies for the last time.

Or if it already had.

Outside, the Evestide night cloaked the world in its darkness. After several hours—the longest period without it for the whole year—the sun would return. The morning would come.

But Penrose feared there would be no end to this night for her.

Malik. Why didn't we get more time? How could this have happened?

She had done it. She'd beaten Cassius.

But for what? Outside, a silent, dark world awaited. The cold logic in her told her that the world would be different—somnus was gone. It would be better.

Better.

It was a funny word.

The world wasn't better without him in it. He was her missing part, and he forever would be.

In the room filled with more departed bodies than live ones, a sharp gasp pierced the silence.

Penrose jerked upright and ran. She slammed into him where he was still sprawled on the ground above his sister. He coughed as she squeezed the air out of him.

She couldn't get the words out, so she was thankful Aisha could.

"Are you hurt?" Her hands ran across his body. "Malik, are you there? Are you with us?"

Malik coughed but nodded in Penrose's embrace. She peeled herself off him to give him space to breathe.

"Yes to all," he said in a strained voice. "But I don't give a damn about that right now." His thumb ran across Penrose's face, and he frowned at what he must have seen there. "What about the others? Cassius?"

Penrose looked at the floor. "Cassius is dead, but ..."

"Henrik," Aisha said for her. "He's gone."

Malik's voice was rough when he eventually spoke. "He was a good man. He did too much for us."

Penrose was silent. There were no words to smother the hurt in her chest for Henrik. Malik was right. She closed her eyes as the tears gathered at her eyelids.

With a low grown, she heard Malik get to his feet next to her. "Mars?"

"Just unconscious, I think," Aisha responded. "I saw the guard knock him out."

Penrose didn't want to look. Instead, she asked Aisha, "And the woman in the dress? Is she ..." She couldn't complete the thought.

"Alive," Aisha confirmed.

But one dead was too many.

She felt a thumb brush away her tear and opened her eyes to see Malik crouching before her. He held her fist in his hand.

It occurred to her then exactly what they had done.

They had done what Henrik had devoted his entire life to. They'd ridded the world of somnus—and the spirit who had orchestrated its spread throughout the kingdoms.

And the hurt wasn't gone, but Penrose couldn't help but smile for the joy of what they'd accomplished.

Penrose squeezed his hand back. She whispered, "Malik. He's gone. We did it."

Malik mirrored her expression, and it was so pure that it did something like the opposite of break her heart to see it.

"I know. You were magnificent."

Suddenly, a torrent of wind filled the room, and an unearthly howl carried on the wind. Shadows coalesced on the ceiling like a storm cloud. Like a strike of lightning, they shot into one of the bodies below.

Chapter Seventy-One

Spirit

Malik clung to her even when the force of the cyclone felt like it was ripping his skin from his bones.

The shadows filled Penrose's mouth, and her eyes rolled in the back of her head. He shouted her name, but the storm of shadows around them swallowed the sound.

Like hell he was going to give her up.

And, just as quickly as it had started, it stopped. Penrose slumped in his arms, her head lolling to the side. His stomach dropped like a stone in a lake.

"Penrose. Penrose," he pled, as if he could fix this by doing so.

Aisha had been thrown across the room, along with the dozen or so bodies that had been scattered about them. The windstorm had kicked up a small flame in the fireplace. Its failing light flickered across Penrose's face.

"Penrose, *please.*" Just as his fingers went to check her pulse—an act that scared him more than anything else he'd ever done in his existence—she jerked upright and opened her eyes.

Her lips curled into a smile, and she cocked her head to the side. Her eyes were black as the Evestide night.

"Oh? Is that what this one is called, then?" Penrose said, her eyes bright despite the black blanketing them.

But it wasn't her. She sounded ... wrong.

Malik's blood punished him, lashing through him like a whip. He didn't even get to open his mouth before shadows pulled her off the ground and out of his arms. With a flick of her hand, a blue pulse of light slammed into his body and sent him flying.

Penrose laughed to see him smash against the wall. She started walking towards him.

"I will finish what my previous form couldn't accomplish," she said as she got closer. "Prepare to die watching your worst fears play out ad infinitum before your eyes."

Malik groaned as he moved. He wasn't sure how much more breakings he could take, though that didn't matter anymore.

He needed to save Penrose from Nightmare.

"Penrose," he said. "Listen to me—"

When he started to stand again, another blast slammed into his side, and he crashed into the chairs at the dining table.

"Malik!" Aisha shouted from across the room, "It's not her anymore."

No. *No.* He refused to believe that.

She was still there. She had to be.

She was the only one who—

A vision rose before his eyes. He was no longer in the castle throne room but at Belnya prisons. This time, he was by himself in line for the executioner's blade. Metal cuffs tore into his skin at his neck, wrists, and ankles.

His father was the only one seated in the stands. He smiled upon him.

"Harder," he commanded someone. "Break him."

It was then that the slice of a multi-headed whip tore into his back. He fell on the dirt, writhing in pain. His father commanded his tormentor to deliver more blows.

"Penrose!" Malik shouted against the sound of the whip lashing the air. "I know you're there," he growled.

Belnya was gone. He was on the floor of the throne room again, though his body didn't feel any better for it. He gasped like a man coming up for air from drowning.

"Malik!" Aisha shouted for him. Tears had streaked her face, but she was alive. "You have to—"

Penrose turned to her. A burst of blue light slammed Aisha against the closest wall, but not before Aisha slid something on the ground to him.

It was the salt-rubbed knife.

She wanted him to kill Penrose.

Chapter Seventy-Two

The Only Answer

Malik grabbed the knife and sprinted for Penrose before she turned around again.

Thoughts fled his mind. He only had one shot at this, and he would not screw it up.

But Penrose had already sighted him and the knife in his palm. She smiled. "Come to kill your lover?" She showed her teeth in a snarl. "Bring it, then."

Before he could make it to her, she dissolved into shadow. Malik twisted, but he was too late. A kick to his chest robbed him of breath, and he fell to the ground.

Only one shot.

Malik rubbed his fingers over the blade of the knife. A small nick drew some beads of his blood, but he ignored that part.

"Penrose," he called. "I *know* you're in there. Please."

"You can't trick me with your sweet words," she said with a smile, lifting her hand.

Before she could hit him again, he flung the knife away from him towards some of the bodies littering the floor.

Her gaze followed it, and he struck then.

Malik leapt the distance between them, and his arms wrapped around her before the spirit that possessed her could realize what was happening.

He'd learned something from watching Cassius take those salt bullets.

Even though Nightmare could shed salt, it anchored it in place and stopped it. It took time to do this, too—unless the salt went through its heart.

Then it killed its host.

But not necessarily the spirit Nightmare.

It had only played at being banished.

The salt grains in his hands did the trick and weighed her to the ground under him.

"Let go of me, stupid human," she said. "You know not what ancient force you play with."

Malik stared into the pitch-black eyes that belonged to the love of his life. Or rather, the eyes that should have been a piercing blue.

What if …

What if it wasn't possible?

What if—just like the blowing wind—she was gone?

Malik held tighter the body of the girl he'd fallen for. "Penrose, please. Please be there." His voice cracked. "I don't think I can do this without you."

Penrose, or the spirit that possessed her, stared at him with a scowl on her face. She snapped her fingers, and the nightmare he had where he lost Penrose started to play before his eyes.

No. I'm getting her back! I'm getting her back, DAMN IT!

He blinked, and the bedroom at the top of the tower was gone.

But she still wasn't where she was supposed to be. She was someone else.

"Penrose." Malik was shaking now. "I—please—I can't …" His voice was raw, but he couldn't stop. "I didn't know how it could be. How emptier it could be without another person. Penrose, *please.*"

The possibility of a world without her swallowed him up. He felt like he was sinking to the bottom of an ocean with nothing but more ocean stretching around him.

"Penrose, *please*," Malik said. Drops of blood and tears fell on her dress, darkening it as it spread into the fabric. He looked into the pitch black of her eyes. They were as deep as a bottomless ocean when they stared back at him like that.

"Penrose. I love you," he admitted.

Malik closed his eyes as he gave in to the sobs that had threatened to wrack his body from the moment when he saw the shadows claim her.

Despite appearances, he wasn't strong like her. He couldn't kill Nightmare. And he couldn't live without her. Not like this.

He was unsure if what he was experiencing was a part of another of Nightmare's conjured terrors or if this was just reality—but he suspected the latter. Well, if he had to die of nightmares, at least let it be one where he knew her.

One in which he loved her.

"I love you," he whispered just to hear it again.

It was then that he got his answer.

"I love you, too."

Malik opened his eyes and saw the love of his life staring back up at him. The skin around her blue eyes crinkled as she smiled.

"Always," she added.

After

The castle's courtyard was overflowing in spring flowers. Purple waves of wisteria climbed most vertical surfaces, including the wooden archway that they'd commissioned for today.

Penrose's friends that she'd made from the bookstore were there—she hadn't told them she was queen when she'd first visited or the fact that she'd been there on the store's opening day one hundred years ago. Their faces had been priceless.

The castle's staff had been given the day off—except for the cooks and necessary guards.

Sorrowtail was happily perched on the edge of a glass bowl, dipping into the mountain of red berries that had been set aside for him. Aisha, Mars, and those friends still loyal to them after the death of Raphael Ezar were there.

Sarina, the woman who had been Cassius's captive and seer, was there with her daughter and mother. Rana hadn't stopped smiling since the day Sarina had come home, or so Rana's grandmother had told Penrose.

Penrose had investigated the matter and had found that Sarina's true service to the king had been kept secret. Officially, she had been his advisor, and Penrose had agreed to keeping her talents hidden.

As it turned out, Sarina had been the granddaughter of an important Karsian diplomat roughly one hundred years ago—one who had been invited to a political wedding in a tower. It was Sarina's theory that the energy of the spell that Nightmare had put on Penrose was powerful enough to seep into the bodies of those who had been temporarily afflicted with somnus that same day. The diplomat's infant son had grown to find that his dreams revealed strange and yet often truthful things.

And then there was the one chair left empty for their last friend.

Last month, Alsra University's library had reopened, complete with the new Renard wing. Among other materials, it contained the complete findings of the university's somnus research team.

Thank you for everything, Henrik.

Penrose walked forward, her lavender dress trailing behind her. That was when he turned to see her where he stood under the archway.

She couldn't stop herself. She ran to Malik.

He took her in like he'd never seen her before. In her ear, he whispered, "I'm still not convinced this isn't a dream, you know."

Penrose smiled. "Why don't you let me show you it's real?"

Before the officiant could start, Penrose pulled him close and kissed him. It felt like flying. Malik threaded his fingers through her hair, causing flowers to litter at their feet, and dipped her low to kiss her more.

Somewhere, she heard cheering. When Malik pulled them upright again, she saw that a crowd had gathered beyond the iron fencing that closed the courtyard off from the streets of Alsra.

She'd chosen this day in part because it was the first anniversary of the end of somnus—the day that, after Nightmare had been banished from their world, the last person sick with somnus had recovered. Every year since, the cities of Aloster had been flooded with garlands of fresh spring flowers and parades.

Penrose waved at them before turning to the officiant waiting patiently on them.

"My queen?" she asked, a smile on her face despite the interruption to their plans.

"Do you think we could skip to our oaths?" Penrose asked.

"Of course, your Majesty." The old woman turned to Malik. "Do you, Malik Ezar, take our Queen of Aloster, Penrose Barinus, to be your wife in wealth and misfortune, to keep and to cherish, and to love for the rest of your days?"

Malik didn't hesitate. "I do."

She turned to Penrose and repeated the question.

Penrose stared into the face of the man who held her heart and had never let go of it.

"I do. And I will always."

The officiant stepped forward and faced those gathered. "I present to you, on the first anniversary of Panacea, Queen Penrose and King Malik of Aloster."

This time, all their guests, both the invited and those uninvited, stood and cheered.

After the ceremony, Aisha squeezed both of them in a bone-breaking hug. Her golden dress had dazzled Penrose since she'd seen it. It must have been a new one.

When she released them, Penrose gestured at it. "You know you're going to have to tell me where you got that." She smiled. "And go there with me."

Lately, she'd been trying out some new styles—with Aisha's help. Penrose would have been surprised to hear that there were clothes stores they hadn't yet been to in Alsra, but Aisha might have been holding out on her.

Malik stared at his sister. "You have to tell her sometime, you know."

"Tell me what? What's going on?" Penrose's gaze bounced between them.

Aisha bit her lip. "I'll be gone from Alsra for some time." She paused and then blurted, "I'm going to Karsia. I'll be going with Sarina and her family."

Penrose squeezed Aisha's hands. She'd been in talks with those who lived in the Karsian slums. From their input and ideas, Penrose had taken a plan to her council.

Karsia was going to gain its independence again.

From Cassius's war on them, the land had become barren and empty, but there was hope. Many of those who had lived in the slums had joined the effort to reestablish its lands, villages, and eventually, cities. This was the first year Karsian lands had supported a successful crop harvest in many decades.

"I'm glad they'll have you, then," she said to Aisha. "They could do no better."

Aisha smiled back. "I promise to visit." She jerked her chin at Malik. "He already told me he'd have my ass if I didn't."

Malik narrowed his eyes at her. But he seemed to give up and shrug. "Would you expect any different?"

"Not really, no." Her face sobered. "Just don't send an army after me. One of us will be busy overseeing a kingdom. And then there's you." Aisha smirked at him.

Malik was certainly about to respond to *that* when a voice interrupted him.

"Your Majesty. The materials you requested to be notified about have arrived at the castle."

Penrose turned to see a courier accompanied by two guards.

It must have been her face. Malik's hand found her arm. His voice was deadly quiet. "What's wrong?"

Penrose swallowed. Whatever they'd unearthed there, she was prepared for it. Though, truthfully, she hadn't prepared for it to arrive on the day of their wedding.

But, standing there with the knowledge that it was all in the same building as her again, she didn't think she could put off looking through it.

Penrose turned to Malik and Aisha. "After we eat, could I borrow the two of you for a bit?"

***

Despite the ridiculous request—seeing as how it was the middle of their wedding—neither of them seemed to mind helping her once Penrose had explained what was going on.

As the three of them sat on the floor of Penrose's bedroom, they poured over the evidence Penrose's soldiers had gathered from Cassius's tower.

There was something she couldn't articulate to the two of them—that she was looking for something specific. It was such a miniscule hope that she didn't dare speak it aloud for fear of killing it before it had a chance to live.

But after finding only pieces of her broken inhalant device from her father, the record of wedding guests, and other pieces of her former life, Penrose didn't think she could look through any more of the hefty trunk of things.

Malik's hand found her shoulder. "You don't have to look through these if you don't want to."

Penrose knew he was right.

But it was what was in Aisha's hands that made her breath stale in her throat.

She looked up at Penrose. "Pen. It's ..."

She passed the slip of paper to her. Even before she put her reading glasses on again, she recognized the handwriting.

It was her father's.

As her eyes scanned the page, a tear dribbled down her eyelid.

She'd never gotten this one. They must have intercepted the message before she received it when she'd been trapped in Cassius's tower.

He'd written back to her in code, asking if she wanted to postpone her wedding to Cassius again.

Again?

Penrose realized then. Cassius must have told them the wrong date for their wedding. That was why her parents hadn't shown up.

Another realization hit her as she read the last line of his letter.

We will always love you no matter what, Penrose. Never doubt that.

It was like she had a hole she'd never noticed in her chest. She gripped the spot where her heart was like it was a physical wound.

"Penrose." Malik pulled her close to him after she showed him the letter.

They'd never wanted her gone. They hadn't thought of her like a bargaining chip.

"It had all been a ruse to fool me into thinking I was alone," Penrose whispered. "He made me thought ... they ..."

Malik whispered in her ear. "They loved you, Pen. I do, too."

"Always?" she said.

"Always."

More Books by Joy Lewis

A Thorn among Fae (Fae Crown Book 1)
A Crown for the Cursed (Fae Crown Book 2)
The War of the Wicked (Fae Crown Book 3)

***

Wither Thorn (The Crest of Blackthorn Book 1)
Soul Sworn (The Crest of Blackthorn Book 2)
Marrow Blade (The Crest of Blackthorn Book 3)
Blood Prophecy (The Crest of Blackthorn Book 4)

***

A Curse of Silver (An Epic Fantasy Short Story)

Acknowledgements

First, I'd like to thank you for coming on this journey with me. I hope you enjoyed this twist on the classic Sleeping Beauty tale. Without you, Reader, there are no more books. I am forever grateful for your support.

I wanted to write Penrose partly because I really craved a heroine who was a bit more like me when I was younger: quite insecure of herself and more than a little shy, and yet carrying around things like the capacity for incredible kindness, a rebellious sense of justice, and an encyclopedic knowledge of strange lore and monstrous fables.

Oh, and someone with a *giant* book practically glued to her hand at all times. Of course.

All this is to say, if you saw yourself in Penrose while reading this book, this one is especially for you.

Thank you to Myriah Webb for lending your support and a listening ear when I needed it the most.

Finally, I'd like to thank Roman Smith, my own forever and always.

www.ingramcontent.com/pod-product-compliance
Lightning Source LLC
Chambersburg PA
CBHW021242190726
48289CB00005B/1450